Lord Vampyre

By

Wendy Rathbone

Lord Vampyre Copyright © 2018, 2021 by Wendy Rathbone and Eye Scry Publications

A publication by:
Eye Scry Publications
www.eyescrypublications.com

Cover by: Wendy Rathbone

ISBN: 978-1942415237
TITLE: Lord Vampyre
Author: Wendy Rathbone

Address all inquiries to the author at:

wrathbone@juno.com

Note to Readers

This novel is set in a make-believe country with an 1800s-ish backdrop. It is more of a fairytale love story, not a historical, and though one main character is a vampire, this is not a horror story. The focus is mm and mmm romance.

-- WR

Chapter One

Ten-year-old Vanni leaned against the cold, damp iron of the balcony rail and watched the carriage, pulled by a team of gleaming black stallions, come up the far lane overlooking the sea. The carriage became invisible for a brief moment as it plowed through hovering fog, then turned into the drive.

The ocean was a low growl to his left. The woods beyond the cliff-road pulsed dark green, almost black.

Vanni shivered in his thin clothes, but secretly liked the feeling. The shadowy foreboding of something new. Cool anticipation.

Father was home and bringing strangers with him to Cliffside Keep.

Now, maybe things wouldn't be so boring.

Vanni rushed from the balcony, through his room and down the vast hall. Orange oil lamps flickered, making his shadow huge on the salt-damp walls. Down the curving line of stone stairs he leapt, taking two at a time. He was at the wide, front entrance before the footman had even opened the door of the carriage to let its occupants out.

Servants had already gathered along the path to the steps to greet their duke's return.

Vanni stopped at the center of the threshold which was framed by a thick, wood arch with ornate carvings of snakes and wolves intertwined, mouths open and showing fangs.

He stood very still and straight, hands clasped behind his back. His chest heaved. His heart galloped with excitement. But he kept himself in check, his muscles locked, his mouth an emotionless line. His blond hair was pulled back in a tight tail, but strands of it had escaped. The sea-breeze pushed the tendrils against his cheek, tickling it. He ignored the sensation and did not move a muscle, only watched.

The first person to emerge from the carriage was the duke. He did not look too different from the last time Vanni had seen him six months ago. His short cloak was black with a crimson lining. His dark head was bare, the hair receding a bit at the temples, pulled back with a dark ribbon. He stomped the ground twice, as if glad to be home to his vast properties, his earth, then turned to the carriage and lifted his leather gloved hand.

A white-gloved hand met his. A lady emerged, dressed all in lavender and pink, the taffeta overflowing in ruffles down to the ground. She looked like a cake and very young, but not too young for the duke, who enjoyed courting women half his age.

Vanni had read the note his father had sent. He knew what to expect. His father was bringing home a new woman named Jessie. Not as a fiancé. Not as a future wife. But as a consort. A mistress.

Being a duke – Duke Andreas of Cliffside Keep – Father was allowed this luxury. But if she was not upper class, he was not allowed to marry her. It had been the talk of the village, the gossip rife with the public boldness of the duke, living with a woman who was not a lady, and more than ten years his junior. And it was not only scandalous because she was young and a widow, but because she had already borne a son to another man who was not the duke.

Vanni could not help but tilt his head, craning his neck to see beyond the massive folds of the consort's taffeta to the darkened chamber of the carriage. Where was he? This boy? For that was who Vanni was really waiting to see.

Finally, a small, dark figure jumped from the confines of the carriage. He had long hair, black as an October night. And large, grave eyes. And a body no bigger than a small hound. He wore gray knickers and a matching gray vest over a white shirt. His knee socks were askew, but his footing was sure.

Vanni pegged him at about eight years old. What a relief!

He had hoped the boy would be younger than Vanni's own ten years. He'd already planned a lot of shenanigans around the Keep, and he wanted to be the boss. In everything.

How he'd longed for a playmate during his lonely upbringing at the Keep.

Now, he couldn't care less about the mistress his father had brought home. He had eyes only for the boy.

"Giovanni!"

Vanni looked up and into his father's gaze.

"Come," his father ordered. "Meet our new friends."

Slowly, Vanni took the steps down to the path, ignoring the servants. He kept an eye on the boy, who stood halfway behind his mother's skirts.

As much as Vanni was thrilled, a part of him was jealous, too. His father had been gone for six months. He'd spent time with these people while ignoring Vanni. Vanni had begged to be allowed to go on this trip with the duke, but was told his studies were more important and could not be ignored.

Hands still clasped behind his back, Vanni stood before his father and raised his gaze.

"Hello, son. I trust you have been a good boy and studying hard while I've been gone?"

Vanni nodded once, trying not to bite down on his lower lip. His father did not embrace him, nor did he give any indication he might have missed Vanni. Instead, he reached for his new companion and brought her a step forward.

"This is the new mistress of Cliffside Keep. You are to treat her with the utmost respect and manners."

"Hello." Vanni's voice came out softer, shyer than he had intended.

"And you are Giovanni!" she exclaimed. "Why, you don't look a thing like your father. You must take after your mother."

He did not know what to say about that. It had been the rule of the Keep never to bring up his mother. He wasn't sure why, but no one talked of her.

She turned to the duke. "Andreas, your son is charming. And he is ten, you say?" She turned back to Vanni. "My dear, you look so composed for ten. I would have thought you were older."

Vanni bowed his head. "Thank you, uh, um, miss..."

"You may call me Jessie."

Vanni only nodded.

Jessie turned toward the boy behind her. "Damion, come forward."

Damion. So that was his name. Vanni watched the younger boy poke his head out from behind the taffeta and take a tentative step forward. His bare knees bent, delicate but sharp, as he took another step.

"Hello," said Damion.

For a long moment, Vanni studied the boy. Damion, dark-eyed, gaze never wavering, studied him in return.

Vanni felt an energy between them, non-verbal and private as they each quietly assessed the other's attributes. He was being examined and judged, the same as he was doing to the other boy. As if their other selves were already having a conversation on another plane in another time.

Coming to the conclusion that this boy was little threat and—thank the fates—two years his junior, Vanni took a step back. Unable to hide his excitement at having a new playmate, Vanni said quickly, "Want to see my room? It's almost as big as my father's room!"

Damion's eyebrows rose quickly. His eyes nearly glowed. "Yes!"

"You may both run along now," the duke said.

Vanni turned and skipped up the steps, hearing the footsteps of Damion already close behind. As he passed through the entryway, he heard Jessie say, "Look, Andreas, I knew they'd get along!"

*

As they ran up the stone staircase, Damion, who had behaved shyly in front of the adults, seemed to lose all his fears at once. He began to pepper Vanni with questions.

"Have you always lived by the sea?" "Will we be sharing a room?" "Are you really ten?" "You seem a *lot* older."

Lonely for so long, Vanni's heart burst open. A smile spread out on his face. He did not remember the last time he'd grinned so wide it hurt the muscles of his cheeks.

He turned and grasped the boy's hand. "You're going to have your own huge room! And yes, I'm ten! And yes, I have always lived here." *And I have always wanted a little brother.* Damion wasn't his real brother, of course, but he was the next best thing.

When they got to Vanni's room and entered, Damion gasped in awe. "This is huge. You live like a prince."

Grateful for the flattery, Vanni gave in to blind trust right then and there. He couldn't help it. After all, even if he looked older than ten, he wasn't. He was still just a little boy himself. "I'm going to show you all my secrets! Everything! I'm so glad you're here!"

"I'm so glad I'm here, too." Damion met his grin and began to laugh.

The roar of the waves was diminished in Vanni's rooms, but he could still hear the distant roll and crash of falling water. The sea sounded like it was laughing, now, too.

Chapter Two

"Did you know," said Vanni to Damion, who sat on the rug before the hearth bent over a checkerboard. "When I was your age I went into the wood down by the cave of the old sea-witches. All by myself."

"Sea-witches?" Damion's eyes flickered in the firelight, growing round and large. "A cave?"

They were in the drawing room with the red velvet curtains drawn against the bleak windows. The fire smelled of cedar. It staved off the almost constant salt scent of the sea.

It had rained hard earlier in the day and they'd been ordered to stay indoors. The sea crashed and roared. Vanni could tell it disturbed Damion, though the boy had yet to complain after two weeks living in the Keep.

"I called out to them. I said I wanted to see them and that if they appeared before me I would give them my soul."

"No! You didn't say such a thing!"

"I did. But nothing happened. The tide was calm in the cave, clear. I could see all the way to the bottom of the pool there. Nothing. Just sand and rocks. And more sand."

"But what are they? Like mermaids?"

"Or mermen," Vanni said smartly. "They're both boys and girls, you know."

"I know. But they aren't real, though. Not really." Damion's voice was almost a whisper.

"Maybe. Maybe not. My father forbids me going there, but I'll sneak you down there soon. Maybe we'll find one leftover from before anyone settled here, before the village. They don't die, so you never know."

"They don't die?"

Vanni came around the sofa to stand on the rug where Damion sat. "Nope."

"How come?"

Vanni grinned. "Because they feed on the blood of little boys!" He reached out fast and pinched Damion on the neck.

Damion flinched, but didn't scream. Instead, he jumped to his feet. "They do not."

"They do."

"You're trying to scare me."

"Don't you like being scared? It's fun."

Damion stared at him. "No. But I don't get scared, either. Not from old fairytales. Anyway, if there are monsters, why would they bother with us? We're just children."

"You're probably right. So you're not too scared to go with me?"

Damion slowly shook his head.

"Good. I'll take you to the cave tomorrow if it doesn't rain again."

"Won't you get in trouble?" Damion asked.

"Who's going to tell?" Vanni smiled when Damion agreed to the plan, but felt a little evil to be teasing Damion who was still so new to the area. But in truth, he was happy to have a companion to play with, and to explore his father's vast acreage.

So far there wasn't anything Vanni suggested that Damion hadn't agreed to. And when Damion followed him everywhere, and gave him devoted looks, something inside Vanni opened to the power of it. He liked being bossy sometimes. But along with that came a feeling of protectiveness, too. Damion was very sweet, and Vanni liked him more and more every day. He would never let anything happen to the boy. Because now, even though they'd only known each other two weeks, Vanni could not imagine life without him.

*

Vanni said, "Come on."

Damion stood back a ways from the lip of the sea cave. Tufts of thin, yellow grass fluttered at his feet from the low breeze. The day had dawned clear. The sky stretched blue over the still angry, near-black ocean.

"Those rocks look slippery," Damion said.

"They have tiny holes in them. They aren't slick." Vanni held out his hand. Damion came forward.

Inside the cave, they could hear water slosh against stone. It took a moment for Vanni's eyes to adjust to the shadowy darkness. It smelled of salt spray, a little bracken.

Damion's hand tightened against Vanni's palm. "Do you think sea-witches actually lived here?" he asked in a loud whisper.

Vanni tried not to smile. "I think so."

When their eyes adjusted to the lack of light, Vanni saw how the rocks curved forming a natural pool. He moved forward, dragging Damion with him, and sat with his feet dangling over the water. The tide shifted, drawing water in and out of another entrance underground. The water level rose, then receded over and over.

Damion sat beside Vanni, who finally pulled his hand away. "I think they swam in here and rested right where we are sitting."

"The witches?"

"Yes. And they liked it so much they stayed. They set up their home here. They brought in their kelp sea-beds, and their chairs made of red coral. And they dined on a table made from a giant shell. They ate sea-bass, mostly. And lobster. And crab."

"How do you know?"

"I just see it so clearly in my thoughts."

"Really?"

"Yes."

"Maybe it's a dream," Damion suggested.

"Then how do I have this?" From his pocket, Vanni pulled out a small abalone comb about three inches long with

11

teeth the length of his pinky finger. He held it up so it reflected the light coming into cave entrance. A rainbow played across the surface of the comb's base.

"I found this in here."

"Wow." Damion's eyes got big. "Can I hold it?"

Vanni handed it over.

Damion turned it against his palm. "It feels cold."

"The sea-witches have long dark hair, sort of like yours, but sleek like a seal all the way down their backs. They used this, I think, to comb the tangles out."

"You really found this here?"

Vanni nodded. He wasn't lying. One summer ago he'd found it after a storm, lying at the edge of the cave-pool, gleaming in the weak light. At first it had scared him. Someone had been in his secret cave. But when he took it in his hand and held it, a tremendous peacefulness surrounded him.

"It's treasure," he said to Damion. "I'll share it with you. You can keep it in your pocket sometimes, all right?"

Damion nodded.

"Do you think the mermaids—or sea-witches—have big tails?" Damion asked.

"Maybe. But I think they walk on land, too. So I'm not sure how that works."

"Why do you call them sea-witches?"

Vanni shrugged. "I heard the word once. I don't remember how. It just seemed right. And real. They would be magic people, right? And witches know magic. And the sea holds magic and secrets. And this is a sea cave."

"Yes," Damion agreed. "It seems right. Sea-witches." He paused, then said, "I wish they weren't all gone."

"Maybe they're not. Maybe they're just hiding," Vanni said.

Damion gave a little shiver.

"Are you cold?" Vanni asked.

"Yes, a little."

Vanni stood. "Let's go back. I'm hungry. Put the comb in your pocket."

When he stood, Damion did as instructed. Then he turned all the way around surveying the cave.

"They would be nice, though, right? The sea-witches?" asked Damion. "They wouldn't hurt people. They wouldn't really drink the blood of boys."

"No. Not unless people hurt them first," Vanni replied.

Just then, the sea gave a roar and dark water rushed into the basin of the pool. The water rose so rapidly, it splashed over the rocky edge spitting its foam on the boys' boots. They both jumped back.

Then, without another word, they turned and ran back to the Keep.

*

Andreas greeted them at the door.

"I've been looking for you boys. Where did you go?"

"Just along the shoreline a way," said Vanni.

"We were looking for lost treasure," said Damion helpfully.

"Vanni, you know you're not to wander off further than within sight of the Keep. And stay away from that cave."

"What cave, Father?" Vanni asked.

The duke raised an eyebrow. "I know you go to that cave. Don't lie to me boy, or I'll certainly whip you and ground you to your room for a week. Just stay close to home. Word is there have been marauders about. The guards for the Keep have been doubled. The village is on alert."

Damion gasped. Vanni frowned.

The duke turned from Vanni and knelt to face Damion eye to eye. "Some chickens were stolen from a couple of farms. And a few sheep have been found killed. But don't worry, little one. Probably it's only an animal, but we can't be too careful these days."

These days. Vanni had heard the phrase before. From the cooks and the servants. *These days were darker. These days didn't feel as safe.*

"As long as you stay in the Keep, or within sight of it, you're safe," the duke said to Damion, ruffling his hair.

A sting of jealousy ran through Vanni's muscles. He stiffened. His father had never been so affectionate with him. He scowled and stomped off into the hall and toward the kitchen. It would be lunchtime soon. He hoped for beef pie today, not fish.

Small footsteps echoed behind him—Damion running to catch up. Still feeling jealous, Vanni jogged faster toward the kitchen. When he arrived, he sat at the table where trays had been set out to bring to the dining room to serve to the duke and his mistress. The boys always got their lunch in the kitchen with the servants. They didn't mind.

Vanni's favorite cook, Tevi, turned. "Beef pie today. Is it what you wanted?"

Vanni nodded vigorously.

Damion arrived at the door a moment later, hair hanging in his face. "I like beef pie, too."

"And so you do," said Tevi with a grin. "My, you look like the wind blew you in!"

Vanni turned away, folded his arms on top of the table, and rested his head upon them. He felt the chair next to him move, and Damion sat.

For the moment, Vanni resented him. Everyone seemed to favor him. Even the cook, now. Even Vanni *liked* him. But it made him sometimes feel as if he was more apart than ever from his father, and from his life here at the Keep.

Damion said softly, "Are you tired?"

"I just don't want to talk right now," Vanni replied, not moving.

When Tevi served them, Vanni ate quickly, burning his tongue on the gravy which was thick and salty and delicious.

He almost asked for seconds but Damion beat him to it. Tevi brought a second helping just as Vanni stood up.

"I'm finished," Vanni said. "I'm going to my room. I have studies."

Tevi chuckled, "Since when do you voluntarily study?"

Vanni frowned. Of course he hated his tutor who was old and wrinkled and boring. But he did like to read.

Without a word, he left the kitchen. He could feel Damion's questioning eyes on his back all the way out. Damion didn't understand that all the Keep and the things within it, including the people, were not his by right. That he was being *gifted* all of it. That Vanni was compelled, now, to think that half of all of it was Damion's. In his heart, he'd always wanted a companion, someone to share all this with. Sharing things wasn't so hard. But sharing attention, now that was harder.

Chapter Three

Vanni had managed to avoid Damion for the rest of the day, keeping to himself, reading in his room, or taking his wooden horses and soldiers out to the chilly balcony to play by himself while he listened to the softly crying wind.

When he peeked over the balcony railing, he saw the setting sun, orange and big, and a lot of purple clouds coming in fast. Another storm was on its way.

The dinner hour came. As it was served in the dining room every night at seven sharp, the meal required dressing properly. That meant a clean shirt, a brocaded waistcoat, and a jacket.

When he was younger, he had a servant help dress him, for his father could never be bothered with such trivial matters. But now he was old enough to dress himself, and he rarely had help. He didn't want it. But at the same time, he wondered if Damion had help, and the jealousy quivered like a mean monster within him.

The duke and his mistress sat at each end of the long dining table. The boys sat facing one another on either side. Sometimes they had guests, and the table became crowded. Elbows bumped. Adults overtook the conversation, drinking wine, laughing loudly. And boys, well, they were to be seen, not heard.

Tonight it was just the four of them.

The duke was meticulous about everything being just right at dinnertime. He fussed over a spoon set too far from a knife, or a candle that had burnt too low, or a spot on his stemware for his wine, or whether or not the food was cooked to perfection. He always sent something back to the kitchen to be re-done, even if it was tasty.

Vanni was more irritated than usual, and would not look at Damion.

16

When Andreas sent back buttered bread for being cold, not warm, Vanni grew even more restless and annoyed, but realized it wasn't really Damion's fault. It was Andreas he was mad at.

"What if *I* like the bread not so hot?" Vanni asked.

"Did I ask your opinion?" the duke returned.

"Andreas," said Jessie softly.

"I will not have my son talking back to me," Andreas said.

Vanni's mind flashed back on the moment Andreas had ruffled Damion's hair. There were other times, too, when Andreas, perhaps coached by Jessie, gave Damion a brief hug, or smiled at him even if Damion did nothing to deserve it.

Vanni stared at his plate and tried not to pout.

"So," Andreas said, in between sipping soup from a silver spoon. "Your tutor tells me you are very bright for your age in your studies, Damion. You are studying at Giovanni's level and yet you are two years younger."

Vanni felt a sting behind his eyes as he glanced up at Damion. Damion squirmed in his seat and did not react at first. His dark eyes met Vanni's. Vanni didn't care that Damion didn't react. He stuck his tongue out at Damion and crossed his eyes.

Damion's face instantly flushed.

"Giovanni!"

Vanni turned to his father in shame, biting his lower lip.

"You are to leave this table immediately and go straight to bed. There will be no more dinner for you."

Vanni pushed his chair back hard, relishing in the loud sound it made as it scraped the marble floor. When his feet hit the tile, he ran. As he turned into the hall, he heard Jessie say, "Andreas, they're just boys. What do you expect?"

Andreas said, "My son is an earl, a lord. He needs to learn more respect. It's not a crime to discipline a child."

Once he got to his room, Vanni tore off his dinner clothes, quickly shuffled into his sleeping gown, and threw himself face down on the bed. On a count to sixty, he let himself cry, his pillow soaking up his tears. After he reached sixty-one, he made himself get up and wipe his face and swallow all the built up tension in his throat.

He had the thought that he hated Damion. But then he realized he didn't. Not really. Damion was brought here to the Keep through no will of his own. He didn't have any choice, at eight, and must follow wherever his mother went. Besides, he behaved like an angel to everyone. Including Vanni.

Then he turned his hatred to Jessie. But she was really very sweet. He had never heard her raise her voice. She always hugged Damion to her waist whenever she saw him. Often, she had special treats for them both, peppermint sticks, or lemon drops drawn from a pretty purple pouch she always had pinned to her skirt. No, Vanni could not hate her.

It was Andreas, his father, he turned his hatred toward now. In Vanni's early years, after his mother died when he was two, he barely remembered him being around. He traveled often, leaving Vanni with tutors and servants. When he came home, he treated Vanni like a stranger. When he didn't travel, he was always working in his study. Always too busy to talk, or to listen to Vanni try to tell him about his day. Vanni learned to avoid the study, and saw his father mostly only at dinner.

When his father left again, Vanni had actually been relieved. But then he'd sent a letter home stating he'd be arriving with guests. A woman and a little boy. He'd found himself another family.

Yes, Vanni decided he had every right to be angry with his father.

Swiftly, he swept more tears from his face. His stomach growled. He slid to the floor and picked up two of his wooden soldiers. He made them talk. One said to the other, *I hate you.*

You're a mean and terrible and cold man. He crashed his hands together, making the two soldiers fight.

The mean and terrible soldier finally fell from his hand, defeated. Vanni picked him up again and stood, facing his nightstand. A servant had lit two candles there. He put the defeated soldier's head into the flame until it turned black. He hoped it might catch fire, but it never did.

When Vanni was done playing, he threw his toys back to the floor, blew out the candles and turned off the oil lamps. He left only one lamp flickering by the door in case he had to get up. That was the only reason. For of course he was *not* afraid of the dark. Not at all.

He dozed after a while, stomach still muttering at his missed dinner. Then darkness rushed in.

Something startled him awake. He lay very still, his heart beating fast. Then he heard it.

The storm had come. He listened to the anger of the waves on the beach, smacking themselves over and over against the gritty sand. The ocean made a sound like a great serpent's roar. Rain pelted his closed windows like gravel. It smelled fresh, not salty for a change. In the distance, thunder rumbled.

Vanni got up from his warm bed and looked out his balcony windows at the liquid whiteness plunging from the sky. Beyond, he saw mostly blackness, but as his eyes got used to it, he saw the sea rolling in its great bed. Different sections heaved up and down, undulating like a giant black bubble that wanted to burst.

The shoreline had nearly vanished at the violence of the water pushing, pulling, back and forth. The normally white beach was dotted with kelp, and narrow in the high tide, nearly gone. He watched the waves pull up and crash forward, and stared at the water turning to froth with its rage. His blood burned like that sometimes, and he liked it.

His little hands made fists. As he continued to watch the storm, something caught his eye. A moving shadow on what was left of the shoreline. Could it be a man? And it looked like it was dragging something.

Vanni squinted, trying to see better through the pouring rain. Just as he thought about opening the balcony door, a great wave crashed forward and the shadow vanished. Nothing was there anymore. Had it only been a trick of the lightning far out at sea that occasionally lit up the sky, blue and green and gold?

Just then, a thump came from behind him.

Vanni whirled around.

Damion stood in the doorway that led to the hall. He looked very small standing there, his white sleeping gown trailing the floor at the hem, his long dark hair scattered all about his shoulders. At a glance, he might have been taken for a ghost.

"What are you doing?" Vanni asked. "Are you afraid of the dark?"

Damion stepped forward, still over ten feet away, and held out his hand. "No."

"What is that?"

"I thought you might like to have it back," Damion said.

Vanni walked over to him and looked into his open hand. There sat the abalone comb gleaming purple and blue and pink.

Vanni said, "Why?"

"Because you hate me now."

Thunder rumbled behind Vanni, far out to sea.

Damion trembled slightly, but his hand remained still.

Ignoring the statement, Vanni said, "You *are* afraid, aren't you?"

Damion shook his head.

"Close the door behind you," Vanni said quietly.

His fingers folding around the neglected comb, Damion obeyed. The door snicked quietly shut.

"Are you cold?" Vanni asked.

Damion shook his head a second time.

"Did anyone see you?"

"No."

"Come on, then. You can climb into bed with me. But only this once. Don't make it a habit."

Solemnly, Damion nodded, his feet silently scrambling across the floor. Vanni noticed they were bare. As were his own. The floor was like ice.

"Get in. It's freezing. Quick," he said, holding back the covers.

Damion hopped up and scrambled under the blankets. Vanni got into the bed from the other side. In tandem, they both turned until they were facing each other.

Slowly, Damion's hand came up and he placed the comb on the pillow between their heads. The oil lamp from the table by the door gave enough light for them to see by.

Vanni stared at it, then back at Damion's dark gaze. "I said you could hang onto that for now."

"But it's your treasure."

"So? I gave it to you."

"But you don't like me."

"Shut up and go to sleep."

Thunder crashed again, loud.

Damion jumped.

"Maybe it's the sea-witches and they're mad," Damion whispered. "Because of the comb."

"Shh!" The boy was making Vanni feel nervous. "As long as you hang onto it, nothing bad can happen."

"Really?"

"Really."

They both stared at the shell comb between them.

"Take it in your hand," Vanni said.

The boy obeyed. Vanni closed his own hand around Damion's fist.

"There. Feel better?"

Damion nodded.

"Now go to sleep."

The dark eyes closed, long black lashes dusting the top curves of his cheeks.

Vanni held Damion's hand and watched him for a long time until Damion's breathing became even. With his free hand, Vanni tucked the covers tighter around them both, scooted a bit closer for warmth, and closed his eyes.

The storm still raged, but more distant now.

Chapter Four
-Seven Years Later-

"Wake up. Wake up! I don't want Father to catch us." Vanni had never been allowed to move about the Keep during the night hours. He was only allowed to visit the water closet if he needed to. The same rule applied to Damion. But for years Damion had crept into his bed almost every night, and left just before dawn so no one would know.

Vanni tossed off the covers and shoved Damion's shoulder, trying to get him to move.

Damion remained steadfast. "It's too early, still dark. Go back to sleep."

"Yes, well *you're* not the one who will get in trouble."

It was true that the duke always punished Vanni no matter who of the two of them found themselves in trouble.

This had become a habit, just as Vanni feared it would when he'd let eight-year-old Damion into his bed one stormy night the first year Damion had lived at the Keep. Damion claimed he couldn't sleep alone. But Vanni was sure he was simply afraid of the dark.

"You're too old to keep climbing into my bed night after night." Vanni had just turned seventeen. Damion was fifteen.

"I'm not," Damion argued.

"I'm getting invitations to balls now. Parties. Dances," Vanni said stoutly.

"Yes, but you haven't gone to any of them. Even after Andreas stopped saying you were too young, and gave his permission, you don't go."

"I will be going. I just don't know anyone in town very well yet, that's all. But some of the invitations are from girls." Vanni grinned as he rolled over to look at Damion. *"Girls!"*

The light from the ever-present oil lamp by the door that burned all night for two boys who swore they were not afraid of the dark made Damion look ethereal. Light and shadow played over his features.

Damion sighed and turned to face Vanni, his long hair rippling over the pillows. The blankets were pushed down. In their thin white gowns, their bodies were almost touching, the heat between them like a fire. "I don't like girls."

"These are ladies with titles and everything."

Damion yawned and stretched his arms above his head. His sleeping gown rode up, exposing his thighs. He was no longer a little boy. Though he was lean, his muscles had thickened and developed in his calves and upper legs. He was gaining in height, but still shorter than Vanni.

While Vanni kept his hair trimmed to just above the shoulders, Damion refused to cut his. During the day, he wore it braided down his back and tied with a thick, black ribbon. He grew lovelier every day, but Vanni didn't allow himself to think about that much because when he did, he felt guilty about the funny feelings that came up inside him, feelings of protectiveness and ownership, but worse, arousal that made him shameful at his lack of control. He worried about what Damion would say if he ever found out.

"Well," Vanni said, "I am going to be courting these ladies. You don't have to. You're still young. You can wait a couple years. But I'm seventeen. And that's almost a man."

"Good for you." Damion sat up, grinning, hair in his eyes. "I don't think I'll be courting ladies even when I'm your age. It's just not my thing."

Just what is your thing? But Vanni didn't ask his question aloud. Instead, he kicked at Damion's thigh with his bare foot and said, "Go back to your room."

Damion slid over the side of the bed and stood. His rucked up gown showed the upper curve of the back of his thigh before gravity dragged it down again.

Vanni would never admit it, but he woke just before dawn nearly every morning with an angel in his bed.

*

Vanni's first ball was at a lesser lord's house in the village which was not as big as the Keep, but still impressive.

The ballroom's floor and walls had been polished to a mirror shine. All the silverware and plates gleamed. Candles fluttered everywhere. People, also shiny, flitted and danced about in fine clothing of brushed wool, satin, taffeta, and silk.

Even the air seemed as if it had been bathed and powdered. It smelled of fresh spring brooks and roses. Wine was served even to the younger teenagers. Buffets of fruits, meats, vegetables and desserts overflowed.

Vanni arrived in the best fashion, allowed to take the carriage and driver alone into the village. He wore fine new clothing, for as a duke his father could afford the best tailors.

It surprised him when he was announced at the entryway to the big ballroom as "The Earl Giovanni of Cliffside Keep."

As the son of a duke, and the richest in the land, he would have that title, of course. But he didn't realize until now how formal and adult it sounded. Vanni watched as all heads turned. The musicians playing on a raised dais by the dance floor paused.

His father had pretty much failed at socializing him. Andreas only had guests a few at a time and never threw balls or parties. But Vanni wasn't stupid. He knew how to dance—his tutors saw to that—and how to comport himself with the best of manners.

What he didn't expect was to be bowed and curtseyed to by everyone he met. It made him feel both important and nervous. All eyes were upon him throughout the evening. He had never been around so many people at once.

The attendees at the ball were all ages, from sixteen to eighty. They represented mostly the upper crust of five or six villages surrounding the Keep. This ball had been given by a lesser lord and friend of Vanni's father for his daughter, the Lady Cecilia, who had just turned eighteen. And it was Vanni she instantly latched onto the moment he'd entered the lavish manse.

She was quite pretty in her bustling skirts and white lace. Her blond hair, a shade darker than Vanni's, was drawn into neat French braids that wove into one and sat in a curve at her upper back beneath a large blue ribbon. Her eyes were a shade of afternoon blue.

Cecilia's hand was cool when she placed it on top of his, ungloved.

"I did not think you would come but insisted Father send the invitation anyway. You've never come down from the Keep, or if you have, no one ever sees you." Her look was mock-accusatory.

Vanni smiled and took her hand, wanting to be seen as gallant, though already he was sweating at his neck and under his arms.

"My father would never allow it. He said I was too young for parties. Until now."

"If you are never seen, it causes rumors. Stories." Cecilia's pout was only pretend, for her eyes smiled at him.

"Like what?"

"That you are misshapen, or sick in the head. But I can see none of that is true."

Really? People talked about him? What about Damion? Did people wonder about him, too?

"Oh, I—uh—didn't know that." Vanni had rarely talked to strangers, but to servants and guests of his father he had never been shy. Now he found himself at a loss for words.

"Well, it's my birthday and I get what I want," Cecilia said. "You shall stick by me this evening and I'll introduce you to, well, everyone!"

26

His heart hammered. All he could do was nod.

He did not get used to the stares. Or the compliments as to his bearing, attire or comeliness. He was not accustomed to any of that. He had never really thought about his looks much growing up. It was Damion who was beautiful, not him.

But everyone seemed to think he was a prize, and many older folks were surprised he had not already acquired a wife, that he had not gotten out more, and was only just beginning to introduce himself to society.

"I am only seventeen." He must have made that statement a dozen times to knowing smiles and nods.

The evening passed by quickly. He danced and drank and ate, and Cecilia truly was a nice girl. He was glad he met her. She seemed to want more from him than mere friendship, and he wasn't quite sure what to do about that, but he liked the feeling of affection, the attention.

As the evening came to an end, she said, "Will you be attending Lord Percy's ball next month?"

He'd never heard of Lord Percy. "I don't know."

"I'll make sure you get an invitation. Maybe you will want to bring your brother."

"My brother?"

"Damion. The people who have been to the Keep and met him say he's a darling, and a beauty. "

A protective surge went through him, along with a feeling of almost-jealousy that people were talking about Damion. *His* Damion. "He's not my brother. He just lives in the Keep. I'm not sure my father would allow it, though. He's only fifteen."

"Fifteen is almost a man. Doesn't he want to make friends? Don't you two get lonely up there at that old Keep?"

Vanni didn't answer the question directly. Instead, he squeezed her hand and said, "We'll see."

Just then, the duke's private carriage arrived.

As Vanni turned to go, Cecilia said, "I'd like to see that Keep some time."

Vanni merely smiled and waved and climbed into the coach.

*

One guard greeted him at the front entry when Vanni arrived home.

He bowed as Vanni came through the doorway.

"Do you need anything?" The guard asked. "I can ring a servant."

"No thank you," said Vanni.

The servants were all in bed. He wouldn't have wanted to wake any of them even if he had wanted something.

The guard nodded, then moved past the door and outside, probably to patrol the grounds.

The duke kept three guards full time. Others came and went. Sometimes Andreas still talked of marauders. But crime was low in the villages. The worst that happened were animal attacks, but even they were rare.

Still, Vanni never forgot that image he'd seen when he was ten years old during a big storm. A shadow on the beach. Dragging something heavy.

He and Damion still told each other made-up stories about the sea-witches, and kept their shell comb hidden in a space under a floor tile in Vanni's bedroom. But they rarely visited the cave anymore.

What they most liked to do as kids, weather permitting, was play in the woods. They even built a tree house together and waged war on invisible creatures from high among the tree's branches.

But Vanni hadn't been out to that tree house in a year. And Damion was growing into the type who liked to curl up with a book before a warm fire, or write and draw. He truly was the smarter of the two of them when it came to books and tutoring. Vanni liked to play games, learn tricks of the hand, or daydream, but he didn't like to write.

28

They were growing up. They had always been different, but now they were becoming two very different almost-adults.

As Vanni took the stairway to his room, he began to wonder about the future. Would he eventually marry and move away? Or move his bride into the Keep? Would Damion go out into the world to search for his own life? He couldn't imagine them being apart. Just the thought made his heart do funny flip-flops.

Outside the sea whispered and moaned, not as angry tonight. Most of the hallway oil sconces had been turned off, or part-way down. The wall shadows looked soft with a blue-black sheen.

It had been a good night. He was happy he'd gone to the ball. But something was missing. It was as if none of it was real, all a neatly staged play. He'd gone through the motions of meeting a girl—a lady, no less--, talking, dancing. And it was all fine, but not real. Not solid. Not something he could sink into without a thought.

And yet, he wanted to go back another night, down the ocean side road, into the villages, and mingle. See more of the world. How could he know what he wanted if he didn't try it all?

He opened the door to his room, a half-smile on his face, veins still tingling from the wine. His gaze came up fast as he saw Damion, white gown, black hair, stretched out on his bed and reading by the light of a pink glass oil lamp.

He shut the door fast behind him.

Vanni tried to keep his voice low. "What are you doing here?"

Damion looked up calmly, his dark eyes sparkling the way they always seemed to whether he was happy or gloomy or bored.

"Waiting for you." He closed his book over a frayed ribbon bookmark.

"You can't just—" Vanni didn't finish. Instead, he let out a huff and started to take off his jacket. Turned away now, he could think better. He said, "We're too old for this."

"For what?"

"Sleeping together."

"Oh."

Vanni heard a small rustle of cloth on cloth.

"I was just waiting for you," came that ever-sweet voice. "I wanted to know how the ball was."

"It was fine."

"Did you meet a lot of people? And eat a lot of food?"

"Yes."

"What was it like? Being treated so fine. Or did they keep away from you? Or… tell me everything!"

Vanni turned, frowning.

Damion had only put one leg over the side of the bed and showed no sign of getting up and leaving. But no matter what, Vanni couldn't stay mad at him. Ever.

"Let me get my dressing gown on. Then I'll tell you everything." He turned toward the water closet.

That night, he let Damion sleep in his room again until just before dawn. They stayed up for hours talking about the ball, the village, and the girl named Lady Cecilia whose father threw the ball for her birthday.

Damion had asked, "Do you like her a lot?"

Vanni flushed all the way down to his toes. Then he grabbed Damion, who smelled of spun sugar and lavender. He put both hands on either side of his face and pushed the back of his head into the pillow. "Not as much as you, idiot! So just shut up about that now, all right?"

Damion lay back and his body went rigid, then very still as he slowly relaxed.

"All right, then," Damion whispered, and his smile made his cheeks dimple.

Chapter Five

Vanni stood in the hot and stifling study of his father and threw a thick, heavy log at his feet.

"Use that!" he snarled, hands on his hips.

He'd been instructed to find a "switch" for his punishment.

If his father was going to treat him as if he was still ten years old, then he was not going to make it easy for him.

Andreas's brown eyes widened and his face reddened. The anger between the two of them was so thick you could almost see the cloud their quick breaths made as they stared each other down.

Vanni's heart skipped wildly in his chest. His hair was sweat-damp, strands of it stinging his eyes. But he refused to avert his gaze.

The truth was, though Vanni really did love his father, the only attention he ever got from him was when he back-talked him.

Today they argued about Lord Percy's ball. Vanni wanted to go, and he wanted to bring Damion with him. Andreas said Damion was too young. And that was all it took to pit them against each other.

The fire in the grate was an all-too sickly orange. The room smelled old and used, confining. Something inside Vanni was churning and whirling, fluttering his stomach with yearning, demanding to be free. He didn't even know how to define it. But it was there. Desperation. Longing. The urge to shout at the moon, break something, run down the beach. Or run through the woods until his lungs gave out and he collapsed in beds of fresh, long grass under trees so green they could make grown men weep.

He had never liked it when he and his father fought. But it couldn't be helped.

He was seventeen. Damion was fifteen. They couldn't be cooped up here their whole lives. What other reason did he need? He'd argued. He'd yelled. He'd stood up to the duke.

"You impudent, petulant child!" Andreas now shouted, staring at the log.

If no switch could be found, a leather belt had been an instrument of punishment with which Vanni was well-acquainted. He saw his father's hand go to his waist in a useless gesture, for today he wore suspenders.

Vanni lifted his chin, did not move. But his resolve was faltering, his stomach a bit green. He didn't allow it to show.

Andreas reached out suddenly and smacked him hard on the jaw. Vanni's head jerked aside but he gritted his teeth, made no sound, and met his father's eyes with a glare.

"You are a spoiled, insolent brat!"

Vanni spoke quietly, trying not to shake.

"I do not regret my words. You aren't being fair. Damion was invited to the ball the same as I was. I'll be with him the whole time. You're the one being irrational when you say he can't go! I could sneak him out if I wanted!"

A haze swept over Andreas's features. Only Vanni could bring on that look, inspiring such contempt, such hatred.

What had gotten into him? He felt out of control, possessed. Suddenly, he turned and ran from the room. Down the stairs he flew, out the double-wide front doors of the Keep. He thought he heard his name; he thought maybe his father was coming after him.

But no one followed and once outside the world fell back into step, green and damp and chattering with life on one side, and salty and misty with the ocean and its constant low grumble on the other.

He took deep, broken breaths as he moved across the path and down to the drive. He smelled the leftover dampness of the thunderstorm that had passed by earlier in the day, saw tulips and yellow lilies that lined the path, and white swirling clouds above.

Everything was a blur at first but slowly it began to clear. The beauty of a May day, the mystery and exhilaration of life. He turned slowly around, twice, hands still fisted, heart still rushing his blood.

Damion stood at the edge of the woods, book in one hand, his homemade butterfly net in the other. He hadn't used that toy in months, but today he must have noticed it was more beautiful than usual outside, and every living thing was awake. Damion had used the net only for catching the colorful creatures, never killing. After naming them and staring at them for hours on end in thick, glass canning jars, he always let them go.

"Vanni!" Damion turned, graceful as a deer.

Vanni glanced away, ignoring him.

"Vanni, hey…was Andreas very mad when you asked him if I could go to the ball?" Damion called.

"Just leave me alone you little imp." Vanni strode down the path and past Damion, heading straight into the woods. He hoped Damion would get the message and not follow. When he didn't hear any footsteps behind him, he let out a long breath.

Silent, still quivering inside, Vanni found a good tree, properly aged and green at the edges, and lifted himself up a few feet on the thicker, lower branches.

Damion came into the clearing below, watching him, eyes big and solemn.

Vanni reached up to the younger branches, found what he was looking for, grabbed and yanked. The branch, thick as his forefinger, tore free, leaving a white scar on the tree trunk. It was littered with stems and leaves. He sat there quietly picking them off.

Damion dropped his net and his book. He crossed his arms, staring up, hugging himself.

Vanni jumped down and moved past Damion so quickly his arm bumped him, shoving him aside. Damion stumbled meekly. In his peripheral vision he saw the boy's eyes get even bigger.

Rapidly, before he changed his mind, Vanni strode into the Keep.

If Damion followed him now, he didn't notice. Or care.

He entered his father's study again. Andreas was at his writing desk. He looked up, eyebrows raised.

Vanni gently set the green, narrow branch on his desk. Without looking at his father, he turned around, and began to unbutton his white shirt.

He heard the chair squeak back on the hardwood floor as the duke stood. Andreas's footsteps rounded the desk. The white shirt pooled at Vanni's feet and his heart thrummed like the ocean crescendo outside.

He was too old for this. But he promised himself he would never close his eyes. He would stand straight and tall.

But as he felt the warmth of his father behind him and the air move just before he was struck, he winced.

The first blow took his breath. The branch was thin enough to have some bend to it; it would make a nice arc through the quiet, warm room.

The second blow, even harder, sent him to his knees. He scrambled not to fall on his chin and caught himself, palms down, as the third blow tinged his vision red. Feeling utterly weak, stupid, useless, he broke his promise to himself and closed his eyes.

At the seventh blow, he stopped counting. His mind whirled. Dizzied. Blackened. There was a mineral scent on the air. Salt on his tongue. He took a deep breath, stayed quiet.

The beating stopped.

Andreas's voice came into his brain as if from some far, distant land. "Leave now. Go and think about your behavior."

Whenever he was beaten by his father, Jessie was never around. He wondered if she even knew. Usually, she stood up for him to Andreas when they argued over the dinner table. But this—he had had to endure it his whole life.

Vanni fell forward once, off-balance, as he tried to stand. His back blazed, skin on fire. When he was on his feet again he did not turn to look at his father. He bent slightly, feeling pain with every movement, and retrieved his shirt from the floor.

He wanted to say he was sorry, but he wasn't. He wanted to look back, beg forgiveness, and hope once again for any approval in Andreas's eyes, even love.

He could not do it.

Clamping down on nausea, pain and a deep devastation at the notion that his own father truly hated him, Vanni hurried from the room.

Damion was in the hall hunched, waiting, his shiny, black hair falling forward and hiding his eyes. He stepped toward him, reaching out.

Vanni side-stepped. "Get away!" he hissed.

He practically ran up the stairway, not looking back. When he got to his room he slammed the heavy door and bolted it. He threw his shirt hard against the far wall, then dropped face-front onto his bed.

He lay like that for a long time, feeling the spring air from his open balcony doors against his scoured skin. At first the pain drew him up and away from his identity, separating him from everything the Earth contained. Later, as the pain became a sting burning him, he curled into himself. He began to analyze it, rocking it inside his mind, taking it all in and using it to fill in all the cracks and crevices of his rage, his frustration, his youthful but unfulfilled desires.

He wanted to break the world open like an egg and drink its very soul. He wanted Damion to have the same. What in hell was wrong with that?

Finally he pulled a blanket up and fell asleep.

*

He woke to darkness. Dim lantern-light from his ever present oil lamp by the door reflected light against his bedroom's thin, silk day-curtains. He could tell by the sounds of the Keep, the silence, and the way the hallways and the rooms seemed to hold back air, that he'd missed dinner.

He got up and put on a clean shirt. He winced only once as he brought the material forward and over his shoulders.

When he went to the balcony and looked out over the shadowy sea, he saw a clear sky with stars. Hands propped on the cold rail, he wondered why Andreas kept him and Damion so close to home. Seeing the people at the ball made him realize a whole world existed not so far away. And his father had denied it to him.

A soft knock came at his door.

He moved to the entrance to unbolt it.

Damion stood in the hall, fist raised as if to knock again. The look on his face was resolute, almost stern.

"What?" Vanni's voice came out a harsh croak.

"I know what happened with Andreas was about me going to ball. I don't need to go. I don't even want to, really. Why do you fight him?"

Vanni's temper surged. "You don't know anything."

Damion shrugged, walked past him into the room and plopped on his bed. He looked up at Vanni, darkly beautiful, innocent.

"Hey!" Vanni closed the door behind him. "Get off my bed. How many times do I have to say you're too old for that now?"

Damion ignored him, propped a pillow behind him and drew his legs up, stretching out.

Vanni said, "What do you want?"

"Nothin'." Damion shrugged again.

Vanni rubbed at his forehead. His head ached. His stomach growled.

36

"You missed dinner," Damion stated.

"So?"

"There are leftovers. I'll go sit with you in the kitchen if you want to eat."

"Maybe later."

Damion glanced away, then started picking at a broken thumbnail. "Are you—are you all right?"

"Sure I am."

Damion chewed on his lip, blinked upward. "I hate him for doing that to you."

"No you don't. Besides, he loves *you*. That should make you feel just fine."

"No. It doesn't. Because of the way he treats you, it doesn't at all."

Vanni sat on the foot of the bed and pulled his legs up. "What do you know about anything anyway?"

"I'm almost sixteen. I know a lot. I observe a lot."

Vanni snickered. "Yeah? Tell me something I don't know."

Damion scowled. "I know that Andreas talks to my mother a lot about things they don't want us to know about."

"Like what?"

"Like marauders and stuff."

"I know all about that. He's always been paranoid. For his family. For us. Like there are monsters in the woods, or something."

"Well, we believed in sea-witches once."

"We were children!"

Damion gave him a half-smile. "You had me believing. I even thought I saw one once, out my window. During a storm. I never told you because I thought you'd get scared."

"Me? Scared?" Vanni made sound of disgust. But Vanni remembered the time he'd seen a figure dragging something heavy across the shoreline, then disappearing. He never knew Damion had seen something like it as well. "Well, you can see lots of strange things during storms. It doesn't make them real." But he could never quite get the image of that shadow on the beach out of his mind.

"Well, anyway, I'm sorry Andreas hurt you again."

Vanni bowed his head and stared at his knees.

"I don't need to go to the ball, Vanni," Damion whispered.

"If you aren't going, then I won't go, either."

"That's not fair to you."

Vanni said, voice a little softer now, "I'm hungry. Come downstairs and sit with me while I eat?"

"Sure!" Damion jumped up and was at the door before Vanni stood. He opened it and they clattered out into the hall.

"Tevi made fried fish. And there's fresh apple pie," Damion said.

Vanni followed him into the hall. "Did she boil enough water to dump you into a bath, too?" he asked.

Damion spun, looking down at himself. "I washed my face before dinner."

"Well, you missed a few spots." He wrinkled his nose. "And what's that smell? All that butterfly hunting in the woods made you into a mess."

"Do I really stink?"

Vanni huffed. "You always stink." *Of lavender. Of sugar.*

Damion laughed. "Do not!"

"Do too."

"Do not!"

"Do too."

They argued like that all the way down to the kitchen.

Chapter Six

Two years passed before Vanni went to another ball. He assuaged his restlessness to see the world by exerting himself more physically about the Keep. He didn't care if he was an earl. He asserted himself with the servants, helping them with household repairs, gardening, and even made them teach him how to cook. In good weather he ran along the beach in the mornings and in the afternoons up into the forest paths that shone with green-gold life. He didn't care that he was an earl; he needed to do something other than sitting around waiting for his life to happen.

He spent some of his time playing board games with Damion, but Damion was growing up fast as well. Though Damion wasn't the duke's real son, Andreas had taken him under his wing and Damion learned accounting and other more elite and officious things. Sometimes Vanni still had anger for how his father preferred Damion, but most of the time he was proud of the younger boy.

It had become much rarer now for Vanni to find Damion taking up space in his bed. He'd said it over and over to him. "You're too old to be sleeping with me!" Maybe the thousandth time he'd said it had sunk in. He enjoyed his privacy, and felt vindicated as an adult at long last. But a smattering of disappointment coursed through him, for he missed Damion's presence at night. His bed felt too empty, too cold.

Though the fancy invitations with gold embossed lettering and lacy edges poured in, he refused to go until the duke allowed Damion to attend with him.

Most of the time the duke remained silent when Vanni refused the offers to the parties. But a new summer was approaching. Life was chaotic and frantic and loud all outside the Keep. It was passing them by.

One day, Andreas said to Vanni, "You are old enough to find a wife now. I insist you go to the next ball held by Lord Durant. I know him and his father. They are upstanding citizens."

"Damion—"

"I don't want to hear it." Andreas held up his hand. "But Damion's birthday is coming up next month and he will be seventeen. So I will allow it."

Vanni could not believe his father's words. His heart leapt up. "I'll go tell him now!"

At long last they were both men of the realm. They would soon be coming into their own. What that future might look like, Vanni could not know. But he was excited for it. And so so ready.

*

The night before the ball, Vanni had a disturbing dream.

He was standing outside the Keep on a clear night looking up. The stars scintillated. The sounds of the sea were soft murmurs. The breeze pushed gently through his hair, summer-dusted, the scent a mix of lilies and salt.

He should have felt safe. But he knew he was not alone.

As if in a trance, he walked toward the dark and silent woods, straying from the path, heading deeper into the twisting shadows. Dark shapes seemed to swoop toward him, then retreat. He kept squinting, trying to see his way better, trying to figure out if he was going in the correct direction. But toward where?

Up ahead he saw a blue glow in a little clearing. It glimmered, wavering like a ghost in his vision. Night drenched him; black-leafed branches stitched the air. The luminescent glow drew closer, rippling like a sail.

40

Vanni felt as if he weighed nothing, almost floating, his skin prickling all over. The breath of the forest blew cool against his hot face.

As he passed the trunk of an ancient tree, a boy stepped into view, eyes dark as the northern hills at dusk, hair the color of wild blackthorn.

"Damion?"

All he wore were black trousers. He was barefoot. He stared straight at Vanni.

Confused, Vanni said, "Hey. Were you lost? What…?"

His voice faltered as Damion opened his mouth. White sharp teeth flashed in the dimness. All the black leaves started to fall as the boy's mouth opened wider and he lunged.

As Damion leaped through the air toward him, Vanni put up his hands and jumped to the side. Damion vanished.

The dream spun and Vanni had a sense of falling. When the world righted itself again, he no longer stood in the dark wood, but on the shore of the sea below the Keep.

The crescent moon had begun to dip into the ocean like a fisherman's dangling hook. The waters were dark and fathomless, except for the edges of the waves that sparked white as they tossed themselves upon the sandy beach.

As he often did in dreams, Vanni kept trying to get back to the landscape he'd just left. Back to Damion. Where was he? Why was he barefoot and wearing no shirt? And more importantly, what was wrong with his teeth?

"Damion!" he called.

The sea winds took his voice and silenced it. He opened his mouth again and nothing came out.

A wave crashed closer to shore than the others and water scrambled up fast, swirling about his booted feet higher and higher. He stepped back, slogging through the churning liquid. When the wave receded a huge knot of kelp caught and stayed upon the damp sand, its limbs glistening.

Limbs?

Vanni stepped back again, realizing that what he was seeing was not kelp. It had arms that moved at its sides, and a long torso. Something flapped against the leftover puddles of water. It had flukes. A tail.

Was this a sea-witch?

As the thing sat up, the top half looked almost human. What looked like seaweed were actually tangles of hair—or something like hair—dangling back from its head. In silhouette, the creature looked made of shadow. But Vanni could make out a round face, too, and eyes, and a mouth.

The tail smacked the sand again, a loud thump.

Then the voice came into his head, softly signing its words.

"You," the sea-witch said. Listening to it was like trying to hear an echo. "I would tell you to turn away and never return to this sea land, this Keep. But you will not obey. So I will say this: Giovanni of Cliffside Keep, your truth will always reside in your heart. You will only lose yourself if you turn away from it."

"What truth?"

"The center of your pain. The center of your soul. For good or ill, it will always be your truth in the end."

"I don't understand. Who are you?"

"Your future is as vast as this briny main. Even as you walk the day, you will not be one with it. This is how it will be. And for Damion as well, whom you will hate equal to your love for him. It cannot be unwoven. The fabric is already set."

Its words made little sense. The beautiful voice made them sound like a foreign lullaby forcing Vanni to hear it all on another level. Something was going to happen. Something tremendous.

But the sea-witch was right. He could not obey its warning, if that's what it was. Vanni could never abandon Damion, or the place where he and Damion had grown up. The Keep, the villages, the beach and the endless forest.

Suddenly he thought of them as his, places where he could recapture himself if he ever became lost. When he found himself too far adrift, alone and aching, this would be the place he always called home.

"I am sorry," the sea-witch said. "There is little I can do. But later I will tell you a secret and maybe it will help keep your heart from growing colder."

He felt a little cold already, actually.

"What secret?" he asked.

"A sea-witch has many talents." It smiled. "We will meet again. Good-bye, Vanni."

"Wait! Wait..." The creature faded right in front of his eyes as if it had never really been there at all. All around him the ocean whispered and moaned. The salt-wind ruffled his hair. The stars began to move in odd, chaotic patterns.

To the night falling all around him, he said aloud, "Sea-witches are real?"

When he opened his eyes again, Damion was beside him in his bed staring at him. Damion had not come into his room for months now. But tonight of all nights, there he was.

Damion's gaze was still and his eyes full in the faintly wavering light of the oil lamp. He behaved as if it were normal for him to watch Vanni sleep. Vanni who was nineteen going on twenty. A man.

"What do you mean sea-witches are real?" Damion asked.

Vanni caught his breath as the dream began to fade.

"What the hell are you doing in my room?"

"I couldn't sleep."

"Idiot." Vanni turned over, facing away from him, and never answered his question. But secretly, he was pleased. So very, very pleased. His bed wasn't so empty now. His heart felt more whole.

Chapter Seven

Lady Cecilia was at Lord Durant's ball. After two years, she looked more grown up but was still unmarried. She recognized Vanni immediately as he and Damion entered the mansion.

Vanni was introduced again as "The Earl Giovanni of Cliffside Keep."

When it came to Damion, the butler hesitated. Finally, he grudgingly said, "Master Damion of Cliffside Keep."

Damion was a vision in his long-tailed red velvet coat, ruffled white shirt and tight black trousers with knee-high boots. His shiny, midnight hair was held back in a tight braid. With his high cheekbones, clear dark eyes, and graceful, sylph-like mannerisms, he took center attention. He might not have been a lord but he had looks to rival any duke, earl, viscount, or even a prince.

Vanni felt a surge of jealousy when dozens of pairs of eyes, both male and female, followed Damion's descent down the marble staircase and into the foyer that led to the vast ballroom. It wasn't jealousy because Vanni wanted the attention for himself. Vanni got almost as much attention just for being the duke's son. No. Vanni realized, not without some guilt, it was because somewhere inside him he felt that Damion was *his*. And what was his he did not like to share with anyone but Damion himself.

It was idiotic to be feeling that, he told himself. Damion was almost a man. He would forge a path into his own life. Vanni had no right to hold him back from that.

Striding forward, Damion in his wake, Vanni took the hand of Lady Cecilia and lightly kissed the skin near her wrist.

"A pleasure to see you again, my Lady."

She curtseyed with her hand still resting in Vanni's palm, then turned. "This must be your little brother?"

"He is not my brother."

"But we are *like* brothers," Damion said, moving forward to bow to the lady.

"We've grown up together as the best of friends," Vanni finished.

"'Tis a pleasure to finally meet you."

The ballroom was all glitter and candles and a hundred lamps making everything bright as day. Lavish buffets holding mountains of food sat at one end. Waiters brought gold metal trays through the crowd, offering wine and punch.

The room smelled of a mingling of sweets and meats, fancy powders and cologne, alcohol and human sweat. People chatted in corners, or danced to the music. Scarves and tails and petticoats flew by on bodies in motion.

Vanni grabbed a waiter with a fancy tray and handed a glass of wine to Cecilia and another to Damion, before taking one for himself.

For a moment, he could not take his eyes off Damion. He glowed. His gaze darted about the huge room, seeming to miss nothing. When his attention finally settled on Vanni and caught him staring, Damion gave him a big smile and mouthed silently, "Thank you."

Vanni looked at him questioningly. Then shrugged. He knew Damion was thanking him for pushing the duke until Andreas finally allowed Vanni to bring him along. And maybe Damion was also thanking him for waiting to go to any more parties until Damion was old enough so they could embark upon the world together.

Lady Cecilia seemed at ease escorting two young men about the ball. Though it wasn't her house, or her ball like the first one Vanni attended, she behaved as if it was. She knew everyone. She conducted herself as if she was in charge.

After she introduced them both to dozens of people, she asked Vanni to dance.

Vanni looked at Damion, not wanting to leave him alone.

Damion said, "Don't worry about me. I'm famished after that long carriage ride. I'm going to investigate the food offerings."

Vanni nodded. But as he watched, before Damion could get half-way to the buffets, he was surrounded by young people their own age, smiling and laughing. He overheard a barrage of questions. "How old are you?" "What's it like at the Keep?" "Don't you get lonely up there all alone?"

Satisfied that Damion would be entertained, Vanni led Cecilia to the dance floor.

It was a lot of fun, and the wine had gone to his head. But still, Vanni had the thought that something was missing. Cecilia was lovely and friendly, but he expected to feel more for her. A heat on his skin. Or a shiver in his loins. Instead, just like two years ago, he was enjoying her as an entertaining friend.

After two more dances, Cecilia decided to stop for refreshment. Vanni snagged them each a glass of wine and escorted her toward the buffet table.

By this time, he'd lost track of Damion. It shouldn't have bothered him in the least, but he felt a pang in his gut anyway. Damion was his responsibility. And again came the odd feeling that he didn't want to share him with the world.

He scanned the vast area, peering over the heads of dancing people, gaze stopping at every brunet he saw. Suddenly, his eyes settled on a trim, exquisitely poised figure at the end of the buffet.

Dark-haired, male, the man looked to be in his mid to late twenties. Startlingly handsome, he stood so still he looked like a statue at first glance. Shoulders back. Chin up. Legs a foot apart, one slightly forward of the other. He had a neat waist, slim hips, and wore the purples and golds of a higher lord. His wavy dark brown hair was pulled back into a black

46

bow. He stared off toward the back of the ballroom, gaze intent, almost predatory.

Vanni said to Cecilia, "Who's that man over there?"

"Where?"

Vanni nodded to the buffet.

Cecilia let out a puff of air. "Oh. That's Lord Neverelle. He's very standoffish and arrogant. He called my friend Daniela a flibbertigibbet at the last ball. And at Lady Serina's birthday party, he called *me* a busybody. And he's even worse to the boys. Calls them names I can't repeat. He comes to all the events around here. He's very rich but he's a little like your father, he never holds big parties of his own."

"Why does he come?"

"He comes to watch the people, I guess. Sometimes he picks a pretty girl to dance with. He moves across the floor like a breeze. He knows every dance. But *I'd* never dance with him if he did ask. He's far too surly!"

Vanni watched the man, assessing him. Something about him made his skin prickle as if in a warning. At the same time, a gentle fluttering tickled deep inside his stomach. The lord's gaze was intent, fixed. Vanni scanned the area to see what he was looking at.

When he found it, his blood surged up hot. Fierce.

Damion stood across the room near a glistening fountain talking with a group of two boys and one girl. He definitely stood out. Unique and darkly beautiful. Even Vanni's heart beat in his throat to look at him.

To see Lord Neverelle stare at him was like watching a panther gaze at a raven.

Beside him, Cecilia gave a short laugh. "Seems your brother…um… I mean your friend from the Keep has drawn Lord Neverelle's attention tonight."

"Uhhh, yeah?" He drew his reply out, voice deepening with displeasure.

"Pay it no mind," Cecilia said.

"Well, what do you think his agenda is?"

Shrugging, Cecilia said, "I don't know. The girls he's danced with and insulted the least say he's exceptional. Makes them almost giddy just with the lightest touch. But later on, even if they invite him for a walk or a meal, he does not call on them again."

"Does he have male friends?"

She shook her head. "Lord Percy told me he and Lord Neverelle shared a carriage home once from a party. Lord Neverelle talked to him of all sorts of interesting things, and Lord Percy thought they might become friends. But after that, they never spoke again except in formal greeting."

"He doesn't make any attachments?" Vanni asked.

"Not that I know about. It's as if the way he socializes is like trying on clothes and none of them fit. So he casts them aside and looks for more."

"Does he live alone?"

She nodded. "Yes, but he has plenty of servants and such. They say he's very wealthy but really not even my father knows where he comes from. Maybe you should ask your father the duke about him."

"I will."

Throughout the evening, Vanni danced and socialized as any proper earl, but he always kept one eye on Damion and Lord Neverelle. Once, Damion accepted an invitation to dance with a pretty young girl with auburn ringlets. As Vanni watched him, he noted that Damion never missed a step. He behaved quite a bit more mature than his seventeen years.

He observed that Lord Neverelle watched Damion dance as well. Right at mid-point, Neverelle offered his hand to a passing young woman who took it right up without a word and without any expression on her face. He danced her to the ballroom floor and made his way toward Damion.

When they were side by side, Damion looked up at the lord. And smiled. They both spun their partners gracefully, but their eyes were only on each other.

Then Vanni saw Lord Neverelle pass close by Damion with his partner and lean into him. His lips moved briefly right by Damion's ear. Damion's cheeks became rosy. His lips parted. His smile stayed.

All of Vanni's muscles tensed. His fingers curled into fists. What had that man said to Damion? He had no right.

But then again— Vanni had no hold over Damion except to make sure he was safe. He'd brought him to the ball to make new friends. To see the world. Why should he care if some mysterious lord said two words to him?

When the dance ended, Damion left the dance floor in tandem with Neverelle and his partner. Vanni started to head their way at the same time Cecilia said, "Let's go back out on the floor."

Taught to be a gentleman, but not wanting to lose sight of Damion, Vanni hesitated.

Cecilia's eyelids closed half-way. "You shouldn't worry about Damion so much. You've barely taken your eyes off him all night. It makes me feel a little left out."

"They're headed to the buffet. Let's go join them."

"But I wanted to dance."

Vanni said, "We will." He tugged her by the elbow and led her toward the food.

"Oh, all right."

Damion, Neverelle and the two young women now accompanying them were still together. Neverelle kept a grip on his dance partner's arm, but edged closer to Damion.

Vanni walked boldly up to Lord Neverelle and said, "Hello. I believe we have not been introduced."

Neverelle looked him up and down, taking his time. His deep eyes glistened, and that's when Vanni noticed they weren't black but the darkest of blues. Like the sea at night. Or during a storm.

As Vanni dropped Cecilia's elbow, she gripped his wrist. He ignored her.

"It is true," Neverelle said. "We have not." His voice was like a slow-moving wind, and seemed to encompass Vanni with sound and words combined.

They both stood about the same height, gazes locked. Waiting. Vanni could feel a strange pull between them, like a competition. A challenge.

Neverelle was mesmerizing. Skin like flawless porcelain painted gold, not a hint of a shadowy beard, and so smooth it seemed there were no pores. He almost did not look real. He was perfectly formed, from his straight jaw and nose to his narrow waist and hips. Lean thigh muscles stretched against his tight black pants. Perfect pink lips met in a straight line showing no emotion. And something was missing from the eyes. They communicated a vast boredom, and a lack of any curiosity. Slowly they raked over Vanni. The eye muscles contracted a bit sleepily.

While to Vanni's mind Damion's beauty outshone this strange man's looks, it was not by much, and mostly because Neverelle looked about as jaded, spoiled and sour as one could be. It was almost unattractive. Almost.

"Very well, then," Neverelle finally said. "Lord Neverelle." He held out his hand lazily, almost as if he could not be bothered, the lace of his sleeve riding along his wrist, showing the edge of a sparkling ruby embedded in a silver cuff.

With his free hand, Vanni met Neverelle's grasp. "Earl Giovanni of Cliffside Keep."

They shook briefly, then Neverelle turned away as if he'd already forgotten Vanni.

Damion, who was watching the entire exchange with wide eyes, became the center of Neverelle's attention again.

Neverelle said to him, "What we began to discuss earlier should be finished in private."

Damion turned to look at Vanni.

Vanni frowned at him, then said to Neverelle, "I'm his chaperone. He's under eighteen."

Mildly irritated, but not turning to address Vanni, Neverelle said, "I have suggested nothing untoward."

"I'll come along, then," Vanni said.

"It's all right. I have no secrets from Vanni," Damion said, always the one to smooth over uncomfortable situations. Which was the very reason Vanni did not want him to go off alone with Neverelle.

Damion had a penchant for letting others take the lead, following without question, giving in. Vanni had always understood that about him, even liked it, but he did not trust others not to take advantage of his beautifully angelic not-brother.

This was Damion's first ball. Neither of them had been about in the villages, or had close friends other than each other. Vanni was not going to trust any of these people at this ball too easily, or too quickly. Especially Lord Neverelle, who made the hair stand up on the back of Vanni's neck.

"What is your definition of 'not untoward'," Vanni asked.

"I asked him to go for a walk in the gardens. I wanted to talk to him about his family... privately."

"I'm his family," Vanni said. His face heated slightly as he realized the three women were staring at him as if he were being rude.

A slight curve came to the left side of Neverelle's mouth. "You aren't, though. Not really."

A slow rage came into Vanni through his solar plexus, up and over his whole body.

Damion stepped forward then, touching Vanni lightly on his sleeve. "Let's all go for a walk in the gardens, then. The six of us."

The women nodded.

Cecilia said, "Yes, that would be nice, I think. I could use some fresh air."

"Then we can talk away from all the music and the bright lights and the festivities," Damion added.

Neverelle gave a small sigh. "Very well, then."

The gardens were almost as noisy as the ball, with a thousand crickets chorusing the group as they walked along the shadowed pathway. Bright colored lanterns lit their way, hanging from tree branches. Leaves whispered in a breeze so light Vanni did not feel it.

The women grouped together behind the men, talking low, softly laughing. Vanni heard one of them —not Cecilia— say, "We are with the three most handsome men of the night."

Vanni tried not to roll his eyes. Wasn't everyone beautiful at a ball? Next to Damion, Vanni sometimes felt awkward and ungraceful. He didn't think of himself as lovely, but others seemed to. He'd only been to two balls now in his entire life, and more people than he could count had complimented him. And Damion? Well, Damion had always stared at him adoringly since the boy was eight years old.

At first, nothing was said between the three of them— Vanni, Damion and Neverelle.

Finally, Damion filled the silence between them. "I love this garden. It's better than the one at the Keep. I smell jasmine, I think. And lily-of-the-valley."

An eight-foot wall surrounded the huge gardens, and latticework arched overhead. It kept them from seeing the moon and stars, as did the lanterns that lit their way.

Vanni had an urge to go further, beyond the wall and into the night.

Where that thought had come from, he wasn't sure. He certainly had not traveled all this way to abandon the party, his dance partner, and Damion. Still, strange thoughts and feelings kept coming into him.

He saw the night-blooming flowers, and the lights, and the trees, but then he saw them weathered and bent, old and rotted.

The noises of crickets and other night-life, including the distant hoot of an owl gave him a sense emptiness and longing. He'd felt those things before when looking at the sea at night, and the stars, but not with such an intense and sudden pain.

An image of the sea-witch from his dream the previous night came back to him. All shadowed and gleaming, the huge tail thumping the wet beach. It had been a male sea-witch, for the chest had been flat, dark and bare. His hair like sea-weed bundled about his head in twists and forever-knots. He'd smelled of brine and fish and salt. And magic.

As Vanni thought that word *magic,* Neverelle stopped and turned abruptly to stare at him. "What did you say?" he asked.

"I did not speak," Vanni replied, confused. "So, what did you want to talk to Damion about?"

The girls had found a well-lit alcove with a pretty white bench.

"We're going to sit and rest for a moment," Cecilia called out.

"We'll just circle round and come back for you, then," Vanni said.

As the three of them moved forward, Neverelle said, "What I wanted to tell Damion does not concern you."

As quickly as the words entered Vanni's mind, in the next instant he found himself leaning against the rough bark of an oak, watching a spider spin its web across two low branches. How he'd gotten there, he didn't know.

And Damion and Neverelle were nowhere in sight.

Chapter Eight

Vanni pushed himself away from the tree trunk, brushing his hands on the outsides of his thighs. The spider in its web bobbed and weaved, making its beautiful trap.

Down the lamp-lit path, some distance, he heard the girls' laughter.

He glanced ahead where the path curved and saw and heard no one. He moved forward, slightly unsteady. Had he drunk too much wine? Just a moment ago, he felt fine.

What had just happened? And where were Damion and Neverelle?

He moved down the pathway where he thought they might have gone. He did not have to go very far before he saw two shadows by a dimly lit fountain. They stood very close together.

As Vanni approached them, he saw Neverelle's head come up as if he had just been resting it upon Damion's shoulder.

He heard Damion say, softly gasping, "Thank you! Thank you so much."

Neverelle replied, "I thought you might like to know. You get your charm from him, and your beauty."

In silhouette, Neverelle's hand lifted to Damion's cheek and long fingers gently brushed it.

Damion gave a soft chuckle, a sound Vanni knew he made when he was nervous, or unsure.

Damion said, "No, I don't think—"

"Never be coy or humble. Not with me." The voice came soft but insistent.

Vanni stomped his foot in the dirt to get their attention.

Damion turned his head rapidly.

Neverelle kept his gaze averted, but lifted a hand toward Vanni, fingers outstretched.

Vanni stopped in his tracks. He was overwhelmed with a sense of dislocation. A moment of dizziness confused him. His vision faded and he saw himself standing in a dark, empty room staring at an oval mirror.

His gold hair was puffed and powdered about his face and shoulders. He wore white ruffles and black trousers and boots. He stood tall, regal, quite handsome except for the blood that trailed in rivulets down his chin dotting his perfect shirt.

The scene whirled and spun and now he reclined naked upon plush blankets in a satin-canopied bed, his legs raised, another body entangled with his. Something long and hard pushed inside of him in his most intimate of places, so smooth, so arousing. There was a cloying scent of roses. The being on top of him groaned.

Vanni heard the sea outside the room answer in the same voice. All he could think was that he wanted to get away. At the same time, he wrapped his arms about the neck of his lover. When the being arched up showing him his face, Vanni saw Lord Neverelle staring down at him.

He heard the sea-witch from his dreams: *Your truth will always reside in your heart. The center of your pain. The center of your soul. For good or ill, it will always be your truth in the end.*

Lord Neverelle's voice said: *Sea-witches are not real!*

But the memory of the sea-witch's words brought Damion to the forefront of Vanni's mind. In a brief moment, he saw all versions of Damion from eight to seventeen. Smart. Loyal. Adoring. Handsome. Waking next to him so many mornings. So warm. So steadfast and true.

He snapped out of his daze and ran to them, shoving Damion back and behind him. "What in hell are you doing?"

Neverelle's dark brows rose. Chin up, he stepped back with the ease of someone who was difficult to startle.

"How did you break my *tempt*?"

"Your what?"

Neverelle shook his head, lips curved but not smiling. "Nothing. As you can see, everything is fine. We were simply admiring the fine marble statues of this fountain, your brother and I."

"He's not my brother," Vanni grumbled. He turned to Damion. "And anyway, why did you leave me?"

Damion looked thoroughly perplexed. He reached up and absently rubbed at the point where his shoulder curved into his neck. "You said you were fine and you wanted to stand under that oak for awhile, to breathe in its fine scent."

"I said no such thing."

Damion's brows furrowed together. His hand dropped.

Vanni wanted to look at Damion's neck but refrained, not wanting to embarrass him. What had Neverelle been up to?

Vanni reached for Damion's elbow. "Come on. We're going back inside."

"By all means," said Neverelle. "I could certainly use some more wine."

Together, the three of them walked toward where they had left their dance partners. Eventually, the girls joined them, laughing and talking along the way.

Vanni's heart would not stop racing. Something wasn't right here. And he longed to get Damion home.

*

Once more beneath the warmth of bright lights and feeling more secure after another glass of wine, Vanni finally relaxed.

But Damion still looked a little addled. His neatly pulled-back hair was mussed, strands waving in his face. And his gaze scanned nervously about the room.

While Cecelia chatted with more friends, and Neverelle pretended to ignore them, Vanni came up alongside Damion.

"Are you all right?"

56

Damion looked up at him with bright eyes. "Is the ball almost over?"

"It's getting late."

"Can we go, then?"

Vanni frowned. "Of course we can. Are you tired?"

Damion nodded his head, his smile a bit half-hearted. "I'm just suddenly quite sleepy."

"I'm sure there's a place you could lie down here."

"No. Home. Please."

"Too much wine?"

"I guess."

Vanni nodded. He didn't want to abandon Cecilia. He'd had fun with her. But after Neverelle's strangeness, he had a great urge to leave. Something was off. And now Damion seemed to be feeling unwell. This wasn't right at all.

They said their goodbyes. Both scanned the ballroom for Neverelle but he was nowhere to be found.

As they walked to their private carriage, Vanni said, "Did you have a good time?"

Damion nodded his head briskly. "Yes. Yes, I did!"

"Good."

The footman opened the door to the carriage. Vanni let Damion enter first, then jumped up and sat alongside him on the sumptuous, red leather couch within. The horses trotted down the drive and onto the darkened road.

Cliffside Keep was over an hour away. Vanni had an hour to find out what Neverelle had said to Damion, but when he turned to begin questioning him, Damion was already asleep, his head slowly sliding along the back of the couch before it came to rest upon Vanni's shoulder.

*

"Wake up. Damion, wake up!" Vanni tugged at Damion's arm.

57

As they exited the carriage, the footman helped them both.

When Damion landed on his feet, he swayed a bit.

Vanni whispered, "Hey, you didn't drink that much wine."

"I—I'm fine." He pulled away from Vanni.

The house was dark but for a few oil lamps flickering in the first floor windows. Behind them the dark woods fell away to blackness and hollowness echoing with the distant bark of a fox. From this vantage, he could not see the ocean, but he could hear its splashing waves, soft tonight, but never calm.

It was late. Even the crickets had gone to bed. One of the carriage horses whickered suddenly. Vanni felt the hairs creep up along the back of his neck.

"Let's get inside. Quickly."

Damion started to stumble when Vanni caught him by the arm and pulled him to the front steps.

"Let go of me!" Damion hissed.

"What's wrong with you?" Vanni asked.

"Nothing!"

But Damion followed, faster now. They took the stone steps two at a time.

Vanni yanked the heavy wooden door open. A guard stood in the foyer, welcoming them with merely the rise of an eyebrow. Still, it made Vanni instantly relieved. His muscles relaxed. His thoughts came more tempered now.

He wasn't sure what he was feeling. He was not normally afraid of the dark. That was Damion's territory. But he was breathing easier. That was good.

Damion stood in front of the closed front door, not moving, staring at the floor.

Concerned, Vanni walked back and stood facing him. "Are you coming?"

"Yes. Yes. I'm just tired." Damion lifted his face. His eyelids were half-closed. He looked paler than usual.

"All right then."

Together they mounted the stairs to their rooms on the third level.

The Keep echoed with the moans and whispers of the sea. Sometimes, when the fog rolled in, or it rained, the humid conditions made the walls and floors slick. To prevent people from slipping, rugs dotted the hallway every few feet cushioning their footsteps.

Every third sconce-light was lit but turned low. The shadows leaped and quivered all around them.

They came to Damion's door first. Vanni opened it for him. "Are you going to be all right?"

"Of course," Damion replied. Slipping inside his darkened room, he abruptly shut the door in Vanni's face.

Vanni blinked a few times, then shrugged. Damion was rarely moody, but tonight may have been a bit overwhelming for him. And what Neverelle had done—had that been a kiss? A first kiss. From a man. That was unexpected. And a big deal.

Vanni's jealousy rose, making his skin prickle. Damion had stated on more than one occasion he didn't like girls. Vanni didn't think much about that, except maybe Damion only said it because he hadn't met many women except for his own mother and the few stodgy friends the duke had as guests for dinner on occasion.

But if Damion really did like men, then this was a major event for him.

Vanni wanted to burst through that shut door now, demand details. He wanted to understand. More, he wanted to be a part of it. He wasn't sure how he could become part of it, but right now he felt rather left out.

Eventually, he forced himself to turn away and take the last few steps to his own room.

The servants had left his oil lamp lit by the door just as he liked it. Another oil lamp stood on the table by the bed, a warm bronze glow. He checked the first and it had enough oil to last the night.

No, he wasn't afraid of the dark, he always told himself. He just needed it to see in case he had to get up for the water closet.

Before undressing, he went to the balcony. The sea-view was smoky and ethereal. The ocean undulated. A stripe of golden moonlight broke it down the middle, glittering. The shore was a line of soft beige freckled with old seaweed. Behind the moon, the sky soared, black and diamond-filled.

Maybe Damion had been confused by the evening's events, but Vanni also had reason to be. He had lost himself on the garden path and he didn't know how or why that had happened. He had had visions. He did not have a fever or feel sick in any other way, so what could be the explanation? Had the wine been drugged?

But deep inside he knew the answer. All the strangeness had something to do with Lord Neverelle. That man was more than a rude snob as Cecilia had described him. His strangeness went deeper. He was definitely an enigma.

As Vanni readied himself for bed, pulling on his white dressing gown, he remembered quite suddenly something Neverelle had said.

*How did you break the **tempt**?*

What a strange word: *tempt*. Temptation. To be tempted. Or tempting. Like a lure, temptation put something in your path you desired. To bait you. To hook you.

Neverelle had accused Vanni of *breaking the **tempt***. Was that why he couldn't remember how he found himself standing beneath an old oak?

He climbed into his warm bed and turned down the oil lamp until it went out. Lying back, hands behind his head, he lay with his eyes open, wondering. His heart pounded a bit too rapidly. It was going to be difficult to get to sleep tonight.

Very quietly, he whispered to the air, "What are you? And why are you trying to take what is mine?"

Though he had been disturbed by last night's dream, now he wanted to dream of the sea-witch again.

"Tell me what to do," he murmured.

His first impulse was to keep Damion safe. But how could he do that? Damion would be his own man in a year's time.

"I need to know what to do." The black air swirled around him, silent.

He sat up, rearranging his blankets and pillows. He turned toward his door when he heard a soft thump.

Damion stood in his white gown just at the entryway to the room, surrounded by the aura of the coppery nightlight. He'd closed the door behind him.

Vanni started to smile, but that would not do. Instead, he rolled his eyes and sighed. "Come on."

Damion padded over to the bed and climbed in. "My neck hurts," he said.

"Well I can't very well see you in the dark, can I? Get up and bring the oil lamp over here."

Damion obeyed, climbing back under the covers and handing the lamp to Vanni.

Vanni said, "Tilt your head back."

Damion did, his dark hair falling like liquid along the back of his white gown.

Vanni held the lamp up. The shadow washed over Damion's face and neck. He held the collar of his gown down and to the side. His skin looked soft, without blemishes. But just at the crook of the neck, Vanni saw it. A line of pink, like a scar.

Vanni reached out and touched it. "There?" he asked.

Damion nodded vigorously.

"Did you ever bump yourself there? Or cut yourself?"

"No."

"Does it hurt when I touch it?"

"A little. More like a bruise."

"Well," Vanni said, "I don't see any bruising. I think you'll live."

"Thank you for looking." Damion leaned back in the bed, staring upward.

"Did Lord Neverelle kiss you there?"

Damion's eyes closed, the thick, long lashes fanning his cheeks. "No."

"But I thought I saw--"

"He didn't. I would remember that, don't you think?"

"Not necessarily. I don't remember how we got separated in the garden."

Damion's eyes opened, dark and deep. Vanni's heart leaped in his chest to look at him as he was right now, reclining in his bed, talking to him about his first adult foray into the world.

Controlling his reaction, he leaned behind Damion's head and set the lamp back on the nightstand. Its flame played along the contours of Damion's gown as if long fingers were pushing beneath the material on their way to doing lewd things.

Now where had that thought come from?

Vanni lay back. Both boys were quiet for awhile. It was Damion who broke the silence.

"I don't know if I want to go to anymore balls."

"Why not?"

"I don't know," said Damion.

"You had a good time. You told me."

"I did."

"And you know how to dance well. You never slipped or made a wrong turn. You made it look natural. Graceful."

The pillows shifted as Damion turned to look at him. "You're giving me a compliment?"

"Well—sure."

"You never do that."

"Of course I do." Vanni frowned. "You always do everything right. You're smart that way. I've always told you so."

"No. You haven't. I never knew you thought that about me."

"Idiot. You know very well I think it. You've bested me in all our studies, and you work for my father now. He never asked *me* to work in his study."

Damion fiddled with the hem of the top blanket that spread across them both. "But you never told me this before, that you were impressed or--. Why now? Tonight?"

Was it true? Had Vanni never paid Damion a single compliment? Ever? That seemed far-fetched. Certainly he had. But now all the memories he could conjure were ones where he'd teased Damion, laughed at his butterfly nets and stacks of books and ribbons for his hair. Or the nights he'd said, over and over, "Get out of my bed. You're too old to sleep here."

Had all the compliments he thought he'd said only ever been unspoken thoughts?

Vanni leaned back, crossing his arms. He did not look at Damion as he spoke. "You know you're amazing. You don't need me to tell you." He gave a sigh, making it loud and extra-dramatic. He added, "Idiot."

In a whisper, Damion replied, "It just—just means more from you."

Vanni huffed. "You don't need my approval." But deep inside, he wanted Damion to keep looking to him for leadership. For guidance. It made Vanni feel important. And more, it gave him a zing of pleasure every time Damion looked to him with hopeful eyes.

He didn't want it out of control, though. Because sometimes in his deepest, most secret thoughts that proprietary feeling made him want to do things to Damion. Unmentionable things. Controlling things. Naked things.

"So," he said, not wanting to think about that. "What did Neverelle want to tell you about your mother?"

"He said he knew her."

"How is that possible? He wouldn't have been grown up yet."

"He says he's thirty."

"Really? He looks a bit younger."

"He said his parents were friends with her. And with my father."

Vanni sat up. The covers came away from them both, bunching at their waists.

"Then why has your mother never invited him to dinner? Or maybe she doesn't want anyone who knew your father to meet her—um, my father." He thought about that for a moment. "Who was your father anyway? I thought you never knew him."

"I didn't. And my mother will tell me nothing about him. That's why when Lord Neverelle told me he wanted to talk to me about my mother, I was interested. I wanted to know what he knew." Damion scraped his hand over the covers back and forth. Nervous.

"What did he say?"

"That my father wanted to marry my mother after he found out she was carrying me. But that he died. My mother never told me that."

"He died?" Vanni frowned. He became instantly suspicious. Neverelle had had eyes on Damion from the start. He could tell him anything to get him alone in the gardens.

"Horribly. He was found in a gutter in North City. His throat was ripped out. That's probably why my mother never told me. Isn't that awful?" Damion's hand moved faster and faster, fingernails catching against the folds of the blanket.

Vanni reached out and grasped that hand, stilling it. "That's terrible. I'm sorry."

"I can't sleep, Vanni. I know you don't want me here, but I can't—Can I just stay here for tonight? Please?"

Why, Vanni wondered, would Neverelle tell Damion such a horrible story?

64

Vanni said, "It's all right. I never said I didn't want you here."

Damion snorted. "You always say that!"

"No. Just that you're too old now. We're both too old now."

In truth, Vanni would have loved sharing a room with Damion when they were younger. Damion was good company. Steadfast and true. The best friend he ever could have hoped for.

Softly, he said, "The best day of my life was when Father brought you to live here when you were eight."

"Really?"

"Yes. So now, shut up and go to sleep."

Damion settled back under the covers as Vanni lay back down.

When they were both still, Vanni muttered under his breath, "Idiot."

Chapter Nine

For the rest of the summer, neither Vanni nor Damion attended any more parties or balls.

The duke received piles of lacy and gold embossed invitations. It confused him when both boys said they would rather not go.

The duke took Vanni aside. "Did something happen at Lord Durant's ball?"

"No. Nothing. We both just found it rather boring. Maybe when we're both older, we'll go out more."

Andreas frowned. "You're old enough now. You need to find a wife."

"I will, Father. But maybe I just want one more summer as a child."

Andreas turned away. "You disappoint me."

Vanni felt a sting begin behind his eyes. Instantly, he thought of a dozen rude replies. He locked his teeth together keeping everything inside. Without a sound, he left the room.

Damion worked for the duke at least four days a week, so it was no surprise to find him in the dank, salt-scented hallway as he exited the study. By the look on his face, he'd heard every word.

With a soft smile, he said, "It's a beautiful day. Want to go out and throw the ball around?"

The sting in Vanni's eyes receded. "Sure."

Warm fingers met his palm as Damion took his hand.

*

Summer gave way to fall, and the ocean reflected the days in dark gold tones. More invitations to social events arrived every afternoon. Vanni and Damion declined them all.

They had their lives at the Keep, Damion working for the duke, and Vanni excelling at more physical activities. He helped rebuild outbuildings. He enjoyed long runs down the beach.

During free days and evenings, Vanni and Damion played games both outdoors and indoors. Croquet. And catch. Checkers and marbles and backgammon. They didn't act like boys on the cusp of adulthood. They enjoyed their freedoms as if they were children again.

The duke had put in tennis courts only a year before. They learned the game and played for hours until they collapsed. Damion looked particularly handsome all in white, the clothes loose but still showing off his slim frame. When he sweated, tendrils of his hair stuck to his forehead making him even more angelic.

They went to the beach often. Though the ocean was always too cold to swim in, they took off their shoes and waded in, racing little wavelets, shouting to the sky, and making footprints in the shining wet sand.

They didn't need anyone else.

For Vanni, it was as if his instinct was to preserve their innocence for as long as he could. Because it wouldn't—couldn't last.

Something waited. He could feel it more and more as each day passed. Something waited to emerge and disrupt their lives.

*

Vanni and Damion whiled away the long, cold winter hours. They read, played games, and laughed like boys before roaring fires. They indulged their appetites on solstice dessert foods: cider, iced cookies, apple cobbler.

The fishing villages supplied them with lobster, crab, salmon. The farming villages brought them grain, chickens, apples. Even in the dead of winter, when snow frosted the lanes, they always had fresh deliveries of food at the Keep. Despite the Keep's constant bluish coldness and echoing unused chambers on the upper floors of the tower, winter was a bacchanal of extravagance for them. Vanni and Damion were always warm and clean and full.

Damion still sneaked into Vanni's room at night. Sometimes they spent half the night reading stories aloud. Sometimes they just slept, practically in each other's arms.

Spring flourished, and the wind and sun warmed them, made their cheeks pink again, their hearts flushed and open.

For one year straight, Vanni had no nightmares.

Those were the happiest of times.

But when Damion turned eighteen, everything changed.

Vanni remembered that day clearly. Damion's birthday. He'd awakened more content than he could ever remember being.

Damion had already risen before dawn, so Vanni had his room to himself. He went to his secret hiding place and withdrew the special gift he'd ordered. A ribboned pack of charcoal pencils and a large artist's book full of empty pages ready and waiting for Damion's excellent drawings. He'd carved curlicues and leaves and Damion's name on all the wooden pencils. He'd written a short note to Damion on the first page of the book in his fanciest, floral handwriting.

Dear Damion:

Do not ever stop creating and dreaming.
You are my best friend.
Happy 18th birthday.

Giovanni (Vanni)

He wasn't the best at expressing his feelings, but Damion would understand.

Vanni did not sign the book with his title. Between the two of them, there were no titles, or secrets. No imbalances of power. They were just Damion and Vanni together. It was enough.

He brought his presents to his bedside and wrapped them together in a piece of velvet folded over and over. He used another ribbon to keep it all together.

He dressed quickly and went out onto his balcony to welcome the day.

The early morning mist made everything white and hazy. He smelled the familiar salt air from the sea, but upon it came something else. Another scent. One that made his skin feel suddenly cold with dread.

Smoke.

Forgetting the present, Vanni ran from his room and straight to the dining room.

The duke and Damion's mother were just sitting down to a plate of fresh eggs and sausage.

"Father, there's smoke on the wind."

Andreas looked up. "I thought I smelled something different from the usual ocean breeze. I'll see if the butler has received any messages." The duke got up and left the room.

Jessie said to Vanni, "You might as well sit and eat. There's nothing you can do until your father comes back to the table."

Vanni sat, picking at his fried eggs with a gold fork.

When the duke returned, Damion followed at his heels.

The duke announced, "There are no messages from any of the villages yet, but the scent is there. Faintly. If it is serious, we will learn of it soon. I've sent a man by horse down to the nearest village."

But of course it had to be serious. The scent would not travel this far if it wasn't. If it had come up over the forest, a small fire already out, the briny gusts and breezes that always rushed the Keep would have already blown the smoke clear.

Vanni met Damion's worried eyes. He gifted him a smile, remembering the day again.

"Happy birthday, Damion."

Damion grinned and took his seat opposite Vanni. "Thank you."

"I have a gift for you, but I left it in my room."

Jessie smiled. "Happy birthday, son. Oh my, my son is eighteen. The years have gone by so quickly!"

The duke nodded his own greeting. "Happy birthday. We have gifts for you, too. In the drawing room."

Just then, a servant entered the dining room with a tray of pitchers. The outer kitchen door must have been opened at the same time, for a strong draft stole in from outside, salt and smoke and cool mist, and rushed about them taking out the flames of the candles in the center of the table and knocking over a juice glass.

"Apologies, my lord," the servant said, quickly shutting the door. He set down the tray, then fumbled with matches from his pocket and leaned over the table to re-light the candelabrum.

For mid-summer—and Damion's birthday—the day was already too gray.

*

After the messenger had returned mid-morning, the duke had gone off in his private carriage, the newest and sleekest black one, to see firsthand the damage of the fire.

All the messenger could report was that one of the minor castles in the hills of one of the villages of the duke's realm had burnt to the ground during the night. The fire had spread to some acreage beyond the castle's grounds. Men were slowly getting it under control.

Vanni and Damion sat on the hard stone front steps, waiting.

Damion had his new artist's book and pencils beside him, but he wasn't drawing. He loved the gift, telling Vanni, "This is my favorite of all my gifts."

Vanni felt a warmth suffuse his entire body, for Damion had received a lot of lavish things from his mother and Vanni's father. A beautiful satin and brocade coat with a furred collar and gold fastenings. A newfangled fountain pen set carved of onyx, inlaid with gold. A ruby on a gold ring just like Vanni's to mark his ascent to manhood. And other things that were luxuries only a prince might have.

The duke had a lot of money, and he didn't go around gambling or drinking, so he didn't spend a lot. He could afford to keep his son and mistress's son in a princely manner.

The smoke did not get worse, but it did not dissipate quickly, either. It had a nut-scented, ashy flavor that coated the mouth and throat.

After a while, Vanni and Damion grew restless. They went for a walk on the beach. There, one could not smell the smoke at all. They threw a ball around for a while, then returned to the front of the Keep.

Back and forth, they threw the ball while the afternoon grew long.

Finally, in the distance, they heard it. The echoing clomp of horses' hooves. Carriage wheels on tight-packed gravel.

The ball fell to the green grass just to the left of the stone path that led to the Keep. It wasn't long before the carriage rounded the bend and they could see it heading for the drive.

Side by side, they stood by the steps and waited for the duke to return.

Vanni had a strange sort of knot in his gut.

The wooden wheels of the carriage clattered on the hard, dirt path. When the carriage stopped in front of them, the footman came around and opened the sleek, black doors.

Damion and Vanni approached the carriage. The first person to disembark was a young woman in a black and white servant's uniform.

"Greetings, ma'am." Vanni's manners made no distinction between people of class.

Behind her, a young man, also a servant, stepped down.

Both Vanni and Damion bowed and said, "Greetings."

The young man turned and helped another person from the carriage. This man was dressed in rich attire, all flashing belts and jewels, silks and velvets. His dark hair was done up in a braid much like Damion's. He tilted his head up, cool and regal, and squinted at the light as if it burned him.

It was Lord Neverelle!

Both Vanni and Damion took a step back.

He glanced at them casually, lips lifting in a smile. "What a nice reception. Two dashing young princes. You would not, by chance, be the sons of Duke Andreas of Cliffside Keep?"

"We've met before. You must remember," Vanni said boldly.

"Then we meet again. Lord Neverelle. But my friends call me Never, and I insist you do as well for I'm sure we shall become good friends."

He held out his hand.

Vanni hesitated. Before he could think what to do, Damion stepped forward and took his hand in his. "Welcome," he said. "Welcome to Cliffside Keep."

Behind him, the footman helped the duke from the coach. As he regained his balance, Andreas said, "I see you've met my son and foster son."

"Yes. I believe we all attended a ball together last summer."

"Father," said Vanni. "What is he doing here?"

"Well, as it turns out, Lord Neverelle's home is the very structure that burnt to the ground during the night. A complete loss. But the fire is under control now. It was almost out as we disembarked."

"Yes," Never put in. "We were glad to escape with our lives, my servants and I. It could have been far far worse if I had not had one of my bouts of insomnia and gone for a walk about the estate."

Andreas moved toward the doors. "Bad business all around. Nothing could be saved. But no worries. We have everything you need here. You are welcome to stay on as my guest here at the Keep until other arrangements can be made."

"My gratitude for your generosity." Never put his hands on the shoulders of his servants, indicating they should follow Andreas inside. "I only hope I can one day repay it."

"I am sorry for your loss," Damion said. Always the polite one.

Never turned his gaze toward Damion, who looked a bit lost and enamored at the same time. Vanni wanted to hit him, knock the silly look off his face.

If Never noticed Damion's daze at all, he didn't seem to mind. He lifted his hand toward him, knuckles up, then lowered it. Vanni could see the pink flush on Damion's jaw at the gesture.

As Never followed Andreas inside, he turned his head all the way around to smile at them again. Vanni could not recall him ever smiling at the ball.

"You're blushing," Vanni muttered.

Damion remained silent.

As Never moved up the steps, Vanni and Damion fell in step behind him.

That was when Vanni saw it. Never's hair was in a braid, yes, but the shorter parts were held back tidily with an unobtrusive comb. An abalone comb. An abalone comb exactly like the one Vanni had found in the sea-cave.

Vanni and Damion exchanged glances at the same time, their mouths open.

Vanni's heart skipped in an erratic rhythm. But no, it couldn't be the sea-witch comb. He and Damion had hidden that safely under the loose tile of Vanni's room. It had to be a copy. Or maybe that type of comb was common. Maybe lots of people had them.

"We'll check our hiding place later," Vanni whispered to him.

Damion's head bobbed up and down, eyes big.

Once inside the Keep's foyer, Never's manner continued in formal mode.

"Duke Andreas, we are in your debt, my servants and I. Thank you for taking us in. One day I will pay you back."

Vanni wanted to ask why a man so wealthy might only have two servants. But everyone was being so cordial. And, well, Never had just lost his home. Vanni held his tongue.

"There is no need to repay me, of course," Andreas replied. "You have suffered a terrible disaster."

Never lifted his chin and turned his head, as if speaking to air. "There are lots of disasters that happen to people. They don't get offered shelter by dukes."

"Yes, well." Andreas cleared his throat. "Though we have never met, my mistress has met you before. She has spoken of you in the past, very highly, naturally. So I do feel I know you. And she would never forgive me if I did not extend myself as a host to you."

"Indeed? And her name is?"

"Jessie—"

"Jessie from the City?"

Vanni's skin grew hot under his shirt. Never was lying to the Duke. Or omitting, which he'd been taught was pretty much the same thing. He very well knew Damion's mother was Jessie. He'd told Damion one year ago at the ball that he'd met her and that he had known Damion's real father.

Damion stared at Never, eyes still wide and dark. There was a flush expanding, just beneath his cheeks. His lips were slightly parted as though he was breathing a little faster than normal. His fists curled, uncurled. His good-natured half-smile turned to a full one. A look of adoration.

Vanni pressed his lips tight, watching him. Feeling betrayed. Which was stupid, as there was nothing to betray. And this was only a look. Only!

Just then, Jessie entered the foyer.

"Madame Jessica." Never bowed his head.

Jessie looked from Andreas to Never, blinking. "Lord Neverelle? It can't be."

"But it is. I am the victim of an unfortunate disaster."

"It is a pleasure to see you. I did not know you had moved from the City. You haven't aged a day in eighteen years! You must be in your forties by now."

"Prolonged youth is inherited. My father saw not a gray hair on his head until he was sixty," Never replied.

But with Never's smooth face and lean frame, there was no way he could be in his forties yet. Age showed in the hands as well, and when Vanni looked at Never's fingers and the backs of his wrists, they were fine and smooth as a sculpture. Jessie had to be mistaken.

"I am pleased you are safe," Jessie said. "You are welcome here."

"Thank you."

Vanni watched this all play out like some strange game. When he'd awoken that morning, he'd never expected the day to turn out like this.

Andreas ordered servants to escort Never and his servants to their rooms.

As Never and his entourage left for the stairs, Andreas turned to Vanni. "Now you boys don't be bothering him with questions. Allow him to settle in and rest."

"We won't." Vanni raised an eyebrow.

When they were alone, Vanni turned to Damion. "He can't be in his forties."

"I know." Damion let the words out fast, as if he'd been holding his breath the whole time.

"I'm not sure I like it that he's here."

"He's kind of amazing, though. It will make the rest of the summer less boring."

"I know you like him. He's your first kiss."

"I told you he never kissed me."

"I saw it."

Damion scrunched up his mouth and glared.

"He left a scratch on your neck. Don't you remember?"

"You're just as intrigued," Damion countered. "Be honest."

"Well, he's not my type if that's what you're asking."

Damion smirked. "He's definitely my type."

They'd rarely talked this way, about secret wishes, or fantasy infatuations. It was as if the friendship they had now as young men was more precarious than it had been in childhood, and could not withstand any jerky motions. It was perfectly balanced, but fragile. For they both knew that adulthood brought with it adult desires and drives, and all of that threatened to break them apart. Any future path that directed them away from each other seemed too painful to contemplate. They were bonded. Yet their love remained platonic.

For Vanni, it was complicated. What he currently had with Damion was perfect. If it wasn't broken, he didn't feel the need to change it. Also, his take-charge nature and feelings of ownership toward Damion made him afraid Damion would reject him outright. For who would want a bossy lover?

He decided Damion must have had similar thoughts about their closeness so as never to pressure Vanni. They rarely talked about sex or future wives. And only a few times had Damion stated he didn't like women "in that way." Damion would close himself off after making such confessions, sometimes laughing it away. He didn't want to talk about such things, and Vanni respected that, for though he'd enjoyed looking at the women he'd met, he had private thoughts about men as well.

76

And about Damion.

But he shut that down because, again, the way he felt sometimes, a bit too protective, a bit too much as if Damion somehow *belonged* to him, as if he wanted to tell him that he had to do everything Vanni said, made him sure Damion would tell him, with that sweet smile of his, to fuck off.

Plus, Damion was too special to him. He deserved to be like the butterflies he'd once chased, beautiful and free. He should be allowed to choose. Allowed to follow the wind if that was his penchant.

Vanni finally muttered, kicking at the rug by the door. "I know he's your type." He did not look at Damion as he spoke.

He felt a soft hand at his elbow and turned. Damion was staring at him intently. Touching him.

"And maybe he's yours, too, just a little? Or you wouldn't be bringing it all up again, how you think he kissed me, how you think he had ulterior motives in the garden at the ball."

But something strange and mysterious *had* happened at that ball. And it had been more than a kiss.

"Well," Vanni said, giving him a private smile. "Something more might be going on. He's wearing an abalone comb. Just like that one I found so many years ago."

"We should go get it right now. I have this urge to make sure it's still where we hid it."

"Yes." Vanni led the way upstairs, trying not to think how strange it might be if the comb was missing.

However, when they lifted the tile from the floor in Vanni's room and unfolded the silk handkerchief they had wrapped the comb in, there it was, shiny and glimmering with rainbows, perfect and new like it had been the day he'd found it. The sea-witch's comb.

Vanni turned it over and over in his hand. It was cold like the sea, and lightweight. A natural shell had dents and seams sometimes, but this one was polished like stone. Beautiful.

"Now we know he didn't steal it," Damion said quietly.

"I never really thought he had. How could he?" Vanni held the comb out to Damion, who took it in both hands, cupping it as if it were fragile as an eggshell.

"Anyway, why would we think such things about Lord Neverelle? We don't really know him." Damion brought the comb close to his eyes, studying it.

"Because, I told you a year ago. Have you forgotten? I don't know what happened in the garden. I can't remember. He did something to you."

"You just think that because you had too much wine."

"Maybe." Vanni went to his bed and sat on the edge, fisting the covers. "But did you have too much, too? Because you don't remember everything. I saw him with his mouth on your neck. I saw him."

Damion came to sit alongside him.

"It was dark. You saw the shadows of the trees moving. Or something. All he wanted was to tell me he had known my mother before. And my father before he died. It was all right before I was born. Then my mother met your father a few years later. And then when I was eight, your father decided to bring us here."

Vanni said, "You can't convince me that was all that happened. I had strange visions that night. Like I was dreaming awake. Maybe he drugged the wine. I don't know."

"He'll be here for a while. We'll get to know him better. Maybe we'll find more answers," Damion said.

"Maybe." Vanni pushed himself up from the bed. "I'm hungry. Let's go see what time dinner is to be served."

Damion held out the comb. "What shall we do with this?"

"I think we should keep it close. Give it to me. I'll keep it in my pocket for now."

78

Chapter Ten

Never walked the hallways of Cliffside Keep in glittering apparel and fresh fragrance. He dressed up, always. As if every day was a fancy ball for him. It was like playing host to a god to have him as a guest. Even the duke did not behave so regally.

The lord's manners were fastidious. He ate with great delicacy and little appetite, like one was taught to do in polite society. He never monopolized conversation. He deferred to the duke at every turn, flattering Andreas and Jessie with his well-spoken words.

The drafty Keep with its salt-coated walls and cold shadows glowing blue from reflected sea-light, seemed brighter, livelier with Never in residence. The oil lamps burned more gold, less orange. The air smelled not of brine anymore, but of candle-wax and amber and roses.

Everything was an intrigue within his presence. He was someone new to talk to, learn from. He knew several languages fluently. He'd read every book Vanni and Damion had read from their father's library.

Lord Neverelle. There was something about him, not just his alluring looks but a charisma. It was exhilarating. It was devastating. For Vanni watched as Damion seemed unwittingly drawn in.

Never's aura seduced everything around it. Flowers in vases bent at his passing. The air puffed sweeter. Wherever he went, servants deliriously bowed deep. The feral cats from the barns ventured indoors and curled at his feet.

Never could make a bland room ornate simply by standing within it.

This man was so different from the man Vanni had met at the ball. And from the way Cecilia had spoken of him as rude to her friends, insulting.

Damion followed him around like a lost boy. Never treated him kindly, so it appeared.

Vanni understood, but also felt left out.

There were so many good things to say about Never that Vanni half-forgot the past strangeness, his discomfort, and the *tempt*.

But then there were moments Vanni's intuition about Never reared up. He noted with some cynicism an edge to Never that was almost crass, but which he hid well with flattery and polite, correct phrasing so the entire household remained enamored.

Vanni, too, was taken in by Never's presence—a fluttering in his stomach, a hotness like a flame all over his skin—but he kept his distance. Maybe he was fascinated because Never was a little like him. Not aloof, but holding something back. He was, Vanni decided, full of secrets. But his dark blue eyes hid them well.

It was hard to get Never off alone. Everyone wanted a piece of him. His servants, Raiden and Anastasia, were always around.

Never flourished under all that attention. If possible, his beauty grew brighter, healthier with each passing day. It did not seem he grieved his former home for one second.

He did not like to go outside during the day, so croquet and catch and tennis were not his forte. He had a condition, he said, where the sun hurt him, burned him. It did not show on his body, but deep inside his nerves screamed.

"It makes me shut down," he told Vanni and Damion. "Have you ever felt such pain that you cannot, for a moment, even breathe?"

He was, in fact, skilled at indoor games, cards and board games and parlor tricks. And many other things as well. He loved the Keep's walled gardens, the trimmed lawns and green knolls, the cloth-of-gold woods that stretched endless and magical. But he only ventured out to see it all at dusk or after dark.

80

One evening in the hearth room after dinner, playing cards with Vanni and Damion, Never announced, "I'm in love with this Keep!"

Vanni could feel his heart bounding, his skin prickling. Over the last three days, Never had been so different from his stoic presence at the ball. He'd been polite, even nice. It was almost unnerving. Was this the same man?

Every night since Never's arrival, Vanni had had dreams he was running in the woods, hair loose and cloak furled behind him. Never was with him. And maybe Damion, too, but he was not sure. It was Never who became the central image. His strangely alluring half-smile. His vivid eyes and wavy brown hair. Vanni always woke flushed.

Something about Never—he had a spirit like no other Vanni had ever encountered. Not quite sweet, not quite scary. He watched as Damion became more and more infatuated as well. He loved seeing Damion so happy.

But he told Damion several times, "Be careful."

Of course Damion didn't understand why he said that. He still didn't believe Vanni about the things he'd experienced in the garden at the ball.

"Please be careful," Vanni said late one night after Never had retired.

"Be careful of what?" Damion asked.

They were in the dim hallway in front of their rooms. Damion had not come to Vanni's room to sneak into his bed in three nights. Vanni only wanted to make sure he was careful. Safe.

"I know you're smitten with him. I know you want more to happen."

"You are jealous?"

"No." But it was a lie. Vanni was jealous. In two ways. He wanted Damion for himself, of course. But he wanted Never, too. Never, who now populated his dreams and made him wake aching and hard. Never, whose gaze trailed over him every morning as he came to breakfast, and every evening before bed.

"You are jealous. Don't lie. He likes me and you're jealous!"

The skin between Damion's eyebrows creased. The edges of his mouth turned down. He was rarely angry with Vanni. But tonight Damion looked like he wanted to punch him.

"I'm not. Honest. I want you to be happy." Vanni suddenly coughed. A lump had formed in his throat. He took a deep breath and cupped Damion's cheek. Softly, he said, "That's all I ever want."

Damion pushed his hand aside. "Then you'll not interfere?" His voice came raspy, untrusting. He had his head turned away.

"I won't. But I want you to come to me if you're unsure about anything. Remember, he had the abalone comb in his hair."

"Oh, that probably means nothing! I'm sure they're common."

How Damion had changed his tune. That wasn't how they had thought three days ago, the both of them holding and touching the comb as if it were some magical object. Suspicious of everything that had happened concerning Never and his quick arrival at the Keep.

Damion looked so handsome, standing in profile to Vanni. His hair was sleek like a seal's. He had worn it down today. It was long and straight. It fell back from his shoulders like a strange, dark liquid, constantly moving but tame, soft.

Vanni noticed Damion always had pink in his cheeks now. A little flustered, his smiles were tight as if he held back many secrets.

Every day Damion wore his best clothes.

And Vanni knew, because he'd peeked, that Damion used his new artist's sketchbook that Vanni had given him for his birthday to draw portraits and figures. All of Never.

82

A knot formed in Vanni's stomach. A combination of pain, remorse, grief. And love.

Damion was falling in love and though Vanni wanted things to be otherwise, he could not be cruel to Damion about it.

"I know that everything seems fine. But I want you to also know that you can come to me about anything. Anything at all, all right?" Vanni said.

"Fine. I'm tired. I'm going to bed now."

Vanni nodded and watched Damion slink into his room and shut the door without a backward glance.

He put a hand to his forehead and rubbed hard. A headache was coming on. He never got headaches.

*

Never's appearance seemed so much younger than Jessie's estimation that he was in his forties. Every day, Vanni looked for some evidence of his age. There was no way this man was older than thirty. However, in his mannerisms and voice, bearing and gaze, Vanni saw experience and uncanny perception. He saw lifetimes in the man. An old soul.

Never had not confirmed his age to Jessie, and it was impolite for Vanni to outright to ask. It was one more mystery his mind mulled over.

Today they sat in the hearth room during the heat of the day because of Never's allergy to the sun. They had plenty to entertain them, though, and buckets of lemonade to keep them cool.

Every subject any of them brought up, Never knew details, history, stories. He didn't try to overwhelm them, but he had fascinating knowledge, and a voice that soothed words, concepts, even other languages into both boys' minds.

He had been to many cities. He had been on ships. He had traveled far and wide.

"I once saw a mermaid." Never lounged on the sofa closest to the hearth, his feet up, hands behind his pretty head.

"I didn't work on that ship, mind you. I'd booked passage to a tropical island. Just for my amusement."

Vanni longed to ask Never where he'd gotten his wealth. He assumed it was inherited, but assumptions could be wrong.

"It was at night. I was on deck. The weather was quiet and the sea so still it was like black glass. There was very little wind, just enough to feel it against the back of my neck, and smell the spice of it clear and tart."

Vanni met Damion's eyes, which were sparkling. Damion looked away, attention—and devotion—completely on Never as he spoke.

"Because the sea was so still, that was how I spied it," Never continued. "First I saw the water move a little, then a little bump. A head popped up. Then the body, long hair like seaweed wrapping it. It did a backward flip and its tail came up, large, long, like a fish's tail. Water spilled along the edges, reflecting green and gold in the moonlight. Well, anyway, it was beautiful. All in silhouette. It could've been male, actually, but I like to think it was a mermaid."

Sea-witch!

Vanni frowned. It was as if Never was telling a story from his own fantasy-version he'd shared with Damion when they were kids. Except for the part about being on a ship.

Coincidence?

He and Damion exchanged a second look.

Never saw them, but said nothing about it. Polite, as always. Pleasant. Alluring. Everything good. Too perfect.

For example, Never had obviously managed to escape the fire with a few things because trunks had been brought to his rooms that first afternoon he'd arrived. Vanni had wondered then, and now, when he'd had the time to pack if the fire was so bad.

His servants were hardly ever seen and did not help with any household chores. They were strictly Never's personal servants. They mostly stayed to themselves on the fourth floor with their master, above Damion and Vanni's floor.

As all three of them sat contemplating the mermaid—or merman—sighting, the duke entered. He rarely socialized with them except at dinner.

When he came into the room, Never stood, bowing his head courteously. Damion and Vanni stayed sprawled where they were, Damion on a fuzzy rug and Vanni in a plush chair.

Andreas motioned for Never to sit again. He walked around more furniture to the center of the room and said, "I have come to inform you that I have been called away on business. To the king's palace, no less." His smile looked aggravated. "I have no idea how long I will be gone. Weeks at least. But I want you to know, Lord Neverelle, that you are welcome to remain under this roof. Vanni is old enough now to be lord of this Keep in my absence. He will be under order to provide you with anything you may need. And Damion understands the running of the household. He does my books now."

Andreas smiled at Damion, who smiled sweetly back.

Vanni was surprised his father put him in charge. Yes, he was the eldest, but Andreas showed very little attention to him these days.

"You will be in capable hands," the duke said.

"I'm sure I will," Never replied, voice low. "Will Jessie be accompanying you?"

"Yes. The servants are packing as we speak. We leave tomorrow at dawn."

"Father, do you have more specific instructions for me?" Vanni asked.

"No. If you have questions, Damion knows just about everything."

Vanni's heart fell. His father had confidence in Damion alone. It was always the case. He was only in charge by virtue of his age.

His fingers pushed at the velvet arm of his chair, making lines. His frustration began to boil up within him. He kept it down, breathing deep. Damion the smart one. The pretty one. Damion the sweetheart. Everyone adored him. Even Vanni himself. But he still wanted to punch something.

Suddenly, a voice came into his head as if from a dream.

Do you know how rare you are with your light hair and your dark eyes? And such a sturdy build, muscles from working outdoors. Skin the color of peaches tanned to a golden perfection. A pedigree of a man if ever there was.

He startled, sitting up. That voice seemed to come from outside himself. Not his usual inner voice that criticized or comforted him throughout his life.

He turned his gaze to Never, who was looking at the duke, nodding at the right moments, still discussing Andreas's departure.

Andreas was saying, "The tailor is returning tomorrow and you are to order whatever clothing you need for yourself and your servants. More are to be delivered today, I hear."

"Thank you, you are most generous. But I have more than I need."

"No," the duke countered. "Since you have arrived, more invitations than ever have come for parties and balls. I want all three of you to attend some benefits in my absence. Show the villages that there is life up here in the Keep. That I care—we care about the people and the land. The disaster which befell you has me thinking that we need more emergency resources for such things. I want to hold my own benefit when I return."

"Wonderful," Never said.

"I can organize the budgets," Damion piped up. "It's a great idea."

Vanni, still staring at Never, still wondering about the voice in his head, said, "Excellent." But his heart wasn't in his voice. What he really wanted to say was: *Are you going to let every stray that has befallen on bad times come stay at the Keep?*

Deep inside, he laughed at his own thought. But also wondered why he was such a grouch. Everything was fine here at the Keep. The duke was leaving for a while but that wasn't a hardship. Still, something churned in his gut.

Just then, Never turned and met his gaze. The hairs prickled all up and down Vanni's arms.

It was as if the man were reading his thoughts.

No one else in the room seemed to notice.

After the duke left, Never turned to them both. "Anyone up for a game of cards?"

Vanni got up quickly. "No thanks." He practically ran from the room.

Before the door shut behind him, he heard Damion say, "Oh, don't worry about him. He gets moody sometimes."

Vanni bristled.

He moved briskly down one flight of steps to the front entrance of the Keep. Once he was outside, he realized he'd been holding his breath. He could breathe again. The air was crisp and fresh and slightly salt-tinged. Filled with life. Indoors, he had felt almost diminished, as if the shadows were sucking him dry of energy, moisture, even good thoughts.

Today the woods called to him, golden in the late summer breezes. He walked briskly down the path that led into them. Once, he looked back at the Keep, scanning the darkened windows. He had such an itch at his back that someone was watching him.

Only when he moved under the welcoming canopy of the trees did he feel better.

He headed for the tree house he and Damion had built together years ago. They hadn't been out there in a long time. The pieces of wood they'd nailed into the tree trunk for steps still held. Vanni climbed them.

The house itself was little more than a few floorboards, a railing and three walls. One of the walls had come loose and looked about to fall. There was a partial lean-to roof.

Vanni sat down near the railing where he could look down and see the pathway. The woods seemed to glow with a jade green aura, and busy insects buzzed all around. Birds chirped, flitting about in nearby trees.

A tremendous sense of peace surrounded him. He had forgotten how much he loved this tree house. In his memory, he could hear the voices of Damion and himself laughing, shouting among the summer leaves.

Something sad awoke in him then. As if he was saying goodbye to it all.

Chapter Eleven

Vanni rose early to see his father and Jessie off for their trip to the palace. They took Andreas's biggest coach and best horses.

Bright pink clouds streaked the newly lit sky to the east. The weather was good for traveling.

Damion arrived after Vanni just in time to hug his mother goodbye.

Never did not show up.

After the carriage left and the echoes of the horses' clopping hooves died away, Vanni turned to Damion.

"Well, the Keep is ours now for a while."

"All ours." Damion flashed a smile.

"What shall we do first?"

"Order the cook to make pancakes!"

"You read my mind."

For a moment, it was as if nothing had changed. As if Never hadn't come into their lives and made them both at odds.

But when they walked back into the Keep together, once they were past the threshold of the entrance, Vanni could feel it in the air. A heaviness as if a storm was on the horizon.

At first when Never had arrived, the Keep had seemed brighter. But the past couple of days the shadows made by the oil lamps looked thicker. Drafts of cold air came and went even though it was still summer. And every room smelled of a combination of brine and roses, a scent that prickled Vanni's nostrils and sent him often to open windows or stand on balconies to take deep breaths of fresh air.

Now, for Damion's benefit, Vanni ignored his foreboding. He patted Damion on the back and said, "Let's go see about those pancakes."

Never made his presence known around noon. He entered the hearth room trailed by his two servants, Raiden and Anastasia.

Damion immediately stood. He'd been at the desk against the wall writing figures in ledgers. "Good morning!"

"Good *afternoon*," Vanni corrected. He was already standing by an open window overlooking today's blue-green sea.

Never spoke quietly to his servants. "You may go."

Raiden and Anastasia moved out of the room and into the hall.

Never strode in a straight line to Damion, immediately taking his hands in his own. "My, look at you today. Radiant. Is there that much excitement to be found in ledger books?"

"Math can be fascinating."

"Oh, how well I know," Never replied. "Equations are like stories. They create life, structure and essentially everything. Without it all we have chaos."

"It's already chaos," Vanni said. "If we only give things meaning through stories, then we're lying to ourselves in a hope for order when really everything is random."

"And yet," Never said, turning his full gaze on Vanni. "If we didn't have some order we wouldn't know up from down, or yesterday from tomorrow."

All Vanni saw for a moment was dark fire after Never finished his sentence.

Damion laughed. "That'd be crazy. What would the world be like then?"

"But if everything is created by and believed in through stories, then everything is a lie. Why bother?" Vanni asked. He had the window at his back now. The breeze was cool but his skin burned.

"Why would you say everything is a lie? Stories can tell truths. Stories can create truths." Never put his foot up, boot and all, on the sofa. The gesture bespoke privilege and bordered on rude. "What you think of as truth, or real, can always change as your perception changes. Reality is not what it seems."

"What's that supposed to mean?" Vanni glanced at Damion, whose eyes were shining and riveted on Never's face.

"We once thought the world was flat. People believed it as a fact. People once believed gods roamed the Earth. Maybe they did. Maybe they still do."

"People believe in mermaids!" Damion offered helpfully.

Or sea-witches. Vanni's mind quipped. *But I made that up.*

Never laughed. His laugh was clear and sonorous like a bell. It swept through the room like an energy being, bursting through Vanni's heart, nearly making him gasp. He could not tell if his reaction was from shock or pleasure—or both.

Damion put his hands to his head, laughing silently, combing his fingers through his long locks. His hair was loose today. A brilliant, polished darkness.

Vanni wanted to be mad at the conversation. Mad at lies. At unreal reality. He did not want to like Never. But something inside him woke up when Never was around. Intrigued. Interested.

"Well," said Never, clapping his hands. "What are we going to do today?"

Damion turned to his desk and gathered up a stack of fancy papers.

"I know. We can go through these invitations and decide which ones to accept."

"Ah, more balls. More socially correct evenings where we can show off our manners, our breeding, our superiority over the world," Never said.

Damion's face fell.

Vanni stepped away from the window and walked to Damion's side. It was time to grow up, go out, and mingle among more people. Time to do as the duke commanded and let people know there was life at the Keep. Besides, it looked as if Damion were suddenly excited by the idea.

All Vanni wanted was for Damion to be happy.

"I think we should. We'll pick the ones we want to accept and go have some fun."

Damion looked up. "Really? You want to?"

"Of course, idiot."

Never sighed. "Your father is most generous in sending his tailor for me. I'll have somewhere to show off my new clothes."

Damion grinned. He got up and brought the stack of invitations to the sofa and sat, placing them between himself and Never.

Vanni followed, then knelt on the floor looking at the lacy cards. And the colorful wax blobs impressed by signet marks that held newer envelopes closed. He picked the first one up.

"This," he said, "seems to be from Lord Percy."

"Again? That man must throw fifty parties a year," Never said.

Chapter Twelve

While Andreas and Jessie were away, the three of them started going out more, to cotillions, garden parties, fund raisers. Damion followed Never all about the events, never leaving his presence even as they accepted invitations from pretty young women to dance. They always danced side by side. Vanni wanted Damion to be happy, so he let him have all of Never's attention. He stayed apart. He tried to have fun.

He hadn't caught them doing anything more than bumping elbows, smiling at each other, or sitting close together on sofas in the Keep. He tried to keep an eye on Damion. So he thought he would know if anything was happening between them.

Never had to notice Damion's infatuation. But he did not appear to make any advances as he had in the garden when Vanni had lost time for a few minutes. If anything were happening, it was behind closed doors, maybe in the middle of the night when Vanni was asleep. But he didn't think so.

Vanni had an infatuation with Never himself, but he still didn't trust him.

So far, he'd noticed no marked changes in Damion aside from a constant blush that came and went along the sides of his cheeks. If anything had happened between them, he thought—hoped—maybe Damion would confide in him even if only in vague terms. He expected shyness and apprehension from Damion. He saw none of that.

After a party at Lord Percy's estate, one late night they all came back by carriage dazzled by too much dancing, drunk on too much wine. The drive was long and boring. Vanni dozed for a while, but though the carriage was top of the line, it was still too bumpy for real rest.

They had a few more miles to go. The night forest slid by the window, all crickets and bullfrogs, honeysuckle and humidity. The horses' hooves clattered. The carriage swayed.

It was just the three of them now. Never sat in the middle, the edges of his fancy new cloak, courtesy of the duke, splayed partway across the laps of both Vanni and Damion. Damion had his arm loosely around Never's shoulders. Friendly. A little too friendly. Damion had drunk a lot of wine.

Vanni sat slouched, his feet up on the facing carriage couch.

Never said, "How fortunate I am. A beautiful boy to my right and to my left." His laugh was low, melodic. It drifted through Vanni like warm liquid, heating the blood in his veins.

There was something about Never's voice that calmed Vanni. Made him almost complacent.

It was stuffy in the carriage. Vanni lifted his fingers to the cravat at his neck, loosening it. A hand reached out, crossing the path of his gaze, and pulled at the cravat until it came all the way off.

In his peripheral vision Vanni saw Never put the silken material to his face and inhale. "You always smell so good, Vanni. What's your secret?"

Vanni blinked. In the darkness he could feel Damion tense.

"I don't smell good. The material is freshly laundered. But I danced and sweated on it tonight. You're teasing me. It must smell like sweat."

"It smells cleanly male. Virile."

Vanni instantly blushed and was glad for the darkness.

"I love the scent of a real man. Shining from exertion. The scent of wine on his lips. Don't you, Damion?"

"Um...um...it's not something I really think about."

Vanni closed his eyes tight, then opened them. Never was being far too forward. And there was nowhere to escape in the closed confines of the carriage.

"Well, you should." Never took the cravat and forcefully placed it over Damion's mouth.

Damion took a deep breath, then pushed Never's hand away. He said nothing. He took another deep breath and turned his head away.

Vanni started to lean forward but Never's fist came up and took hold of the shoulder seam of his jacket.

"Have you thought about it, Vanni?"

"I think sweat smells like sweat," he replied. He kept his voice steady and neutral. But his heart quickened.

He blamed it on the wine but he knew better. Being near Never made his skin prickle. He felt verbally outmatched, and Never had the ability to physically disarm him. He was the stronger one here, the older one. Vanni may have been the earl of the Keep, in charge now that his father was away, but Never had the commanding aura to take it all, Damion included, and make Vanni feel like he was a child again. A child who believed in sea-witches.

"Do you, now? Well, I love the scent. May I keep the cravat? Just for the night perhaps?" He smiled at him with mock innocence.

Damion, seeming to muster some personality at last, said, "I don't like it at all."

"What don't you like, my dear?" Never asked.

"The smell of sweat."

"Perhaps you have never been in the right circumstance to appreciate certain lovely flavors of nature." Never finished with a soft chuckle.

Vanni's heart skipped. Never's flirting should not have bothered him. It was overt but poetic. But he was flirting with both of them. After Vanni had promised Damion he'd step aside.

He did not like this at all. Never had already come between them. But now he was sabotaging what was left of Vanni and Damion's trust in each other. Already, Vanni heard Damion's breathing increase. Was he fuming? Damion didn't *fume*. But lately, after Never had come into their lives, his moods had shifted. Damion was no longer a sweet little boy. He was a man now in his own right.

Hell, they both were.

That did not seem to matter at all to Never. His hand fell gently against Vanni's thigh.

In the dimness of the carriage's tiny lamp, Damion could see everything.

Vanni pushed Never's hand away. But not before Damion turned his head abruptly and stared out the window.

Never merely tilted his head further toward Vanni, the cravat now draped over one shoulder and against his neck. He'd pushed his cloak all the way back off his shoulders.

"What do you think, Vanni?" Never asked.

"About what?"

"About the natural essence of *human*. Men specifically."

Damion's voice interrupted. "He doesn't like it either."

"I'm not asking you, Damion. I'm asking Vanni's opinion."

Vanni did not like the way things were going one bit. Never was being completely unfair to Damion. Yet he could not deny the rush that went through him. Never stirred him up so quickly.

Safe in the shadowy dark of the carriage, he smiled.

"It's fine," he said, voice bold. He leaned his head back.

"Have you ever had a moment to partake? More intimately, I mean?"

Vanni felt sly, challenging. Everything inside him pulsed, wanting to burst free. That included an inner strength, his will. Even his proprietary nature toward Damion came from that force. He liked it. It made his soul bristle. It felt great.

He's asking if you're a virgin, his inner voice teased.

Vanni laughed. Yes, Vanni was a virgin. He'd done nothing more than kiss Cecilia. And that without passion.

After a moment of drowning in his own weird amusement, he decided to answer with a question of his own. "Have you?"

Never said, "I would not be having this conversation if I hadn't."

After some moments of hearing just the clip-clop of the horses' hooves and the rumble of the carriage wheels on the road, Never said, "I'll interpret your silence as disapproval of the subject. And confirmation that you have not engaged in the natural intimacies of men."

Vanni flushed all over. He thought over the years of how his bed was often occupied by another male. Sometimes that male nearly slept in his arms. It was innocent even if his thoughts, as he grew older, often weren't.

Vanni said, "You make assumptions based on nothing. Maybe I don't kiss and tell."

Never acted as if he had not heard him. He turned to Damion, taking his cravat in hand, untying it.

Damion made a little sound of protest, but did not push Never away.

"Much too cumbersome, darling. It covers your beautiful gold-brown skin. I would like to see the top of your chest above your ruffles."

Vanni heard Damion's sharp intake of air. The bronze-lit lamps of the carriage put everything in silhouette. Never held Damion's cravat up to his nose. It was almost the same as Vanni's blue one. Except for the color. Damion's was red.

"Yes," said Never. "The mix of you two is quite heady."

Never put the second cravat on his other shoulder. The cloak still fastened about his neck, but it was bunched behind his back in favor of the scarves that now draped him.

"Are you going to wear both our cravats now in a twist?" More boldness from Vanni.

"You're stunning no matter what you wear." Damion complimented him.

"Or what I don't wear," teased Never.

Damion's gulp was audible. "I'm sure, although I wouldn't know that, my lord."

Never laughed low again, obviously pleased. His hand on Vanni's thigh returned. A shiver curled down Vanni's spine.

He was pleased and angry at the same time. Damion had never called him "my lord." But why should he be jealous? He had never wanted Damion as a servant.

Sarcastically, Vanni said, "By all means, more wine for all of us as soon as we get home. We most certainly have not had enough."

His body was on fire. As things stood, he felt far too wild for the moment. Definitely, more wine was a great plan. If he couldn't knock some sense into himself, he might as well knock himself out. It was Damion who was falling in love—or lust or whatever it might be called—with Never, not him. No matter what, Vanni had made a promise not to interfere.

As the carriage pulled up the drive, Never returned the cravats, each to its proper owner, as if by way of apology before they disembarked the coach.

As they got out, everything was back in place. Nothing had really happened anyway. Nothing at all.

Damion, the first to step down, waited to the side as Never lowered his booted food on the little footstep. When Never had his balance, Vanni saw that he reached for Damion's arm but Damion pretended not to see. Damion moved swiftly forward alone, toward the Keep's dark entrance.

Vanni, the last to disembark, glanced quickly at him.

Damion's eyes flashed in the dimness as he turned to glare at him. Vanni hurried forward to catch up to his friend, leaving Never behind.

As they met, Damion took a step toward Vanni, leaning forward until their shoulders almost touched, and said in a hollow, quiet voice, "I hate you."

Abruptly, Damion turned and moved alongside Never who had now caught up, and ascended the steps.

Guilt flicked knifelike through Vanni's chest.

"Wait!" He jogged up the steps until he was alongside Damion, letting Never go through the open door first. He saw out the corner of his eye as Never's servant Raiden met him, taking his cloak in hand as Never removed it, murmuring low to him.

Again, for a moment, Vanni and Damion were alone.

"I know. I know. I deserve your hate. I'm sorry," said Vanni.

On the salt-damp landing of the entryway, Damion halted. "You're jealous, Vanni! It's not fair. You know how I feel about him. You have known all alone!"

"I know. I said I'm sorry. I've been trying to stay out of your way and let whatever is going to happen happen. He--he just grabbed my cravat, like he was playing some game."

"Well don't play. Just don't."

"I won't. I promise."

But it wasn't his promise Damion needed to be worried about. Never was pushy when he wanted to be, rich, entitled. He had a predatory aura about him—yes, that had been the word Vanni was looking for, predatory—and a hungry and selfish glint. He could not trust him. *They* could not trust him.

And yet it was the very thing Vanni liked about Never. Mystery. Danger. Who wouldn't be enticed?

Chapter Thirteen

When they got inside, under the oil lamps Damion's face was drawn and dark; he looked entirely disappointed and depressed. Vanni felt responsible. He wanted to talk to him again, but before he could make a move, Damion had bounded up the steps toward the third floor. The door to his room closed, echoing distantly.

Never had disappeared through the kitchen door.

Vanni went after him. He wasn't sure what more he wanted to say to him. He was seething and excited, angry and in awe.

He entered the kitchen in long strides. It was darker in here but one lamp was still lit and there was a low ashy-orange fire in the biggest stove.

Never was at the main pantry opening cupboard doors. Raiden had vanished.

Beyond the shuttered windows, a rattle. The wind came up. The ocean seemed to growl.

"I'm ravenous tonight," Never said without bothering to look at who came through the door.

The polite host and earl of the Keep and the angry son of the duke warred inside Vanni. Because he was Andreas's guest and an old friend of Jessie's, the host won. "What would you like?"

"Anything." Never turned, dark hair loose from his usual braid, falling across his white-clad shoulders. Vanni had the sudden urge to brush that hair back, to feel the bouncy silk of it against his fingertips.

"I'm hungry for a midnight snack," Never added. As he spoke, his face seemed to take on an inner glow. "Aren't you?"

Vanni had yet to see Never eat much of anything. He never gobbled his food. He took small bites. He fiddled with the flatware. He'd never been a big eater.

Vanni stepped up to the shelves. He'd eaten many midnight snacks on his own for years and knew where everything was. He grabbed leftover breakfast rolls from the morning, butter and preserves. As he placed them all on a tray on the side-table he felt Never come up behind him.

Vanni turned to face him, stepping to one side. Never's body followed him.

Vanni's skin shuddered cold, then flushed hot. He could not catch his breath. "I think--" He swallowed hard. "I--I..."

Never kept staring at him, a smile shifting at the corners of his perfect pink lips.

"Lord Neverelle—" Vanni backed up until the small of his back pressed the edge of the wooden counter.

"I told you to call me Never. You can't deny there's a spark between us," he said huskily, his body moving closer, almost pressing.

"No." Then quickly, Vanni said, "I mean yes."

Never pressed just a little.

"Stop."

A little more.

"Wait." Vanni wanted to push him away but didn't.

Never's body was full up against him now.

"What about Damion?" Vanni whispered.

"What about him?" Never's breath fluttered against Vanni's neck and chin.

Any more distraction and his mind would stop working. Vanni raised his hands to Never's upper arms.

Never let out a small grunt of surprise as Vanni pushed him away.

"Don't do this. Damion likes you. You know this. I thought you were, you were—"

"What?" Never asked.

Vanni wasn't sure how to describe it. They weren't a couple. He'd seen Never kiss Damion in Lord Percy's gardens a year ago. He'd seen how Damion's entire demeanor shined. "Damion's in love with you!"

"You thought I would court him."

"Well. Sort of. Yes!"

Never's mouth opened a little. He eyed him mischievously. "Yes, I suppose I am courting him."

"You suppose--"

Speech knotted Vanni's throat. Dismay caught him, followed by returning anger. "You can't say it like that. This hasn't happened to him before. He's never...no one has ever affected him like this. He's--he's..." He took a deep breath.

Never said, "You affect him."

Vanni frowned. "It's not—not the same thing."

But part of him wanted it to be. The slow burning away of the last moments of innocence. Rushing into adulthood together. But it was the deep bond they had that prevented it. As if they were hanging onto old ways, clinging to old behaviors for their dear lives. They enjoyed their childhood together so much they never wanted it to end.

Quietly, Never said, "How do you think it's not the same thing?"

"He doesn't want me. He wants you!"

Never laughed.

"Stop laughing. He's only eighteen," said Vanni.

"And a virgin, I know." Never actually seemed to hum as he talked. "As are you. Am I right? It's all very delightful, don't you think?"

Now Vanni glared. "It's why you can't play games like this, or treat him like a toy."

"What about you? How may I treat you?" Never's smile was close-mouthed.

"I won't hurt him."

"That's not what I asked."

Vanni's breath shuddered in his lungs. He could not deny he felt attraction toward Never despite lack of trust, and Never's forward manner. And Never's cool regard for Damion's feelings.

"You may treat me only as a friend," Vanni finally answered.

The muscles of Never's face tensed. The smile fell away.

"You are not being the gentleman here. It's quite rude of you to talk to me about Damion's first brush with love and assume that I, on the other hand, am experienced. How presumptuous."

Vanni stared him down with a slick smile. "What? You are expert at flirting. You are so sure of yourself. Besides, you told us both in the carriage you knew about the scent of men—and intimacy, so don't even try to play that game with me!"

Never's eyes widened at Vanni's boldness. "Perhaps I should be insulted."

"Or perhaps you're enjoying every bit of this. And that's why I'm telling you. Damion isn't a game piece."

"Vanni, are you jealous?" He asked the question with such a sneer as his body swayed forward, that Vanni reacted by instantly grabbing his arm and pushing him further away. Hard. Then he took a step forward and pushed again.

Now Never was backed up against the pantry wall and his smile widened. "Well, well. The head of the house while Daddy's gone has decided to play master, after all."

"I mean it, Never. Do. Not. Hurt. Him."

"How can I ever guarantee that?" he asked haughtily. "What if I have fallen in love with someone else through no fault of my own?"

Confused for a moment, Vanni started to step back.

Never reached up and touched his palm to the side of Vanni's head. "What if that someone was you?"

"I--" Vanni stumbled back a step. "No. You can't just—No!"

He put his hand under Vanni's chin. "Now who's acting virginal?"

Vanni still had the focus of mind to push his hand away. "This is about Damion."

"Is it?"

Vanni's vision was a blur. "Don't you have any feelings for him at all?" His voice sounded hoarse to his own ears.

"Of course I do."

"Then...why?"

His brows narrowed. "Try to understand my dilemma. I have two beautiful men, one on each side. I like men. In every way you can think of in that curious young mind of yours. How do I choose one over the other? Whom do I choose?"

Vanni's mouth dropped open. He had promised himself he would step out of the picture and not become involved in anything Never was doing.

Never took one step back from him, his clothing rustling, and looked Vanni up and down, head to toe. "I'm afraid it's a terrible plight. My heart aches over it. I'm suffering, Vanni. Can't you see?"

In fact, Vanni couldn't see it at all. Never was having way too much fun to be suffering. "You are anything but suffering."

Now Never actually pouted. He looked very much the pampered lord.

"If I told you," Never said softly, "that it was you who made my blood flame, you I'd been eyeing ever since I arrived, would that not have any affect on you?"

This wasn't good at all. Vanni stared at him, speechless.

Never reached out and cupped Vanni's cheek again. Suddenly, his entire body flowed with fever, as if tiny flames licked up and down his skin underneath his formal clothes. The arousal heated him so quickly, and with such strength, he felt behind him for the counter to steady himself. It was too far away and he almost stumbled.

Never reached out with his other hand and put it on Vanni's shoulder, steadying him. He leaned in slowly, his warm breath like autumn roses against Vanni's face.

Every calm cell in his body experienced an upheaval. Pleasure coursed through him untamed, as if some door had opened inside him and could not close against the rush of energy that came pouring through.

He'd never had physical, erotic pleasure consume him so fast. His body thrilled to it. He was so hard now, all embers, kindling, and Never knew it. One touch and Vanni knew he would explode. Still, through the haze of his desire, he refused to forget Damion.

"You have to tell him," Vanni said firmly, pleased that his voice remained even and somewhat calm through gritted teeth.

"Oh. He knows how I feel about you." Never's smile was downright annoying.

Vanni was sure he was lying, or Damion would not have been so angry on the carriage ride. "He doesn't know. Or he didn't before tonight, until your flirting on the carriage ride home. And now? I won't let you play this game with him or me. No one is sneaking around in this house behind anyone's back."

"I'm not sneaking. I've been very open with you."

"And you're going to break Damion's heart."

"We'll see. Maybe you're right, maybe you're wrong. Maybe Damion and I can come to an understanding until I decide what—or who, rather—I find the most delectable of you two. He's stronger than you think."

Against the will of his body, Vanni backed away a few inches. His hands were fists against his sides.

"Do not tell me about Damion and his strength. I've known him my whole life. I know how he is."

"All right, then. I won't."

They were still incredibly close, foreheads almost touching. Finally, Never straightened and turned. "There is no reason under the sun and the moon why I should even have to choose between you two. To court only one person at a time. So old-fashioned."

Vanni swallowed hard. His whole body was tense. Thrilled. Mortified. Flattered. Insanely aroused. He closed his eyes, trying to gather his control. He heard Never's boot step shift upon the kitchen floor, the shift and drag of his ruffled shirt and stiff black trousers as he moved toward the door to the staircase.

"Goodnight, Vanni."

Vanni did not open his eyes, did not reply.

Jaw set, body coiled, still raging, he finally turned toward one of the kitchen windows. He pulled back the shutter. It squeaked and strained, the only sound now but for the wind humming up from the sea, singing in the voice of a male siren.

Vanni stared out the kitchen window into the night.

For a long time he watched the play of shadows in the distant trees as he calmed himself, as his brain worried the problem of Damion. Damion was still so young. A part of Vanni loved his childhood companion more than anything in the world and knew this was so unfair to him. But another part, after his body's fierce and sensual betrayal, didn't care.

Chapter Fourteen

The night after the ball when Never had pushed Vanni up against the kitchen counter, Vanni slept fitfully. He was tired all the next day.

He stayed indoors and watched Damion. Watched Never. He said nothing to Damion, who still seemed to be ignoring him. But Never was friendly and encouraging. He insisted they all play games of cards.

Never was dressed in a crimson shot silk waistcoat with scattered black rhinestones. At his throat he wore a red cravat tucked into his ruffled shirt. A Celtic cross of platinum embedded with a flawless diamond at the center swayed against his chest. His long hair, the color of rain-drenched mahogany, twisted back in a massive braid that caressed his neck and upper back. Tucked against the braid at the back he wore the abalone shell comb.

Despite Never's arrogance and forward personality, Vanni could not look away from his beauty. Neither could Damion.

Never met their eyes with lingering looks as he dealt the cards. He ordered his servant Raiden to bring them bottle after bottle of wine from the cellars.

Vanni drank because it made everything seem easier. He did not know what else to do.

Damion drank probably because the other two were. He wasn't as fond of wine as Vanni was, but he emptied glass after glass without a word.

With the wine, the world shifted. The tension in the room subsided. Suddenly it seemed they were laughing, all three of them, and actually having fun.

Vanni had already decided to slow down his drinking when Never cut them off. He made Raiden take away the glasses and bring cool pitchers of water.

Never said, "It's easier if we're not all too drunk."

"What's easier?" Vanni asked, staring blurrily at his cards. He had a bad hand. He didn't care.

"Playing the games I like to play."

Damion instantly smiled.

Vanni frowned. Even drunk, his muscles tensed, his breath caught.

"You will like these games. I promise," Never said softly.

Damion nodded, still smiling.

Vanni looked up into Never's dark blue eyes and trembled. But not from fear. The ocean roared far away. Sent a singing wind. And everything Vanni was or ever believed began to fall away. Any residual child self tumbled into dust and was blown out to sea.

Something strange happened when he looked into Never's eyes. His body experienced a total relaxation, almost like sleep but he was still awake. It was different from being drunk. And when Never raised his arm, Vanni followed the motion, leaning closer.

"What games?" Damion's voice held a trace of past innocence, but was filled with wonder, too.

When Never turned his gaze on him, Damion took a deep breath and held it. Then he closed his beautiful dark eyes so that the lashes fringed his cheeks.

What is this? Vanni wanted to ask. Instead, he heard himself say, as if from faraway, "Teach us these games."

"Let's all move to the sofa."

Vanni realized he'd been wanting Never to say that.

Damion stood, slightly swaying. He did not have to be asked twice. He lay back against the cushions and pillows, his hands up and under his head.

Vanni and Never approached him.

Damion turned his head slightly to look at Vanni. Those dark, sweet eyes. Big. Full. Brimming with anticipation.

But the gaze hardened. He pressed his lips tight as Vanni approached.

Vanni remembered his words to Damion just last night.

I deserve your hate. I won't. I promise. He had promised to stay out of the way and let Never pursue Damion.

Vanni stopped.

Never turned. "What is the matter? Don't be nervous."

When he looked up at Never, Vanni lost himself again. As if time had no meaning. As if he could not think beyond want, need, passion. He smelled roses. He shook his head. "I don't—"

Never held up his hand. "You do."

"I do," Vanni repeated. But it seemed he spoke not of his own will.

Damion made a fast hissing sound.

Never turned to him. "Stop that. You are going to enjoy this."

A strange, obedient smile broke out over Damion's face, transforming it into an almost-grimace. "I already am."

"Come." Never held out his hand to Vanni and escorted him to the sofa, making him sit with enough room for Never to recline between them.

A fog entranced Vanni. He could see everything, but as if through a lens of fine lace. The air was smoky, misty. But not from the salt air. His body moved, almost sluggish, yet he was wide awake. And incredibly aroused.

Every move Never made Vanni sensed with hyper-awareness. Such as when he reached out slowly and drew his fingers up Damion's smooth-shaven jaw to cup his cheek.

Vanni felt as if the hand touched him as well.

Every sound amplified. Outside, the crash of the waves was no longer a roar but like bells as if he could discern every single drop of water drip into more water. He could hear it—billions of water drops scattered, obliterating themselves through every moment. Breaking away and rejoining in an ever-moving body of water.

Vanni's own heartbeat pounded in his ears. His blood, like the sea, wanted to froth and churn. He was about to explode.

He heard Damion's breaths come faster. And the rustle of Never's clothing as he bent at the waist toward the younger man.

Vanni's own breath became a wind. Hot and fast. Light and dizzying.

Everything was liquid here. Melting. Flowing. A dampness against his trousers.

He heard Never's quiet voice like a distant rain. "Here you have been all along, the two of you, like beautiful trapped princes under a spell, waiting for me. Waiting for me to claim you."

Vanni winced inwardly at the poetry in Never's words. But he loved it, too. More than anything. Who spoke that way? Who had ever spoken that way to him? Not even Damion, who loved him. Not even the voices in his dreams.

"You want my kiss more than anything, yes?" Never asked Damion.

"Yes," came the answer, a faraway voice, needful and drunk. "Yes."

Vanni felt himself lurch.

Without looking back, Never's left hand came back and cupped Vanni's knee, steadying him. For a moment outside of this moment, Vanni wanted to yell, grab Damion into his arms and pull him up. Wanted to run away with him into the woods to hide. Back to the tree house. To boyhood when they innocently and only belonged to each other.

Tears started in his eyes, stinging, coming fast to wet his lashes.

Never said, "Vanni, you are with me. With me. And together we will make him ours. You will have everything you ever dreamed."

That heavy fragrance again. Roses. And Vanni felt himself drift into full compliance.

110

He had no will against this man. But found he didn't want it. Not really. Not the way his body was burning.

However, though Never had his hand on Vanni's knee, all his attention focused on Damion. Vanni could not help but feel left out. But he wanted Damion to be happy. And Damion had been enamored with Lord Neverelle since the first time they'd walked in the gardens at Lord Percy's a year ago.

Vanni closed his eyes and concentrated on the weight of the elegant hand against his knee. He listened to all the sounds that were heightened now in his slowly whirling mind. All the individual drops of the sea. The doleful and defeated whine of the wind. The candles that smelled of beeswax, ancient and bronze.

He heard the rustle of clothing again. A soft quick groan. He opened his eyes to blue-edged shimmers of candlelight, and beside him on the velvet sofa, Never bent over Damion and finally gave him the kiss Damion claimed he'd never gotten in the gardens.

Vanni wanted to look away. Something stirred inside him, a dangerous excitement that made him want to push Never aside and pull Damion to his own mouth.

His breath hitched. He watched, head back, warm flurries inside him pooling at his groin. He could see only the side the Damion's face, his long hair curving back, loose, eyelashes fluttering, cheek pink, chin up to receive the kiss with full wonder.

Never's perfect mouth pressed to Damion's, lips moving against lips, noses pressing side by side, chins touching. Never's free hand pressed the side of Damion's head where Vanni couldn't see. He imagined those long fingers combing through Damion's silken hair.

One of Damion's hands came up to touch Never's chest, then grab tightly with his fist at the ruffles there.

Vanni heard another groan from Damion, a quick breath through his nose. Their mouths opened.

Vanni's mouth parted as well just to see it. The depth of contact. The intimacy of a simple kiss that was, in truth, not simple at all. It was a first kiss. It was a deeply passionate kiss with a sort of wet devouring sound.

Vanni's heart pounded. He thought he could hear Never's and Damion's hearts as well, their pulses mixing with his in a sort of drumming beat, a chant, a spell.

A spell.

That was what was happening. A part of him knew it. A bigger part of him didn't care. But Never wore an abalone comb.

Vanni reached, as if in a dream, into his pocket and touched the shell comb he'd found so long ago. The smooth cool sea-glaze of it. The thrill that it might be magical treasure. For it was an exact twin to the one Never wore.

Vanni had become so entranced staring at the comb in Never's hair, and tracing the one in his pocket, he'd lost track of time. Until he heard Damion's small voice echoing in his ears.

"Wait, not yet—"

Vanni glanced along Damion's face to his chest and saw Never's hand there, undoing the top button of his white shirt.

"You are ready to begin a new journey," Never said.

"We're not alone."

"I know. That was my intention."

"But I thought—"

"That I could not want you both? That societal rules for lovers might hem us in?"

"But I don't want Vanni to—"

Vanni shut his eyes again. But his ears still heard. The words were hurtful.

Never said, "To what? See? But you love each other very much. There is no problem here."

But Vanni knew the problem. Damion wanted Never all to himself. Love was greedy that way. Especially new love.

And why should he have to share? Except this was Never's game. Never was in command.

He had put his hand on Vanni's knee, had looked at him with hypnotic eyes and filled him with the scent of roses. Vanni couldn't have walked away if he'd wanted to. He couldn't move.

Vanni's desire for Damion to be happy and his own lack of will to leave him alone with Never were at war. In the end, his body won out over his mind. The prickling of his skin. The heat building like a sea-tide within. It was as if his heart were made of hot liquid that melted throughout his limbs.

A surging warmth pooled in his belly. It started as a small ache but soon became pure pleasure sending wave after wave of arousal through his system.

He had the urge to rub himself against Never's side. He tried not to move, his fingers curling into fists. The candles filled the room with their honey scent. The thick aroma spread through the air. His senses became overloaded. He leaned forward so he could see better the remnants of that first kiss.

A kiss that should have been mine!

But which man's kiss? Never's? Or Damion's?

His body wanted Never. That could not be denied, the way the man moved and spoke and beckoned. The way he looked at Vanni with sea-deep eyes that drew him inward, made him feel languid with need, heavy, needing some sort of release.

But his mind… his mind was not so easily turned. While he could become lost in Never's eyes, and in how the man moved and coaxed with the secret promise of sensual touches, it was Damion Vanni wanted to clutch to his chest, hold, find solace in.

His feelings were conflicted deep inside.

Damion was like a favorite treasure he wanted always to own. To savor. To save. Forever.

Never was the unknown. Something to reach for. Someone to make the assembly of his desires complete. Outside the Keep, Never represented new growth. Damion was the heart. But Never was the adult form of himself, darkness to Vanni's light, risk and thrill and adventure. The promise of a bigger world, vast and new and carefree.

Vanni turned his head and swayed toward Never, who bent to Damion and, with slightly parted lips, again took Damion's mouth. Vanni could not have had a better view. The way the muscles of Never's mouth molded his lips to Damion's. The way his cheek hollowed just a bit as he drew Damion's lower lip between his, a gentle pull.

Damion's beautiful lashes fluttered. His cheeks glowed with a warm flush. His entire body tensed, back beginning to arch. His fingers clutched at air, then one hand found Never's shirt sleeve just below his elbow and curled about the material, pulling hard enough that Never's shirt, loose at the neck, drew away from his upper shoulder and revealed his clavicle.

Two dark heads, their hair spilling together against the back of the sofa, bent together. The beauty of their continuing kiss coursed through Vanni as if it were happening directly to him. He could feel their lips touching his, and the pressure where the bodies touched as if he reclined between them.

Vanni had never seen a man kiss another man before. At the parties he'd attended everything had been perfectly paired, the girls with the boys. But of course the idea that anyone could romance anyone had seemed normal to him.

Of course he had secretly wanted Damion's touch from the time of his first wet dream at the onset of puberty. But the special bond between them had been enough. Damion sneaking into his room at night had provided enough of a forbidden thrill that it was sufficient for the child that still resided within.

But now... Now they were both older. Both adults.

And that kiss. It made the room so hot, as if the Keep itself were on fire. As if the sea and its wind song outside were boiling, churning up the world with a molten lure to match his own inner burnings. Right now, the world was made up of nothing but this.

This.

Damion's mouth opened under Never's and a small groan escaped. Touching, their chins, their foreheads, they were so alike, but so different. Damion had the olive complexion of the northern lands. Never was paler, with a coppery tint, but their hair swirled with similar brilliant dark inks, catching the blues and purples of the interior lighting. If they merged, Vanni thought he could love them both as one.

Damion's eyes flashed open in that instant, the whites catching the flicker of the candle flames, the dark irises deep as wells between stars. Sideways, his gaze caught Vanni's.

Vanni's blood went suddenly cold. For he could read Damion well, every nuance of body language and the flicks of his every look. From the time Damion was eight until now, he could see what the younger boy was thinking from the cast of his eyes. He had known him happy, sad, angry, calm. But this, this was something else. Arousal and rejection. For this was something Damion wanted all to himself.

The blade of that gaze went straight to Vanni's heart.

For a moment, the room blurred. Vanni rocked on the edge of the sofa, thinking he might fall. All his balance disintegrated. He almost cried out but at the very last moment when he thought he might come apart, Never reached up and put his arm along his back, curving up from the waist. His hand grasped at Vanni's shoulder pulling cloth, raking skin, until Vanni came forward and fell into the embrace of the lord.

Never drew away from Damion's mouth and captured Vanni in a swift, first-for-him kiss, damp with Damion's moisture, sweet but not quite gentle. It happened so fast Vanni had no time to think. His body swooned.

And the cold of Damion's look filtered away as if it had never happened.

With that one strong arm, Never pulled Vanni partway onto his lap.

Vanni struggled to find a new balance, one hand scrubbing against Never's ruffled shirt, then pressing hard to his chest, the other finding purchase, palm down, against Never's hard thigh.

Never held him tight to keep him upright.

Flavors of wood smoke and loam and lonely November nights. Wild roses. Wild spices. Wild seas.

All Vanni wanted was to get closer as he felt that hot tongue probe his mouth. Claim him.

His trousers dug into his groin, his cock so stiff and full it hurt. He pushed his tongue against Never's, and the dance of their kiss began.

Was this what it had been like for Damion?

Vanni had never done this before, but he didn't need to know how it was done. His body knew. His mouth knew what it liked and sought more, as if to drink from Never's offered intimacy the way he'd drink a glass of rare, aged wine.

Colors played behind his eyes, all hues of molten orange suns and the redder depths of pure lust.

As if from far away, he heard a murmuring. The wetness at Vanni's mouth receded. His stomach cramped in a kind of panic until he looked beyond the ruffles of Never's shirt which his cheek now rubbed and saw Never claim Damion yet again. Damion who closed his eyes as if he didn't want to see, but who arched up again to meet Never's demands.

For a fleeting moment, Vanni wondered what would happen if any of the Keep's servants wandered into the room. And where were Raiden and Anastasia? He'd lost track. His stomach fluttered, sending adrenaline like ice into his veins.

What was happening?

Vanni started to turn away so he could see the room. Was the door open or closed? Should he get up and check? Should he leave? Damion didn't want him here, that was for sure.

At the thought, Never hugged him tighter and lifted his head from his kiss with Damion, who was even more sprawled now, ass toward the edge of the sofa's seat, one leg straight, and the other bent at the knee.

Vanni had the urge to go to his knees.

Never caught Vanni's gaze with his, and for a moment Vanni was lost, swirling on nothing but mist. Then Never spoke.

"You will stay."

Well, of course he was staying! He didn't want to leave. Not now. Not ever.

"On your knees," Never said.

Vanni wanted to smile, because he'd been thinking just now of doing that very thing. Sliding from the sofa's soft cushion to kneel at Never's feet. Right there. Between his long, black-clad legs, the heavy boots on either side of him holding him in place.

Yes, that was exactly what he wanted to do.

Vanni slid to the floor. Never parted his legs, and Vanni fit just right between them. He put both his hands on Never's waist and arched his back so his head tilted up. His hair, just above his shoulders, fell away from his neck.

Never raised his hand and stroked the side of Vanni's head.

"That's it," Never said. "See me. Feel only me. Until I tell you otherwise."

Damion began to speak. "Why does he—"

"The same goes for you, sweet boy," Never said, turning to Damion. "See me. Feel only me. Until I tell you otherwise."

"On my knees?" Damion's voice came out soft, low.

"No." Never shifted his upper body. He turned toward Damion. "Rest against my chest."

Damion curled into him, head on Never's shoulder. His dark hair curved against Never's shoulder. Vanni knew how that hair felt, like brushed silk. So soft for a boy. Or a man. So cool against his fingers when he'd dared to touch it while Damion slept upon Vanni's pillows in Vanni's own bed, the boy sneaking into Vanni's rooms even as late into their lives as a couple of weeks ago.

Vanni kept looking up, watching the way Never coerced Damion. He wanted to ask something but forgot what it was as soon as he thought he might have a question. His hands stayed firm on Never's waist.

"Beautiful," Never breathed, looking from Damion to Vanni and then back to Damion again.

Never kissed the top of Damion's head. Damion kept his eyes shut as if hiding his own ardor. But it was too late. All the telltale signs had arrived. A slight sheen of sweat against his hair line, the way his skin looked so taut and warm from the fever of awakened passion burning its way through his body. And the tremble of his fingers as they tapped at Never's chest.

Vanni glanced lower and could see that Damion's thighs trembled. In the middle the trousers were tented where Damion's genitals had hardened, no doubt pulsing as fervently as Vanni's own.

Vanni did not know how long Never kept them that way, both pressed to him hard and trembling, one at his chest, one between his legs. As if the boys of the lonely Keep had become his. As if they no longer had any other life and this was everything. Everything at once.

A euphoria suffused Vanni like he'd never known before. The colors of the room deepened. He did not move except to breathe.

It was as if Damion slept against Never's chest, and yet Vanni knew he was wide awake. He could tell by the stiffness between his legs, and how both of them remained tense and waiting.

Waiting.

As if in a dream, Never moved so fast Vanni could not see how it happened. One moment Never was relaxed, eyelids half-closed as if in a doze, and the next he was nuzzling Damion's throat. That nuzzle, like a neck kiss, reminded Vanni of the time a year ago when he'd seen Lord Neverelle make that very same gesture in the garden at Lord Percy's ball.

Damion's hair was in the way, curtaining the kiss, but Vanni could hear a suckling noise that made him even harder. He wanted to join in; he wanted to move but couldn't.

After a while, Damion's head fell back on his shoulders and his hair spilled behind him leaving only a thin veil caught upon his chest. Vanni could see the skin of his neck revealed now, dimpled red, a small pucker. It was like a wound already closing as Never licked and licked it.

Damion moaned, eyelids opening and closing. A small smile curved his lips as his pink tongue came out to lick them. He still clung to Never, but his head was back.

Now Never was on Vanni, and Vanni could not recall him moving at all. His mouth was to Vanni's throat, licking, kissing, and Vanni swallowed, moving the muscles there to entice him more.

Never's mouth made a sliding motion against the side of his neck. Vanni felt the bite before it registered that, yes, Never was indeed biting him. It was more of a nip, though he felt a sharp needle-like pain at first. But after that split-second of icy shock, the bite became a suck that went straight to his groin. No pain. Just endless falling into pleasure, white and feathery, with a red core of desire like a hot coal.

The sensation seemed to last forever. And it was over far too quickly.

The next thing Vanni knew, he was leaning back on the sofa still aroused, the heat beneath his skin a fever still unbroken.

Damion still sprawled on the other end of the sofa, eyes closed.

Never stood before them. He handed Vanni a chalice. "Drink," he ordered.

It was not wine but pure grape juice. He drained the entire contents of the chalice before he realized how thirsty he was.

Never said, softly, "Go back to your room. Sleep until you are no longer tired. Then you will have a meal."

Vanni stood, unsteady at first. Still impossibly aroused. He righted himself, then realizing how sleepy he was, he headed for the hall and the staircase. A nap sounded perfect. He would rest to clear his head and then find out what this was all about. He would tell Never, firmly, that Damion was who he should be courting. That Damion had been Never's first choice, and should be his choice this time as well.

For Vanni, with all his heart, could not ever bear to see his childhood companion and best friend hurt.

Chapter Fifteen

When Vanni woke, he listened to the wind sigh against his windows for a long time. There was salt in the air, and upon his lips. His genitals still tingled, though he hadn't touched himself at all.

Everything came back to him slowly, piece by piece, image by image. Damion's beautifully flushed face, the spill of his hair, Never kissing Damion like the sweetest of angels. The sound of the sucking against his neck. And Vanni's own neck, still itching from a similar kiss.

He reached up to touch the spot where Never had bitten him. The skin was smooth. No pain.

Dryness roughened the back of his throat as he tried to swallow. He sat up and reached for the pitcher of water and a glass at his bedside table. He drank two glasses of water without thinking.

When his thirst was quenched, he pushed his legs over the side of the bed and stood. A sudden dizziness overcame him, gone as quickly as it came.

Still fully clothed, he slid his feet into his boots, adjusted his hair and left his room.

Damion's room was one door down, shut tight, silence emanating from within. Vanni approached the door. He stood facing it for a long moment before quietly knocking.

No answer.

"Damion."

Silence.

His hand reached for the doorknob, gently turning. The door snapped open. Vanni pushed it until he could peer in only a few inches. He saw curtained windows and the light gray shadows they made on the floor and the soft red rug by Damion's bed. He saw shelves of books and notebooks, a desk with quills and brushes. And the bed itself, with oak posts and white curtains held back with black ribbons.

On the bed, Damion sat motionless, still wearing his black trousers, his white shirt. The shirt was undone almost to his navel, revealing the tender, young flesh of his slightly muscled chest. And the hairless, light brown bud of one nipple. Damion sat so still that Vanni thought he was dreaming him. But when the glare met his, he knew Damion was awake. Wide awake.

"Get out," Damion said, voice low and even.

Vanni took a step into the room.

"Get out!" Damion's voice rose.

Vanni took another step toward him.

A third time. "Get out!"

"I swear," Vanni said, moving quickly toward him. Damion didn't scare him. "I didn't mean to interfere. You saw what he did to us. How he controlled us. You felt it. I know you did. I wanted to leave. I swear!"

Damion took a deep, unsteady breath. His chest trembled. "You promised."

Vanni came close enough to the bed that now he stood before him. "I know. And I meant it. I will stay out of your way. I swear. I didn't mean for him to pull me in. I didn't instigate it. He's different. There's something about him--"

Damion's hard glare softened. But barely. He bit at his lower lip, his eyes moving about the room, not meeting Vanni's.

"Damion—"

"Quiet! Don't speak." His mouth turned down. He blinked quickly. Finally, he looked back up at Vanni. "I know what it's like," he said. "I know he's different, not exactly like you and me." His voice had become a whisper. "But I don't care. And I don't want him to want you."

Guilt and hurt surged through Vanni. All he wanted was to protect Damion. To give him whatever he desired.

122

"I know," he finally answered. "I'll make myself scarce. I'll take my meals with the servants away from you both."

Damion sighed. "That's ridiculous. You don't have to go that far."

But Vanni knew short of leaving the Keep, his absence needed to be extreme. "I do need to go that far. I should. I will."

"But I don't want you out of my life," Damion protested. He moved his legs against the side of the bed as if he couldn't decide whether to get up, or stay put. "You're like a brother to me. I want you to be—here."

Vanni frowned. "I don't think you do."

Damion frowned back. "I need you. But please, just don't kiss him again."

Vanni nodded. Relieved that Damion didn't hate him. "I won't."

"But he's very persuasive," Damion said. "You must be on guard."

"I will be. But Damion, I'm not sure what happened. Don't you think it's a little strange that he—that he—" He couldn't finish. Swallowed hard. Finally he said three words like a question. "Both of us?"

"Yes. That's why I'm going to tell him tonight."

"Tell him what?"

"That I'm in love with him."

It was devastating to hear those words. Yet, he was sadly happy for Damion. That boy should have everything good happen to him.

Vanni came to the side of the bad and sat next to Damion. "So soon?"

"I need to tell him. So I can know. He'll either reject me, or give me all of his attention. Don't you think?"

Vanni didn't know what to say, so he nodded, blinking hard.

"I never felt this way before." Damion turned to look at him, eyes dark and unguarded now. So handsome the way his hair fell against his left cheek, still sleep-tousled. He smelled of camphor from the snow-white sheets of his bed.

A stabbing pain sliced at Vanni's heart. Then was gone.

"I understand." But it was a lie as much as the truth. Had Damion never felt a thing for Vanni? His chest felt like it wanted to cave in at the thought.

"Thank you for understanding. I knew you would, Vanni." Damion's smile came so bright onto his face that for a moment Vanni thought a servant had entered and opened the curtains on one of the windows.

Quite suddenly, Never stood in the open doorway of Damion's room, flanked by his two servants, his clothing unwrinkled and crisp. He'd changed into gray trousers, a clean white ruffled shirt, and a red jacket. All his tailored styles hugged his slim figure, tracing into a "V" at his waist and giving him a tall, impeccable presence. His unlined face, dark long lashes and pink lips painted him with the look of a youth, but the way he held his mouth and jaw, tight, angular, made him seem older. He had the look of a man in charge.

Vanni glanced away, frowning. It felt to him as if Never were intruding. And yet, the duke had given him free reign here at the Keep. And Damion was in love with him. Of course, Damion would give Never an open invitation to come into his room.

"Lunch in the dining room is being served now," Never said. Then he gave them a sly smile.

Vanni's heart skipped a beat when he saw him wink. Never looked directly at Vanni and said, "Aren't you hungry?"

Damion pretended not to see the exchange, and jumped off the bed, bending and sliding his feet into his boots.

"I am!" he said, and hurried to the door, following Never down the hall.

Vanni took a deep breath, blinking hard. He looked at Damion's back with a sinking feeling of longing. But with Never, there was a quick fire, and he could not get the

124

memory out of his head of Never forcing him against the counter in the kitchens, or Never's kiss this morning that sent his body into a blaze that even now was banking again, storing heat for the next time. But there would be no next time.

He clamped his teeth down on his bottom lip. He'd promised Damion. No more Never. No more.

*

The rest of the day unfolded fairly normally, considering what little intimacies had happened between the three of them. They were back to their games, although somewhat subdued. Back to entertaining each other the way they had when the duke had been home.

Never played classical piano and cards equally well. He quoted speeches from famous plays, entertaining them with nuance and style. After dinner, he even agreed to go for a walk about the grounds at dusk where he picked wildflowers and poured them over Damion's hair where they tangled and sparked their white petals, making Damion smile and laugh.

Vanni trailed behind them, the sea-wind whipping about his locks of blond hair. He smiled to see Damion smile. But inside, he was all shadow and no grace. Bereft. Left out.

The wind rippled through the trees at the edge of the woods. It shot cold air straight to Vanni's heart. They all wore their cloaks even though it was summer, but the breeze could not be intimidated.

Never's black cloak, lined with red, rose up behind him like great wings. Damion chased the flapping material, laughing, before Never whirled about and caught the edges himself, whipping them around Damion, pulling him into the folds of the cape. He bent his head.

Vanni stopped, turned his head to look away. But he couldn't see anything anyway. No doubt a shared, secret kiss. A touch to his cool cheek. A stroke to his silken hair.

Vanni could almost feel it himself, how Never's lips massaged the mouth. How the hot tongue delicately invaded private space.

Vanni heard Never say, "Are you cold?"

Damion's reply: "A little."

Vanni had already begun to head back to the front entrance of the Keep. He didn't want to hear or see any more. Tonight the ocean wind would be relentless. Even now, the sea gave off a shuddering roar. He'd add an extra blanket to his bed. Have some hot mulled wine.

"Vanni, wait for us," Never shouted above the increasing gusts.

Vanni pretended not to hear them. That wine sounded better and better.

Once indoors, with the latches shut securely behind them, Never became even more presumptuous. To Damion, he said boldly, "Go to your room and wait for me there." He did not even smile.

Damion seemed not to notice. His eyebrows shot up. His face sweetly darkened and his eyes became glazed. "Yes!" was all he said as he bounded up the stone stairs.

Never turned a cool, storm-blue gaze on Vanni. One side of his mouth quirked. "What?" he asked.

"I didn't say anything." Vanni replied. He wanted to punch that look off Never's face. Or kiss it. He was so confused.

Never approached him. He ran his hand gently down Vanni's back. For a moment, Vanni could not breathe but covered it well. Never's hungry smile gleamed in his eyes. Vanni felt empty inside, waiting for something to happen. Waiting for—for what? The moment he could freely touch him, hold him, have him?

But that was not going to happen!

Yet at this juncture, more than anything in the world, he wanted to make love to Never, take him away from his

126

goal for the evening, from Damion. He'd never felt this dizzy and senseless in his life.

"You don't like what I'm doing with him?"

"He's sensitive. I've told you over and over, I don't want him hurt." It was the truth. The fact that he wanted Never for himself was only a side-effect of what had happened that morning.

"I will not hurt him."

"Oh?" Vanni huffed a breath of disgust.

Never raised an eyebrow.

"He's just very young—" Vanni began.

"So are you," Never countered.

"Not like that." He gulped. "Just be good to him."

"Look at my eyes, Vanni."

Vanni could not look away, those depths of intimate whirlwinds, as if the ocean itself came to life and made itself manifest in Lord Neverelle.

There was a giant mirror on the wall over the couch. His reflection in it dazzled Vanni; in the glass Never shone even brighter, a man of tidal waves and stolen secrets.

Never leaned up and kissed him, a feather-touch to the lips. His hand pressed the back of Vanni's neck. Vanni wanted to yell, "No!" Or moan in pleasure. He could not decide which. Instead he swayed.

Slowly, Never backed away.

Hunter. Wolf. Sea-Witch. What in the hell was he?

"Come," Never said.

Vanni watched, as if mesmerized, as Never took the stairs two at a time, his boots tapping, making stark echoes.

Vanni shook himself, the kiss still singeing his lips. All his resistance left him. All his will.

At a run, he followed Never, who seemed not to notice. At the third landing, the door to Damion's room stood open. Never's two silent servants came out and met Vanni's eyes once, then moved quickly down the hall.

Damion's room glittered with candles. There were lilies on the desk and white roses in glass-mirrored vases on the nightstand and bureau. The hearth snickered with warm, golden flames. The room captured summer, sweet and satin, liquid, hot.

Damion stood in the middle of the room, glancing about, mouth open, skin glowing.

At the door, Never turned, looking once toward Vanni. "Satisfied that I intend to treat him well? To spoil him?"

Vanni nodded as Never's free hand pushed the door closed right in his face. Vanni put his palm against the wood to prevent it from closing all the way.

"Never?" To his horror, his voice sounded far too earnest in his own ears. What was he doing? Why had he followed?

Never turned a wicked smile upon Vanni. The pupils of his eyes dilated brightly as he said, "Vanni, go to your room and stay there."

"Bu--"

"Go!"

The door slammed in his face.

Nausea churned inside him. And a kind of furious sorrow took him up into a white cloud of shock. Sorrow that Never might still hurt Damion with his strange games. But also, sorrow that Never had pushed him away.

In spite of this, he found himself obeying his command without hesitation, entering his own room, going to the bed, lying down on his back and staring up at nothing. He didn't even see the ceiling. It was, in fact, nothingness that consumed him, gray-edged, sunless, mindless.

He did not know how long he drifted like that. The room spun darkly around him. The wind wailed.

A knock came at his door. He roused himself from his stupor, got up and opened it.

Never stood before him, night-bright tempter, and lunged into Vanni's arms.

128

"Well?"

"You were with Damion. What are you doing here?" said Vanni.

"You do realize that it is you I want to be with."

"No. I don't." But his heart beat in a wild frenzy now.

"But I couldn't say it in front of Damion, now, could I? And you had made your own wishes very clear. You wanted me to court him. And so I am. But for my own wishes, I am now here." There was no friendliness to Never's tone. No nicety. Just a bold statement of desire.

But for Vanni, it was everything. Despite his promise to Damion. His guilt. It was that sudden, his shift from abject devastation to now, to this thrum of life standing before him, this throbbing ecstasy, this man. It was all he wanted in this moment. It was everything. And more.

His new promise to Damion had lasted less than a day. He would chastise himself for it later.

"You're the one, Vanni," Never said. "You're all I want."

Still, the tone deflected emotion. Vanni wondered at that, but his body didn't care. He stepped out of Never's arms, back from the doorway, allowing Never entrance.

Never came toward him. Not knowing why he did so, Vanni took a step back. Then another. Something wasn't right. And yet his body was so fevered he could not deny his desire. That Never had come for him. That Never wanted him.

When the backs of Vanni's legs hit the bed, he almost fell back. He managed to hold his ground. Even as Never wrapped his arms around him. Even as Never bent and kissed him.

Everything turned red.

It wasn't just a fire between them. It was an explosion. Urgent. Untamed.

What is happening? The small voice in the back of his mind was easily silenced.

His hands went everywhere and he was afraid he'd tear Never's newly tailored clothes. Never didn't seem to care. He was already tugging hard at his own shirt in his waistband, then pushing Vanni roughly down on the bed. Vanni landed on the mattress face up and Never straddled him, holding him down hard by the shoulders. Rough. Frowning.

"You do everything I say. Am I clear? No questions. And you will never, ever again tell me how to handle Damion."

Through the haze of arousal, body raging as fervently as the winds outside his windows, Vanni nodded. There was no other option. Like a dream, there was no other course to take. All paths were blocked now. Everything but the path to Never.

He was surrounded now, by Never's hair, the silk of his white shirt, the warm wool of his gray trousers. The intensity only increased as they wrestled.

Vanni shifted beneath him as Never fumbled with Vanni's clothing, ripping away his shirt, pulling down his trousers and revealing bare skin.

He had never felt such a fierce desire. The chance for shared love or lust with another had not come for him. He was as virgin as Damion, simply older. More wary. But in this heady moment he had no cares, not about the Keep, not what Andreas might think or do, not Damion.

He didn't even care when Never bent his head and bit him firmly on the neck. A warmth trickled up, immediately obscuring any pain. His skin felt wet, slightly itchy. Never seemed to be drinking. Just like this morning. It was strange but he liked it. No, he *loved* it.

It was all that mattered. He had him. He had Never in his arms.

In a fever, his body strained. Ripples of arousal tremored through him, pooling at his groin, aching.

130

Naked underneath Never, he pushed up, wanting friction on his erection, on his whole body.

Never pulled back and stared down at him. Then he did something very strange. For a long while after, Vanni thought he'd dreamed it. Never bit down hard on the fleshy part of his palm and held his hand to Vanni's lips.

Warm blood dripped into Vanni's mouth. Only a few salt drops, pungent as a sudden mist from the sea. He breathed in cool air. Everything in the room brightened. Though there was no light, no candles, he could see. The walls, the ceiling, every vein, every tiny pucker and crack in the structure. The room glowed. Everything on his shelves, books, statues, boxes, and old toys had a golden halo.

"It's beautiful." The salt was still upon his tongue.

Never made a sort of bored groan. "Of course it is like that at first." He moved back, looking down at Vanni's naked body. "And you will feel it intensely. How easily you fall into this swoon and become mine."

"Yes." He didn't care that Never seemed irreverent. That his hands running up and down Vanni's chest were almost rough as if immune to his virginal sensitivity.

"Any liquid you have to give me is what I like."

"What?"

But before Vanni could try to comprehend that statement, Never's mouth lowered to his chest and moved down, down. Rapid and hungry. Tongue and lips.

Vanni felt the dampness at the tip of his cock, and suddenly Never was there as well, licking fast, sucking him into his mouth.

Euphoria ripped through him. The mouth pulled, hot and wet. Seeking his completion. He couldn't hold back. This was the first time anyone had ever touched him like that. This was the first time anyone had touched him at all, save chaste kisses with Cecilia at a couple of balls.

He cried out, his insides surging forward, burning. Throbbing. His cock pulsed again and again. He came hard, felt himself spurt into Never's suckling mouth.

When Vanni had nothing left to give, Never pulled up slowly, letting his spent cock flop back onto his abdomen. Then he roughly pulled Vanni up and turned him on the bed until he was on his stomach.

Sharp fingers stroked and pulled at Vanni's buttocks. That was when he felt Never's hardness, bare and stark and hot against his hip.

Never leaned forward, and in Vanni's ear he whispered, "Lift up. Lift your hips to me."

Vanni wasn't sure. Everything was happening too fast. He was not like Damion. He'd said so. But maybe in more ways than he realized, he was like him. Not just virgin. But innocent. Maybe even more than Damion. And this was the end of all of it.

"Now. Do not defy me."

The voice went into Vanni's mind like a snake, making a curving path, winding him up, speeding, slowing, undulating. Vanni lifted his hips.

"You want me," came the whisper.

"I want you," Vanni echoed.

Something wet touched him between his buttocks in his most intimate space, probing. Like the tongue in his mouth. Like the teeth in his skin. Like blood and biting, an invasion to the system.

The slickness increased. Then a hardness pushed into him without warning. Shock. Euphoria again. Mixed with pain. His hips rode back on it as the whisper in his head grew and grew. *You want me. You want me.*

"I want you," he cried out, and Never breached him, impaled him. His cock fully inside him now.

So this was it. The last edge of innocence fallen away like a crumbling cliff, down down to the sea. To the salt. To the gray storms and the waters and sea-witches who had all gone away, died off. Extinct childhood. No more fairy tales. Only reality.

This dark hand. This sex. This desire. Trembling through him like a nightmare broken into a million shards of beautiful iniquity and darkness revealed. And though it hurt, the pleasure was like nothing he'd ever imagined. The sweetness of the forbidden uncurled within him. So good.

Hand on Vanni's back, holding him down hard, hard, Never began to fuck him.

Tears rolled down Vanni's face.

When Never began to slow, Vanni said, hoarsely, "More."

Chapter Sixteen

Vanni woke to the metallic scent of blood and the musk of semen, still dazed. He half-remembered the sound of rustling clothes, Never dressing, Never leaving as swiftly as he had arrived.

The room echoed with the crying wind. Emptier than ever.

Was that it, then, for them? Would tomorrow go on like before, with all three of them pretending nothing had happened? No discussion. No acknowledgment of vulnerability, or the unprecedented closeness of intimate acts. This was Vanni's fear. And his hope.

For as he recalled what Never had done to him, and how he'd cried out for more, shame rushed to heat his cheeks.

And there had been blood. A cut on Never's palm. Drops of salt on his tongue. He'd swallowed blood! Or maybe it had all been a dream? Because that was completely unexpected.

He could not imagine wanting what they'd done spoken of aloud.

Nude, covered in semen and dried sweat, Vanni went to his balcony window and drew back the curtains. Dawn light from the east made the sea look cast in molten silver, wrinkles of brilliant whiteness falling back upon itself over and over.

For a long time he stared at the wildness, constant and real and moving.

After a while, he rang for a servant to bring him a bath. He took his time in the hot water, examining his body for wounds, scratches, abrasions. He found none. Even when he felt between his legs at the sensitive entrance to his body, he felt nothing unusual. No sting. No bruising.

Maybe it all had been a dream!

But then, why did he feel so banged up within? *That* was real. Guilt. Shame. Disgust for breaking his promise. For liking—no *loving*—what should have been Damion's alone.

Added to that, it seemed Never didn't care that he might have broken Damion's heart last night. No, not one bit. And his rough treatment of Vanni revealed no true soft side. No tenderness for Vanni, either.

Maybe he'd saved all that for Damion. Vanni hoped so, because Damion deserved to be treated like a prince, petted, stroked, held, loved. He deserved to have someone soothe away his nightmares, and look after him when he was feeling alone, scared, and maybe a little empty like Vanni felt all the time lately.

Never had promised to treat Damion well. Vanni would make sure he kept that promise.

He got out of the bath dripping, and stood in front of his private hearth to warm himself. He took his time getting dressed. Breakfast was still a couple of hours away.

Through the long, salt-laced halls of the Keep, Vanni wandered. He could scent and feel and hear things he hadn't noticed before. The sleeping breaths of Damion, and even Never on the fourth floor, barely breathing, sleeping as if dead.

The kitchen was three floors below, but he could hear the servants talking as if the floors and walls were made of paper and not wood and stone. He could smell the bread dough rising, the wood stoves puffing, the dish soap bubbling.

In some parts of the Keep, he could hear rats scuttling under the floorboards. Spiders ticked as they walked the rock walls. A shingle far above on the topmost tower rattled in the wind.

The rock walls made faces at him. He'd never noticed that before, how the random designs formed eyes, noses, ears, and open mouths. The stone froze time and all those faces were caught in it, forever and ever unending.

Vanni wandered the floors and when he got tired he sought more civilized surroundings, and warmth.

He entered the drawing room where they had played their games, shared their kisses. Candles glinted from every surface, corner and shadow. Everywhere he went now, there were candles. More and more of them to match Never's tastes.

Never liked candles better than oil lamps. In his first week as a guest at the Keep after the duke's absence, he'd ordered them by the box-load from nearby villages using the duke's money, and had them delivered.

On his orders, the servants kept them lit from early morning until late at night. Their flickering light and cumulative heat made the drafty Keep seem drier, almost warm.

Vanni still preferred the salty air. He was constantly opening shuttered windows during the day only to find them closed again. He now knew Never closed them when he wasn't looking, preferring in his dry, cool lordly nature the way a room became more intimate in candlelight.

For he was in high seduction mode. Had been from the moment he'd set foot in the Keep. Now Vanni knew-- it could not have been anything else.

Candle wax had melted along the room's shelves, a frozen dripping like out of place icicles. The servants had not yet had time to clean this room so early in the morning. Later, the wax would be cleared and fresh candles set into holders for the new day.

Vanni sat in a cushioned chair, making himself comfortable, and tried to read. His mind moved at a languid pace. He was awake, but still dreamy.

Servants had lit the hearth, yet the room retained some chill, and Vanni draped a day-blanket over his knees. He sipped a glass of water and tried to concentrate on the words of his book.

Time passed. Finally, a servant called him to breakfast.

To Vanni's surprise, Damion and Never were already seated. Neither of them had come looking for him.

Never nodded, when Vanni sat.

Damion would not look at him. Said nothing.

Breakfast was a quiet affair. Never ate delicately, as always. Vanni and Damion had second helpings, both apparently ravenous.

Upon finishing, Damion excused himself, saying he had a few hours of work to do in the duke's study.

Vanni went back to his chair in the drawing room, feeling overly full and suddenly tired again from his night's antics.

Never followed him. He picked up a book and reclined on the sofa where just yesterday all three of them had—

Vanni took a breath. Finally, he found the courage to speak.

"What were all the candles and flowers in Damion's room about? What did you do?"

"What did I say last night about questions concerning Damion?" he replied, not looking up from his book.

"But--"

"Do you think I de-flowered him as I did you?" Now he looked at Vanni over the spine of the book.

Vanni shrugged.

"But he's so much more delicate than you," said Never. "And you did want me to treat him well. I'm taking my time with him. Distracting him."

Vanni did not believe him. His book fell to his lap. He crossed his arms in front of his chest and lowered his head.

"Oh-- Did you want candles and lilies, too, my sweet? How romantic. I'll arrange it."

"It isn't that, it's--"

Never's eyes widened, the pupils expanding. "We need to be discreet. I need to make him feel like the center of all my attention, don't I? If I told him you were my choice, as you said just yesterday, it would break his heart. You understand this, don't you?"

"Yes. But you--?"

"Slept with him?"

Vanni swallowed hard, said nothing.

"Don't worry so," Never teased, running his fingertips over his mouth. "I was very gentle with him. Very considerate. And I did not penetrate him as I did with you. If I treat you roughly it is because I know you can take it. It is what is solid between real men, less coddling, more fucking. I prefer you. Don't you realize it?"

A compliment, to be sure. But Vanni did not feel it.

"No need to be jealous." Never's laugh came hollow.

In response to Never's strangely seductive harshness, Vanni found his eyes warming. "We can't hurt him. I won't have it."

"Of course, darling Vanni. We are of the same mind in everything. Including Damion."

Vanni nodded, the emptiness within warming a little.

*

The day passed quietly. Damion joined them after lunch and they played cards and checkers. Never commanded the piano for almost an hour.

The winds had stopped for a while. The ocean lay calm and blue in the late afternoon. The temperature was cool but not chill.

They decided to have dinner on the veranda and watch the sunset.

Nothing more was said about the past day's events. After Vanni and Never had discussed Damion and his more sensitive nature, the subject became closed.

After dinner, Damion stood by the railing looking out at the still calm sea. He looked taller, shoulders a bit further back than normal, chin held high. Or maybe it was Vanni's hope for him. That Damion was happy. That he was healthy, well, and not upset with Vanni. Not worried.

Vanni kept watching him. He didn't stare, but he kept an eye on him.

Damion had attention only for Never, so he did not notice Vanni's interest. That was good.

When Never went to change from dinner attire to evening wear, Vanni went to stand beside Damion at the rail.

Voice low, Vanni said, "I want you to be happy."

Damion turned to him with a shy smile. "I am."

"All right, then." Vanni turned to go back into the Keep.

"Vanni." Damion's voice was pitched slightly high.

Vanni's heart lurched to hear him call his name. Stupid, actually. He turned. Beyond Damion, the sea shifted in a dozen shades of blue and gray. "What is it?"

"I'm—I—I don't know."

Vanni took a step toward him. "Tell me. I'm here for you no matter what."

"It's just—" Damion looked down, then up, his brown eyes wide, young. His beauty emanated through his skin, his features, his voice and bearing and Vanni felt a knot form in his throat.

"What? You can tell me."

Damion nodded. "Sometimes, I'm still a little afraid. At night. You know."

Vanni frowned. "Of what?"

"Everything." He took a deep breath and twisted his mouth as if making fun of himself. "Time to grow up, right?"

Vanni said, "It doesn't have to be so fast if you don't want it to be."

But it was happening fast. Vanni almost winced as he remembered Never roughly flipping him over, barely preparing him before he thrust into him, taking him, claiming him. Yes, Vanni wanted it. But it all happened so fast.

Today was the first day of leaving his childhood behind forever. His first time was over. It had been a tumble: hard and dirty. It had hurt. There had been no sweet words. Not before, during or after the act.

Like Damion, he felt that maybe he was in love. But he could not have that love. No matter what Never said, that he was the one, that Damion was a dalliance, Vanni could not allow it. That pain for Damion would be too much. And he loved Damion too much. More than he loved Never, though he had never said it.

But could he resist? Either man? Both men?

Even now, Damion's smile matched the one in his own mind. Full of wonder, but also smug.

"Damion—" Immediately, Vanni's throat went dry.

"What?"

He took a deep breath. "I will always be here for you. Always." *Even if you get scared and want to climb back into my bed for old times' sake. Even if you break my own heart now and forever.*

Damion's smile grew, shining. "Thank you."

He longed to hear Damion say the same words in return. But like a gossamer curtain, the silence of growing up too fast draped itself between them.

*

An evening of wine. Too much wine. They played charades. Tongues loosened. They could not continue without laughing, falling down, speaking when they were not supposed to speak per the rules of the game.

Even Never laughed more than usual. His temper grew casual and fun. Excited, even. His gaze met Vanni's often, hot and red, but it was Damion he touched. A hand to the shoulder. Fingers brushing back the hair from Damion's face where it had loosened from his braid. Quick, twirling dances when Damion had correctly guessed his gestures for the name of a play during the game.

When Vanni guessed correctly, he received a verbal reward only. "Good thinking there!" "Quick-witted, aren't you?"

But he didn't see himself as quick-witted. Because where quick wits really mattered he didn't have them. Something was going on here and he needed to figure it out. Something more than two boys falling for the same man. More than the need for Damion to be happy, and a fear of being left behind.

The candles told part of the story. And the way Never's servants rarely spoke and kept to themselves. And how Never barely ate, and took advantage of the duke's generous nature, and was now taking advantage of his boys.

It was not lechery, or a bad influence. But more.

It was in the way Vanni felt drunk even when he had not had that much wine. How his desire flared so quickly and so hot. Again he thought of the blood. How Never had bitten his own palm and put it to Vanni's lips. That was no common practice. As naïve as he was about the ways of the world and affairs of the heart, he did know that blood-drinking was more like a fairytale. If people actually did it, it had to be a rare fetish, or possibly something associated with mental illness.

Never was up to something more than just deflowering two lonely young men. But Vanni's mind grew foggier the more he tried to think about it.

After the charades, Never caught Vanni's gaze and held it longer than was comfortable. He said, firmly, "The hour is not late, but I want you to sit here and read for an hour. Then go up to your room and wait for me."

Vanni glanced at Damion on the other side of the room. He could not hear them.

"Why?" But already he knew he would do it. His hand was reaching for the book he'd been reading that morning. He was intrigued to get back into its pages.

"Look at me. And only me." The dark blue eyes seemed to swirl. "Why do you always question me?"

Vanni started to look away and found himself frozen in place. He could not move his eyes. "I don't." His voice came out meeker than he'd intended.

"You want us to be discreet for Damion's sake, do you not?"

Vanni nodded. Yes, that was it. Of course. Never wanted Damion to think he only visited him at night. He only kissed Damion. And Vanni wanted that as well for his best friend. So like brothers they were. That loyal bond. For Damion's heart was bonded to his, and what hurt Damion hurt him as well.

In truth, Vanni shouldn't be sneaking around at all.

Vanni started to speak but his words stuck in the back of his throat. *Don't come to my room tonight. Don't touch me. Don't want me. Don't—fuck me.*

As a true friend, he should have said all those words and more. But he didn't want to. He didn't want to be left out, forgotten. Just the thought of Never returning to his rooms tonight set is body ablaze.

And there was some jealousy as well. That fact that Never put his hands on Damion. He wasn't jealous for himself. He was jealous of Never. For Damion was and always had been Vanni's, and to see him taken away by a man with such an elegant nature and beauty continued to grieve him.

"I know you feel protective of him. And maybe more." Never smiled as if he knew all the secrets of the Keep.

"No—I—" Vanni struggled for more words.

"I promise. I won't hurt him." Never's lips parted. His teeth caught in the candlelight, neat and straight and white. It couldn't have been those teeth that nipped his own hand before putting it to Vanni's mouth. No. They were too perfect, too clean.

But he couldn't help but wonder, did Never feed Damion his blood as well? And why?

142

He felt the fog come over him again as Never turned away. But a part of him vowed to ask Never about this fetish when they were alone. Tonight. In Vanni's cushioned and beckoning bed. Where adult secrets came unraveled to the ever-moving sea shadows.

Chapter Seventeen

Vanni lay on his back listening to another calm night. The darkness ticked with echoing creaks and groans. His ears were sensitive now, more than he'd ever remembered. His eyes saw colors through the shadowed dark, as if his bedroom walls glowed crimson edged in deep topaz. He could smell the sea mixed with the dripping timber of the woods all the way up here in his stone room. He could almost hear the leaves shedding from the trees. The loam they made left a sweet aroma on the thin air currents.

Beneath a furred blanket, he lay naked and waiting. His skin tingled up and down his arms and legs. In his stomach, a heavy knot of longing formed. He was already hard, his erection pressing up to bob against his abdomen.

He strained to listen through the yawning tides of the sea and the whispering wood, all the rustles and whispers of the Keep. Strained to hear Damion in his own room and Never with him soothing, placating, kissing, loving.

He heard everything around him but that. Servants muttering in their sleep. Candles sizzling, guttering. And outside, owls and the hoof steps of deer. He even heard the fish gliding through the sea.

Damion, he thought. *Damion, are you happy? Is he kissing your neck again the way you like? Is he treating you like the prince you deserve to be? Are his hands hot as they smooth over your hair and cheeks and chest? Please be happy. Please let your lovely soul fly free.*

Even though his imagination enjoyed the view, and Never was gentle with Damion, Vanni kept thinking: *I can do it better for Damion. I know what he likes. I care.*

A single knuckle-rap on his door startled him from his reverie. Never did not wait for Vanni to speak. As Vanni raised his head and looked, the wooden door had already swung open. A lean, dark shadow entered his room.

For a quick moment, everything went red. Ridiculous. He was already swooning?

But of course. This was Never. And of their own accord, Vanni's hands pushed the blanket away from his body, down. Down. Revealing himself. Offering himself to this man who had taken over every cell in his body.

Never hovered above him, a static energy almost touching but not quite. A presence that lent a flow to the air that had no weight but exuded a heavy force.

Vanni reached up.

Never was in his arms at once, pulling him tight to his still-clothed body, nose and mouth nuzzling at his neck.

No words. Just action. Vanni wanted it like this. He'd waited for more than an hour. He'd been jealous of both Never and Damion long enough tonight. Now this was his time. His hour with a man who could make him soar.

There was no preamble to the biting this time. To that strange blood fetish. Now Vanni was sure—though his thoughts didn't seem to care or worry about it—that the fetish did not involve only himself drinking blood from Never's wrist.

Never drew blood from Vanni's neck. That much became evident this second time around. The bite stabbed sharp upon his skin just to the side of his throat. He had an idea it should have hurt more than it did, but his foggy mind numbed the pain. The dampness on his neck beneath Never's mouth smelled of hot metals and salt, and quickly thickened; Never licked and licked.

Yes, this time there could be no mistake. Never was drinking his blood.

Vanni loved it. His body arched at the pleasure of Never's mouth attached to his neck. Vanni clutched at him with all his strength, knees bending, legs spreading. Never smelled of deep wells and candles and an ancient soft dust-like perfume that turned Vanni's heart from calm to rage to undaunted passion in seconds.

As he pressed himself against Never's center, the surge of pleasure increased, his sensitivity multiplying. It was so abrupt he had no time to do anything but groan aloud.

Never pulled back. "Wait! Don't come yet—"

But Vanni was already lost. He could not control the ecstasy that came over him. His cock pulsed even as he tried to obey the command. He wanted to obey, but his body had already gone too far. His mind splintered at the conflict. *Don't come.* His essence shot onto his stomach and chest. *Don't come.*

Never sat back between Vanni's legs. "What a waste."

Vanni blinked back tears even as the pleasure continued to send white lightning through his limbs.

Never bent to lick the spendings from his chest. The tongue lapped like velvet. Vanni's heart hummed.

Never raised up again, smacking Vanni hard on the flank. "Turn over!"

Still dazed, Vanni tried to obey, his knee bumping Never's thigh.

"You will not disobey me again!"

"I won't." Vanni heard his voice say it as if he had no will of his own.

Rough hands spread him. Sharp fingers poked him. Vanni gasped. Shut his eyes. He wanted this. He'd laid himself out like a sacrifice for this, waiting for Never to arrive.

Yet, a wave of grief and mortification washed over him. Such cold regard held love in its gestures of quick commands and smacks to his ass, the tugging of flesh, the biting. He remembered that Never had said Vanni was more mature, that this was about them being men. What happened between men did not need candles or flowers.

He believed him. He wasn't a little boy anymore.

Between his buttocks came a slick warmth. The sharpness receded. He heard the whisper of soft cloth being undone, the scrape of nails against wool. Felt the hard tip. Never's cock, ready for him. Damp and needful.

He liked it that he made Never feel this way, that Never needed him. Even as Never plunged into him, taking no time to let Vanni become used to the invasion. The burn made him cry out. He bit his own tongue. His eyes closed so tightly, his forehead began to ache.

Never fucked him, two fast thrusts, then leaned over him and said into his ear, "What are you thinking in that witty mind of yours?"

"That I want you," Vanni stuttered.

"Say it again."

"I want you." In an amazing physical response, Vanni's cock hardened again despite the bunching of his stomach muscles and the stabbing fire of Never's cock as he moved in and out of him. In and out.

Maybe this act could be different. Then again, maybe this love for Never who commanded with such force was enough, but without reverence Vanni felt lost.

His cock didn't seem to mind, all the aches of his body now feeding a second round of pleasure.

Never continued to fuck him, but said in a low voice in his ear, "You lie. Tell me what you are thinking. Tell me why you are so tense."

If Vanni told the truth, he would look like a boy, not a man.

"Tell me. You are not to disobey me. If I command you, you do as I say. If I ask a question, you answer."

Vanni was so full inside, as if Never's cock kept expanding, forcing him to give way. In a small voice, he said, "It hurts."

"Do you want kisses and compliments, then?"

Vanni frowned. That question had nothing to do with pain.

"Answer me, boy!"

"I'm not a boy. But I—I haven't done this before last night. It's too fast, too much."

Never slowed. But still he kept up his thrusts, lazier now, softer. He ran his fingers down Vanni's spine. "It's just that you make me crazed. Your blood is pure euphoria."

Vanni managed a deeper breath just as Never thrust a little harder. The air came out of his lungs in a whoosh. His skin was on fire.

Never said, "You're tight. So tight. We fit so well."

Vanni wanted Never's attentions. His affection, even. But the fit? His cock was hard but his heart bereft. And the pain—was it always such? Did Never make Damion feel this way?

For a moment, Vanni panicked at the thought. Damion should not be made to feel this. All that kissing at first on the sofa in the drawing room—that was all good. Sweet. Mesmerizing. Arousing.

This was different. The warm reds of passion but mixed with a kind of predatory need. It was as if Vanni were being held immobile by invisible chains, and even his words did not seem like his own. He did not want to be coddled, but he felt he should be able to participate a little more.

"Do you not like it, Vanni?" Never asked, his thrusts gentler now.

"I do." It was a truth. He wanted this. Even if it was painful.

"You humans are so sensitive. Let's see what I can do."

Humans? But Vanni had no time to think of that strange phrasing.

Never, so large, so hard inside Vanni, changed the angle of his thrusting. Sudden pleasure filled Vanni's veins, a different fire now, passion-laced but tingling so good. Never's cock passed over that place inside him again and again, and Vanni forgot everything else but that sensation.

"I'm going to come again," he hissed.

"No. Not until I do. Not until I say!"

The desire to obey formed a hard tangle of will deep inside him against the onslaught of pleasure. That will, snarled and burled, belonged to Never in this moment.

Even as the pleasure foamed for release, as he wanted to come, something blocked him. Something deep. A resonance toward Never's body, not his own. A timing within that had nothing to do with himself. He waited. And waited.

Never continued to torment him, brushing that sweet spot inside over and over, thrusting, groaning. Vanni pushed back onto him, jerking his hips up, bending for him, spreading for him, ass high as he could get it on his hands and knees.

Never growled. Hot liquid filled Vanni's insides, the pulsings strong. Never came for a long time deep inside him. Moaning in ecstasy. Making Vanni ache even more.

His cock was so hard now. Jutting between his thighs, angling toward his belly. "I need to—" He was practically sobbing.

Never took his time withdrawing from his body. Finally, he flipped him onto his back and leaned his body over Vanni's.

He was still clothed. Only his cock was exposed, and Vanni could barely see it in the dimness. His own body was taut with need. He was panting hard now.

Never said, breath gusting over Vanni's stomach, "You can come now when I suck you. You can feed me now."

A hot mouth engulfed his hard cock, wet and strong, the suck sending him reeling over the edge.

He came hard in a white frenzy, fists gripping his bedcovers, feet stomping the edges of his bed. He thrust up into that mouth and emptied himself over and over. Never spilled not a drop.

When he was dry, Never leaned over him and put his hand to his mouth the way he had the night before. Vanni tasted tart salt and sucked. It was only a small amount of blood, but what he took onto his tongue and swallowed made him feel like coming again. His body's heat increased; the pain stopped.

After a moment, Never took his wrist away and moved back on the bed.

"Tight and sweet," he said, as he did up his trousers. "You've done well." He turned and patted Vanni on the stomach.

Vanni's body jerked. He watched Never get up and head for the door. He longed to say something. Anything. *Stay. Sleep with me. Let's do it all over again.*

His body, even through all the memory of aches and exhaustion, wanted him again. His mind wanted to call out. *Don't leave me.*

But it seemed Never did not want that.

There was a held-back lump in his throat as he watched Never step into the hall and close the door softly behind him.

*

At breakfast the next morning, Damion looked bright-eyed and shining.

Though the remnants of euphoria still coursed through Vanni's body, he did not feel like talking. The sun against his eyes hurt. He found himself craving more candlelight, like Never, and he picked at his breakfast as if it might be poisoned.

After they ate, Damion bounded off to the drawing room, saying he was taking the day off from the duke's business, and shouting, "Anyone up for more charades?"

Vanni followed. It was nice to see Damion happy. But so much was based on a lie. It made him sick inside to think it.

"The Earl Giovanni," Never said from behind him.

Vanni froze, turning in the long hall. Damion had disappeared at the far end into the drawing room.

Quickly, Vanni said, "He's happy. Thank you."

Never raised both eyebrows. "And you?"

Vanni nodded, looking down.

"Have I not told you how special you are to me? That you are the one? The one I choose?"

"Yes." Vanni's voice came out higher than intended, sounding too much like a boy's.

"You deserve this," Never said.

"So does he."

"But not more than you."

"Why?" Vanni asked. "He's the more beautiful. The one who is the sweetest, the rarest… like a gem—" He stopped, feeling inane, stupid.

"Is that how *you* feel about him?"

Vanni took a breath but did not answer.

"I see. And you think you are not as lovely as he is? And that he is not as infatuated with you as you are with him?"

"No. He relies on me. He is loyal to me. That's all. And I know I'm not as beautiful."

"Do you ever look into mirrors?" Never asked with a sly smile.

Vanni wanted to ask, *Do you?* But held his tongue.

"You need only ask around the villages to those who have seen you at the balls. You are truly a golden prince. You don't even see it, do you?"

"I'm an earl, not a prince," Vanni argued.

"Ah. But they think of you as a prince. And so do I. In your lovely ocean-dark castle."

Vanni's mouth dropped open. Never strode by him. Before Vanni could take another breath, he'd disappeared down the end of the hallway.

Chapter Eighteen

For more than a week the night visits continued. All dreaming and a little madness and physical trysts that involved both pleasure and horror. Never took as he pleased, when he pleased, pleasure and blood at his command from both Vanni and Damion with no protest on their parts.

The days remained languid, calm. But the nights came with storms of passion for Vanni, blood-drinking, and hard, fast sex that left him a bit empty, gasping and hurting but euphoric.

Daily, Vanni grew more enraptured. His body craved Never even through his guilt and shame. Damion's own glow increased in brightness. Looking at Never and Damion, from one to the other, Vanni had a hard time deciding which man was more beautiful, more perfect.

Damion had stopped glaring at Vanni. He no longer said any harsh words to him, or asked him to leave him alone with Never. They accepted each other's presence, and Never's, as they did the air.

And Damion smiled a lot. Those smiles knifed straight to Vanni's heart. For he still didn't understand what was going on here. And he didn't believe Never would stay good to his promise and not hurt his best friend.

No one bothered them as they went through their days like spoiled princes in a castle keep. The servants made no comment; they all saw to their chores but remained scarce, silent.

Never had them all order lavish new wardrobes, jewelry, books, games, candles, incense. Damion, who did the ledgers for the duke, insisted there was plenty of money to go around. He seemed unconcerned, less meticulous about the household, and he often stared off into space as if dreaming awake.

Everything seemed normal, and yet nothing was normal. Vanni could not seem to muster the energy to worry about it, though.

Never often met his eyes. Vanni felt held in place by those depths of ocean-blue with hints of hidden storms.

One evening, just after dinner, Vanni and Damion were in the drawing room alone together. The fire spit and hissed. Amber incense burned at the base. Vanni sat slumped on a plush sofa. Damion was standing by the flickering hearth. The sea-winds had gotten colder in the last few days and the Keep's fires burned night and day.

Often when they found themselves in the same room and Never was not around to buffer them, they ignored each other. But this evening, Damion broke the silence.

"I am sorry if I acted mad at you."

"It's all right. I understand," Vanni replied.

Damion walked to the end of the sofa. He'd grown into such a handsome young man. But now his head lowered. Shadows crossed his face.

"I'm afraid."

"Of what?" Vanni sat up. A surge of adrenalin shot through his body because Damion's words echoed something similar, but muffled and contained inside him.

"All this." He swept his hand through the air. "It's good but so different, like everything's changing. And I'm afraid. Just afraid."

"You know I won't ever let anything hurt you."

Damion's dark eyebrows lowered. "But also, I'm afraid that a rift will come between us so deep we'll never find each other again. I—I can't imagine a life without you. Never tells me not to worry, but I do."

"That's ridiculous." But Vanni's heart soared to hear those words.

"Then promise me right now that whatever happens we won't ever stop being friends. Brothers."

The twisting ache in Vanni's chest did not surprise him. He'd been feeling it forever. He motioned with his hand. "Sit down beside me for a minute."

Damion stared at the cushion beside Vanni as if it might be filled with rocks.

"Never went to change his outfit. Again."

"I know."

"So we're alone. You can talk to me. You know you can."

Damion nodded, sitting but keeping his body upright, muscles tense.

"You're being morose," Vanni said. "And too sentimental. We'll always be best friends. You know that. More than brothers, right? Nothing like any rift will happen."

But he knew Damion was right to be concerned. His broken promise to Damion sat between them, tangled evidence of the confusion wracking them both. For Vanni had promised Never would be Damion's. And now Never had been saying Damion was merely a dalliance.

"Even though I said I hated you when he flirted with you in the carriage—and you promised you'd stay away, I don't hate you, Vanni. And I know what he does at night. That he still visits you. That you—you try to hide it. That you want everything to be all right between you and me."

Vanni glanced away, more than uncomfortable. He wanted Never. He wanted Damion in his life. How could he have both?

A quick sea breeze blew against the windows, rattling; it whistled softly about the Keep. The evening was still early, still light through the curtains, but inside candles furiously danced, making the room like the center of a gemstone.

"I do want everything to be right between us, Damion. You have to believe me."

"I believe." Damion nodded. "I know something is different with him. That he's very difficult not to obey… to resist."

Damion had both hands palm-down on his thighs. Vanni reached out, touching Damion softly on his forearm. He leaned forward, trying to will him to look at him. But Damion kept staring straight ahead, as if waiting for something. For some*one*.

"Damion, can I ask you something?"

Damion nodded again.

"Look at me."

The beautiful face turned to his, the brown eyes clear and sparkling.

Vanni gave a little moan of longing. Damion. This boy should have been his! "Tell me the truth. Does he treat you all right?"

"Yes." The full, pink lips curved up.

"He doesn't hurt you?"

"No. He wouldn't. He's so gentle."

Vanni blinked to keep the warmth behind his eyes at bay. It was not how Never was with him. Rough. Rude. As if Vanni were a toy to be tossed about.

Working to keep his voice steady, Vanni said, "I'm glad."

He leaned further toward Damion, his arm going about his waist. Finally, Damion relaxed a little and leaned back into Vanni. He smelled so good, like soap-cleaned skin and firelight and childhood. The embrace was everything. Warmth. Hope. A swelling in the heart. They stared into each other's eyes. Damion's smile widened.

"If he ever *ever* hurts you," Vanni said, "you tell me. Promise. If you are ever unhappy, you must say so. Because I can't bear it. I can't take it if you aren't. If anything is wrong for you, I will make it right."

"I know you will. And I know he visits you and I'm not mad anymore. He has reasons. He told me. So I accept it. And I'm even glad. Because I don't want to leave you behind."

Vanni smiled. Now his chest trembled. Because he had that very same thought in the other direction, that he did not want to leave Damion behind.

"I will never leave you behind. I'll always be here for you. Loyal." Then he hugged Damion tighter and bobbed his head, leaving a quick, chaste kiss to his glowing cheek."

Damion took a deep breath, starting to say something before a voice broke their focus.

"Ah, this is too sweet. My boys finding their way to each other again. Well, I for one am glad that tension of the last couple of weeks is gone!"

They both looked up.

Vanni thought, *My boys?* A protective surge of heat began in his chest. His fingers gripped Damion's shirt at his side. How long had Never been standing in the doorway watching, listening?

Damion put a hand on Vanni's thigh by his knee, making a fist.

Never stepped into the hot room and moved toward them. His eyes seemed to spin and spin and Vanni became dizzy as he heard him say, "Two little sparrows, waiting to be plucked. You're going to be good little birds, aren't you?"

Vanni's head nodded as a familiar fog came over his brain. Beside him, Damion nodded, too, but his hand clutched at Vanni's knee tighter and tighter. And Vanni had the strange impression that everything these past two weeks had been unreal, like watching a play. Only now, the actors had forgotten their lines.

Chapter Nineteen

As Vanni climbed the stone stairs, his body seemed heavy, slow. He tried to remember why Never had called him and Damion sparrows just moments ago, but his mind kept letting go of the thought before he could try to make sense out of it.

When he reached the third floor, he started toward his own room where he always went, where he always waited, but Never, walking ahead, beckoned him back to the stairs. Up and up they went to the fourth floor landing.

Damion shuffled silently behind them.

But why were they going up here?

Never approached the open door to his room. Vanni came up alongside him. Never's servants were still lighting candles. The room smelled of roses, though Vanni did not see any. What he did see was the bed. Huge, ornate—as all the guest beds were in the Keep, but this one was awash in red satins and black furs. The red pillows were edged in black lace. As he recalled, the guest bedrooms were decorated with far less ostentation. Never must have ordered all these items, no doubt with the duke's money.

The room was otherwise neat, thrifty.

Never ushered Vanni and Damion across the threshold. All three watched as the servants finished lighting all the candles and exited the room. The door closed with a loud thunk behind them.

"You haven't invited us up here before," Vanni said. His voice sounded far away.

"No, I have not."

Vanni turned. "Damion, have you—?"

Damion shook his head no.

"But—" Vanni frowned. He was not naïve. This was something new and secret, and his whole body shivered.

"Vanni, are you nervous?" Never asked, head tilted.

Vanni frowned. He wanted to leave but something inside him wouldn't let him. He walked to the hearth which had been freshly lit. He would stand here and stare at the flames. All night if need be.

A short laugh came from behind him.

Damion had just confessed to him that he was afraid. Was he afraid now? He turned his head just in time to see Never bend to him and whisper something in his ear. He lifted his hand and brushed Damion's hair, which he wore loose now most days, away from his shoulder.

Damion smiled and glanced at Vanni.

Vanni inhaled long and deep.

"Vanni," Never said, voice echoing off the stone walls. "Go to the bed and take off your clothes."

His mind knew it was not a reasonable request, not in front of Damion whom they were trying to protect. But his hesitation dissipated and his body was eager to obey.

He went to the bed and leaned against it, blankets brushing his thigh, and began to undo his shirt and waistcoat. Laces tied the ruffled cuffs of his shirt to his wrists. He undid them, fully aware that Damion and Never were watching but not once did he glance in their direction.

He pulled the shirt over his head and tossed it on the floor. Would Never object to the mess? But no word came from the other side of the room.

The air played cool about his shoulders and naked chest. His nipples hardened to small, round nubs.

"The boots," Never commanded.

Vanni's heart raced for a moment, then calmed.

He leaned down to take off first his left boot, then his right, and straightened. He must have paused for too long, because Never's impatient voice accosted him again, along with a vision of that infernal gaze.

"The rest, now. All of it."

158

Vanni's hands went to his trousers and belt. First the belt came off, the leather sliding cool against his palms. Then he attacked the laces, and the small hooks holding his trousers together in front. Loosened, they fell in an accordion of soft cloth about his shins and ankles. He stepped out of the puddle and kicked the cloth to the side.

That left him in only his white drawers, which reached mid-thigh. He started to sit back on the red bed when Never said, "Drawers, too."

Vanni gulped. Even before he could think about a response, his hands went to the four ivory buttons on the left, undoing them deftly. The folds of the gauzy cotton fell back, revealing the juncture of his thigh and crotch.

"Lovely," Never said. "All the way now."

Vanni's cheeks burned. He refused to look up. He'd never disrobed in front of anyone but servants in full light before. Not even in front of Damion when they were small. All his trysts with Never had been in shadow and gray darkness.

Vanni put his hands to his hips, pushing down. He stopped, finding the courage to look up. Never's eyes were like gleaming light from across a vast ocean. Ship lights from a land far away. Fairy lights.

They took him up into a dream where feathery hands of cloud turned his body, touched it, breezing all along his arms and thighs, taking away any extra accoutrements he might be wearing. The final cloth of his smalls was whisked away. The air tingled against the insides of his thighs, and breathed with long exhales upon his tender genitals.

He blinked as he lost track of the last of his coverings. He was aware of Damion and Never, still on the other side of the room. But he did not look directly at them.

"Lie back," he heard Never saying. "Lie back."

He looked down at his side, turning, and the bed was before him, huge and glimmering. Red satin sheets spilled like liquid across the frame and mattress. He'd never seen anything like them. Where had Never ordered such decadent items?

As Vanni slid his body against the bed, the sheets of red were cold, so cold. His backside slipped up the smooth material as he scooted until he was at the center of the bed, all legs and arms, his skin tawny in the candlelight and against the red sheets. He pulled his knees up to his chest and waited. His hair fell forward against his jaw.

Again, his mind wanted to question what he was doing here. But every time he tried to think rationally, he could not grasp onto any solid question or reason for his mental discomfort.

Besides, he loved Never. He wanted anything Never wanted. That was key.

"Truly the golden prince." Never's voice was closer now. "Don't you think, Damion?"

"Yes," came Damion's small voice, young, almost shrill.

Vanni should not have been surprised at the answer, but he was. He peered through his curtain of hair. His shuddering was for Damion now, not himself. For what was Never up to?

Never stood at the side of the bed, as if he'd moved in a blink, his form outlined in bright, white candlelight. There had to be fifty candles burning in this room alone. Bright as stars against the black of Never's dark-clad silhouette.

"Damion."

Never held out his hand. Damion came forward, boots knocking against the stone floor. Vanni saw him take Never's hand, palm to palm, and press his fingers around the edges until the tips were almost white.

Vanni could do nothing but watch. And wait. He was always waiting.

"Now, my dear," Never said to Damion, "be a good sweet thing and climb up on the bed beside Vanni. I want to see you side by side." He glanced back and forth between Damion and Vanni. "And Vanni, lower your knees."

160

Vanni's breath caught. His bare feet slipped against the satin, so darkly crimson against the heels, the soles, his clenching toes.

Damion climbed up onto the bed on his hands and knees at first, then sat close, but not close enough to touch.

Vanni was trembling now. *It should not be this way*, he thought. But it was going to be, and there was nothing he could do.

"You two have great loyalty to each other, and that makes my life here a bit more difficult, yet exciting as well. So tonight, in celebration of that, things will change. No more jealousies, for that is the destroyer of the flavors of the heart. And no more hiding and secrets. Why should we hide from each other? Why should loyal friendship ever create an enemy? It is all to be savored. And I mean to savor it fully."

Damion made a strange sound, almost like a whimper.

Something in Vanni broke his internal haze. Concern. Maybe empathy. Certainly abiding love for the young man at his side.

"You are right," Vanni said hotly. His hand came up and smacked down on the bed, right on Damion's wrist. He gripped it tight, connecting them. Damion's body shifted, but stayed put.

"You are right," Vanni said again. "I would not betray him for anything." *Even you.* But he left that notion out. "I will not hurt him, ever!"

"Yes, I know," Never said. "Excellent. Your love is not a question then. Things will be so much better from now on. So much more pleasurable for all."

Vanni's love was not in question. For either man. But he had not been sure of Damion, so shy, so quick to deny what might be seen as weakness, to be feverishly sensitive and angry, to be jealous. And Damion, so gentle, had every right to be. Never was his first blush. First love. Where Vanni had wanted to be, but it had not come to pass.

Toying with them even further, Never said, "What do you think, Damion?"

Softly, "About what?"

"Your love is no longer a question."

"It never was," came the reply.

Vanni looked at him.

"For you, my lord," Damion added, staring straight at Never, unflinching.

Vanni's chest ached.

Never smiled until his white teeth showed. "I know. And for Vanni?"

Damion's breath hitched. "I—I—"

"I see," Never said. He leaned in close until Vanni could smell the roses and the ancient dusty sweetness and fresh spiced earth scent of him. "It is overwhelming, I know. Love. From all angles a twisting road, an agony of easy bruising for want of simple pleasure. An opening, a vulnerability that leaves you in weeping pieces not from pain, but unbridled rapture. The bliss of the body. The ecstasy of the mind. It is a risk to take that road for fear you might never reach the end. Or if you do, the fear is you will never reclaim that moment again, seeking your whole life for one more taste and always falling short. That is the agony of it, that the yearning cannot be stopped."

Vanni swallowed hard. His muscles were bunched beneath his skin. He was hot and cold at the same time.

"Vanni, I want you to kiss Damion."

His mouth opened. "But he doesn't want me—"

"He does. Here and now. A little push is all you need and I am here to ease you through it. To taste the new flowering of all you are. It is better this way, all of us together. You will see."

Vanni loved Damion. But this wasn't the way he wanted it to go. Not the way he'd imagined, if he'd ever allowed himself to daydream about it: Damion in his bed as more than just friends. Damion in his arms as a lover.

162

"He loves you!" Vanni whispered, harsh.

Never seemed to ignore the outburst.

But Damion heard it. His breathing began to catch in silent sobs.

"Damion, love, you must not think you are anything but the wonderful man you are. I am not rejecting you, but embracing you and all that is about you. Inclusive to all you love. You and Vanni. This is not reflective of a judgment on you. Or on Vanni. Do you understand? My loves, you are so precious, so sweet to the taste, and I only want us all to share in that again and again. It is what is meant to be."

Never knelt on the edge of the bed and placed his hand against Damion's forehead.

A placid look instantly came over Damion's face. He nodded. Only one tear had escaped, and Vanni watched it trail away to a diamond spark in the low light.

Watching Never with Damion, Vanni frowned to see how easily Never placated him, manipulated him. He had expected a fight, a drama, more tears. But Damion looked almost hollow-eyed, devoid of any emotion.

A quick chill washed over Vanni. For a moment he was frightened. It passed.

Vanni's mind refused to read anything into Never's hypnotic tone or to think any more about it, for the words were like music to him. They spoke everything he'd ever longed to hear.

"Vanni, I will not ask this again. Kiss Damion."

He turned to see his beautiful friend, dark hair tangled against his shoulders but still gleaming. Soft and deep. He tugged at his wrist.

Damion turned, eyes round, large. Vanni leaned in. He wanted to say something comforting, something endearing. Instead, he held his breath. He tilted his head. And pressed his lips to Damion's full and waiting mouth. Sparks of pleasure within let go and flew about, igniting his whole body.

"Hold there," Never said. "Feel it."

To Vanni's surprise, Damion's mouth moved. His lips parted, but only a fraction.

Vanni hardened so fast he grew dizzy. Was it possible to come from a kiss?

"Let the sensation envelop you. Open to it. It is the one thing life gives us that is grander than itself."

Vanni let his hand wander up to the side of Damion's head. His fingers touched the silken locks there, the tips seeking more sensation.

Damion tilted his head back. Vanni's heart went from cold to hot to liquid. He was shaking again. But not from worry. The pleasure struck him over and over, deep and hard.

Never was almost chanting. So soft and constant, Vanni blocked it out. But now he heard, "Good. Good. Now you will undress him, Vanni. All the way now. Slowly so I can see. Do you understand?"

Vanni felt Damion jump. Lip to lip, Damion's pulse flexed. His held breath came out fast and warm.

"Damion. Lie back now, sweet. Head on the pillow, that's right," Never said.

Their kiss broke. And for Vanni the world seemed to tumble and fall. All the thread and mortar and earth and nails holding it together broke, crumbled, melted.

Damion gasped aloud as he fell back, knees apart, hair everywhere, over the pillow, tangled at his throat, strands caught against Vanni's fingers. Somewhere in the room, Never was laughing. Low and deep. A slow rumble.

All of Vanni's attention was on Damion. Never commanded them, but Vanni could decide how he wanted this to go. Either forced or more flowing.

He touched Damion's shoulders, his arms, a non-verbal reassurance.

He leaned down and said, "It's all right. I'll take care of this. I'm here and I won't let anything bad happen."

Damion stared at him, up and down, reminding Vanni of his nakedness. His cock was hard—so hard—but he ignored it.

"He's making you," Damion whispered.

"No, it's not about that. Just look at my face."

"It's not right, but I can't say no to him. He's too strong."

Vanni felt his eyebrows rise. Damion had a strength of mind to be aware, and that shouldn't have surprised him but it did. It was why earlier Damion had confessed he was afraid.

"You see him, don't you?" Vanni asked.

"Hush!" The bed shook as Never's weight settled upon it beside them. "My sweets, less talk, more undressing." He reached out and untied the shirt at Damion's throat.

Damion shut his eyes, hands grasping at the slippery sheets.

Vanni knelt, the hardness growing more rampant between his legs.

Never looked at him with a languid stare. "Pace yourself. He's not going anywhere."

Flushing all over at the criticism, Vanni wanted to reach out to Never, beg him to stop, take him back to his rooms, have his rough way and leave Damion alone.

"He's not as innocent as you may think," said Never, as if reading his mind. "Now push his shirt up."

Vanni did, revealing the olive brown of Damion's belly and young, hairless chest.

"There," said Never. "That's right. Lift it over his head."

Never pulled Damion's arms up as Vanni tugged the shirt over his head and off. It caught at the wrists where they'd forgotten to untie it. Never took the left wrist, Vanni the right.

Damion lay still, arms over his head, eyes closed, smooth chest rising and falling. His lashes glimmered as if damp with tears.

When they got the shirt loose, Never took it in hand, folding it neatly, placing it on the table beside the bed.

"Boots," commanded Never.

Vanni moved down in the bed, lifting Damion's left leg.

"The candlelight plays so beautifully across your skin," Never said.

Vanni looked up. Reminded again of his naked body. Hot all over. He looked at Damion, shirtless now, making his heart thump hard in his chest, and lost his focus.

"The boots," Never reminded him.

He pulled one off, then the other, and tossed them to the floor. Damion bent one leg, settling himself.

Quick thoughts entered Vanni's mind. It was too cold. It was too hot. Maybe this was all a dream.

Seated on the side of the bed, hand pressed to the covers by his thigh, Never watched them. All the light in the room rushed to make his features more angular, his skin almost bluish as if he weren't human at all. He looked starkly handsome, a statue made of enticement and secrets and the hunter's pose.

This shouldn't be, thought Vanni. And yet he wanted everything in this room just the way it was with a rampant hunger. His body betrayed his every inner desire. He could not hide himself. Even the fever of shame dissipated leaving him open to anything.

He heard the command before Never said it. "The rest goes, too. All of it."

Vanni's hands shook as they reached for Damion's belt. He pulled it loose, then tackled the laces and hooks.

Where Vanni's fingers touched bare skin, they felt the flame beneath Damion's skin. Never helped him slide the garment past Damion's hips, leaving behind his buttoned up smalls, the same style of white shorts that Vanni had been wearing.

Damion was hard beneath the lightweight material, arousal making a v-shaped hill at his groin. To see that, Vanni's body gave single surge, freezing him.

Never said one word. "All."

Damion made a small sound. Maybe contentment, or maybe fear.

Vanni said, "No rush," and was surprised to hear a grumble to his voice. But Damion's well-being superseded everything. Even Never's commands.

Never commented. "Your will is strong, but I have you where you wish to be, do I not?"

He could not deny it. But Damion—Damion was too vulnerable lying before them, eyes closed, and it was not natural. He wasn't reaching for Vanni or Never. He wasn't moving at all.

"Damion, it's all right," Vanni said. He put his arms around Damion's waist, hugging him hard. He leaned his head down and placed his cheek against Damion's naked stomach.

Damion shifted until he lay partially on his side. The white undergarments barely hid a thing. His body was motionless, waiting, but Vanni could hear the pulse thrum through his body and feel the constant tremble beneath the skin. He kissed him softly, just below the bellybutton.

Damion groaned.

"Push the cloth down his hips now," Never ordered.

Vanni raised himself up enough so that he could get his hands under the cloth. At the same time, the buttons popped through their holes. The material gave and slid as he pushed it down Damion's hips.

With a tug it was around his thighs, then his ankles, and finally free. Vanni dropped it to the floor and turned back to look. Damion's cock arched dark pink against his abdomen, fully erect, damp where the rounded tip swelled past the foreskin.

Never sighed and angled his body closer to Damion's side.

"Come." Never held out his hand over Damion's body. "Be with us."

Vanni crawled up Damion's other side and settled himself against him, his cock brushing Damion's thigh. He took Never's hand and together they began to caress Damion's chest.

Damion's breathing quickened; his chest moved up and down.

"Vanni, I know you cannot resist him. That you love him more than life itself."

He wanted to tell Never to shut up. He wanted to hide his head in the pillows and sleep, wait for another day when he didn't have to reveal so much so fast.

"Kiss him again, Vanni."

Already he was doing it, without thought now, nothing but desire welling up, his lips meeting Damion's with the heat of all the years they'd known each other.

"Damion," Never whispered. "Do not deny him."

Damion's lips parted beneath Vanni's. He brought his arm up, putting it around Vanni's neck, and pulled him closer.

Never's hand trailed over Vanni's shoulder and arm, down to Damion's chest, then back to Vanni again. He caressed them as they kissed, as their mouths opened wider and their tongues clashed.

Damion did not resist. It was like a dream come true.

Damion tasted of sweet air and summer heat. Vanni put his arm over his waist and the skin felt like velvet, warm and tight and smooth. He wanted to cover him with his body, wanted to press and rub and hold him tight, never to let go. But he went slowly. To savor. To revere.

It could not be happening. But it was happening. Damion in his arms. The falling into passion for one he'd loved since the first time Damion crawled into bed with him afraid of the dark. The beauty of this boy, now a man, earned all his devotion.

"It is my pleasure for you both to take your pleasures," Never said in a surprisingly soft tone.

But Vanni was afraid to move further than kissing. What to do next? Would he make a wrong turn?

And the kissing was so good. So warm and intimate with Damion's hand on the back of his neck and the new demands of his willing tongue. Vanni pressed his erect cock harder against Damion's thigh. Damion bent his knee and gave him friction.

He gasped into that hot mouth.

"My beautiful sparrows seem to need me to tell them what to do next," Never said. "My blushing, innocent boys. The two bright angels of a dark, dark keep."

Damion's hand gripped Vanni harder at the neck.

"Vanni, take a breath," Never said.

With a pang, Vanni pulled himself away, mouth drawing in cooler air.

"Can you not see Damion is ready to explode? I have not gone as far with him as you think. His blood, yes, I have tasted it, but nothing more. My caresses have led only to his embarrassed releases beneath his clothes. He remains untouched. I have done this for you. It is one of many gifts I will give you."

Vanni met Never's eyes. He wanted to curse at him. He wanted to thank him.

"You can do more for him," Never said. "Make him yell out loud, then taste the result."

He looked down at Damion's cock, so perfect and sweet, so hard as it arched up toward his navel. Surrounded by tight black curls, it was full and taut and ready.

"Damion," he whispered.

Damion reached for Vanni, moaning. His hips thrust up, making his cock bob. His sac was tight against his body, two nodes stretching the skin tight beneath the base of his penis.

Vanni lowered his head, kissing Damion's stomach, licking. A whine escaped the boy's throat.

"Touch him at the base; cup his balls." Never's orders need not have been so gruff. Vanni wanted to do it.

His fingers brushed the root of Damion's cock.

Damion yelled. "Vanni!"

Vanni held the balls in his hand, so firm and soft at the same time. The pressure of his palm brought the cock upward slightly from where it rested against his abdomen. He opened his mouth, stuck out his tongue and licked the head. Tang of ocean. Magic nights. A dream made manifest.

Damion groaned, squirmed.

"Relax, angel. Just a kiss, Damion, just a kiss," Never murmured.

Vanni put his lips to the tip, licking the small crease where liquid pooled and dripped. Damion sat up and cried out and his cock began to spurt white stripes of semen against Vanni's lips. Tart. The sweetest of seas.

Vanni sucked down on him taking it all. Thirsting. Wanting. Oh, how he loved Damion. Why had he never done this before?

As Damion fell back in unchecked pleasure, Vanni felt Never move over him and he knew that Never's mouth was on Damion's neck. He felt the bite as if it were happening to him. Then the suck of blood as he sucked the semen, keeping Damion hard, needful, in the midst of ecstasy for as long as he could. Then he licked up and down the still-hard shaft, letting Damion remain on the edge of ecstasy. For he was young, and a virgin, and could probably stay hard for hours if they let him.

Damion's cries receded to more moans. Non-stop. Vanni gave him a little break and nuzzled his belly again, then kissed and stroked the insides of his thighs. He licked those beautiful balls. Suckled them. Wanton, Damion's knees spread wide, allowing it all. He was the loveliest vision Vanni had ever seen.

Never spent a lot of time at Damion's neck. Vanni saw red about his lips being fastidiously licked clean. A small bruise decorated Damion's throat.

"My saliva has healing properties. And my blood," Never said when he saw Vanni watching from his vantage between Damion's legs.

"How?"

"Mind your business." Never made a shushing gesture with his hand.

Vanni licked slowly back up Damion's cock. Kissed the tip.

Damion sighed and squirmed again. He never said a word, lost in some dream.

"I love the insatiable energy of youth," said Never. "And how quickly the blood replenishes itself."

Vanni watched as Never nipped at his own wrist and pushed it toward Damion's lips. Damion suckled.

Vanni went back to work below. He loved the taste of Damion. He could not get enough.

"Now my angels," Never began after a few minutes.

But Vanni didn't want to listen. He had just begun a slow suck down the length of Damion's cock again.

Damion's hips trembled. His cock throbbed in Vanni's mouth. Never touched the base of Damion's cock where Vanni's mouth descended, and manipulated it away. The tip left Vanni's mouth, dripping.

Never stroked the hardness, squeezing just a little, and said, "Turn, Damion. Onto your stomach. Now."

Vanni's eyes widened. Never was *not* going to do to Damion what he did to *him* every night. There was no way he was going to allow that rough treatment!

Damion rolled. He opened his eyelids and Vanni saw his pupils were wide and black. There was almost no iris left in his eyes.

Vanni felt drunk, but not *that* drunk.

Never's hands, elegant and graceful, were not gentle as they tugged Damion's body in the position he wanted it. He pulled Damion's bare hips, so that his curved rump was in the air.

Vanni's cock throbbed. He slid back on his knees, unsure, slipping on the satin sheets.

Damion squirmed as Never pushed his knees apart and put a small, fringed pillow beneath his stomach. His buttocks parted, revealing more of him, the shadow of the crack receding straight to a puckered bud surrounded by a halo of short black hair.

"Wait." Vanni struggled to find his senses.

Damion lifted his head as if Vanni's single, sharp word awakened him from his stupor.

"Vanni?" he asked, his voice shaking. His big eyes filled.

"Hush, the both of you." Never's voice floated about them, a salty flavor in the mind, a craven, illicit magical song the blood, the body and the brain could not resist. He placed his hand on Damion's left buttock.

Vanni held his breath as he saw that hand find Damion's entrance and slick it with something in his hand.

Damion jumped, then moaned.

Never looked at Vanni. "Come here."

Vanni stared back, wanting him, wanting Damion, but for some reason unable to move.

Never's fully clothed body kneeling next to the fully nude body of Damion made his passion flare even harder.

"Come here," he repeated, firm.

Vanni scooted forward, slipping, sliding. Those sheets!

Never reached out and grabbed him by the cock. The shock of it reeled through Vanni. He yelled as if in pain, but it felt so good, Never's hand on him, sliding the oil all over his hardness. He almost came just from that.

172

Never laughed. "Don't come yet. You need to be hard to fuck him."

Damion turned his head again. "What? No—Please!"

"Such surly boys, my sparrows, my angels. What is wrong?"

"I don't—" Damion stopped.

Vanni shook his head. "Don't."

"Vanni, it is such an easy thing. And what you have always wanted, is it not?"

His cheeks flamed.

"And Damion!" Never smacked him on the ass, the sound echoing through the room. "You wanted *me* to take you. You begged me. But I made a promise to this one." He flicked his finger at Vanni.

Damion gave a small sob.

"Why are you crying? Vanni loves you. He will be much sweeter at fucking you than I. For I am old and jaded, and take more than I give. But Vanni is young and he's never done something like this before. And you, my sparrow, my angel virgin, you will take him into you with ease because you want it. Have always wanted it. Yes, your secret is known to me. And, my dearest Damion, you will like it."

Vanni couldn't believe it. Damion had most certainly *not* always wanted this. Not this! And not from Vanni. Did he?

Vanni looked at the door only ten feet away. He could easily get up and leave. But his body would not obey. He looked back at Never, his eyes—they were deep as time itself, and he felt himself falling, falling.

Never's hands were on him, then, one on the hip, one on his arm, fingernails digging in, and he urged Vanni forward with sharp tugs.

Vanni slid closer to Damion, looking down. Damion was ripe, so sweet to look at. His dark skin taut and lean.

His hands shook as he laid them on the small of Damion's back, the heat of the boy rising up through his fingertips and palms. His cock bobbed and brushed at

173

Damion's crack, so aroused it surged with its own lubrication in addition to what Never had rubbed all over him.

Never said, "That's it. But he needs to be more open." He took his hands from Vanni's body and placed one on Damion's buttock, pulling it aside to reveal more and more. His other went to the bud, the hole that seemed too small, and Never pushed into it with one oiled finger.

Damion gasped.

Vanni gasped.

He wanted everything to stop. Or to never end. He could not decide!

Never thrust in and out, dilating the hole, then without warning his finger left the hole and grabbed Vanni's cock and rubbed the tip of his erection over the hole.

"Push," he ordered.

Vanni closed his eyes. The tip of his cock burned and burned in pleasure, wanting, needing.

Never said, "Good grief! Get to it!"

Vanni felt a slap to his buttocks and jutted his hips forward. His cock, still in Never's tight grip, breached the entrance.

Damion yelled. "Oh god. Oh—oh—"

"You remember how it is for you with me," Never said. "If you want it to be different for him, hold back. Take your time. For love can be sweet or harsh, comfortable or terrifying. Your choice."

Your choice, too, Vanni thought, surprised he still had any capability to think at all. *But you chose harsh with me for my own first touch. Why?*

But then he was lost in sensation again as Never smacked him a second time. More than the tip of him was encased now, tight, so tight, and Damion was gasping. From pleasure or pain?

The pleasure for Vanni was like having his entire body ignited by flame. Tingling and tickling. Both inside and out. It was the most exquisite feeling. Damion's inner warmth surrounded the center of him, the root of his physical pleasure.

He held back because he did not want this to be like it was for him with Never. He held back because he was already becoming lost and it would be so lonely if he didn't take Damion with him. He held back because he wanted to love Damion, not just fuck him. He wanted to make love.

He pushed deeper, inch by slow inch, taking his time, until finally his balls rested against Damion. He wanted to reach under and between Damion's legs, feel if he was still hard. Touch him. Love him.

A rustling sound of cloth parting came from behind him. He felt Never's heat at his back.

Never's breath ruffled the hair behind his head. "Spread for me."

Never put his hands between Vanni's legs and slapped the inner thighs. One finger pushed at Vanni's ass, a slick quick entrance.

The pain and pleasure stung him both at once. Vanni pressed into Damion making him yell again.

"S—sorry!" Tears quickened in Vanni's eyes.

Damion continued to moan.

"He loves it. Pull out and push in," Never whispered in his ear. "Give him what he needs. What *you* need."

Slowly, Vanni stroked his hands down the plush, firm buttocks and pulled back. As he did, Never impaled him. And not with a finger this time.

He threw his head back and hissed as Never's erect cock stabbed deep. His own cock jerked in response, and he could not help but thrust, burying it in Damion again.

"That's it," Never coaxed. "We'll get the rhythm right soon, my angel. Soon."

Vanni could not hold back a loud moan.

Never said, "Damion, are you with us?"

"Yes." A dreamy voice buried in a pillow.

"I want you to stay very still," Never ordered. "Still and open. Relax. Feel Vanni move within you, in and out. He's going to move between us. Each time he pulls back, I'll be deep inside him. When he thrusts into you, I'll be pulling out. We will be playing a sensual game of catch. He will be the ball between us that we are tossing back and forth."

Flames wracked Vanni's skin at Never's debauched description. It turned him on more than he could stand to admit. Still, Vanni moved slowly, not wanting to hurt, but hoping to give pleasure. He stroked Damion's buttocks, then boldly reached between them and rubbed Damion's balls.

Damion arched and Vanni thrust. As he did, he felt Never pull back, leaving just the tip of himself in Vanni's ass.

Then Vanni pulled back from Damion and impaled himself on Never's cock to the root. It took the breath right out of him.

Back and forth between them he rode, fucking Damion—no, making *love* to Damion—then fucking himself on Never's cock.

If he'd been aroused before, he'd never known anything like this. A cloud of golden euphoria engulfed him. It was a place of purity, a state of idyllic bliss.

Damion's buttocks dimpled right where they met his lower back. Vanni touched him there. He reached with his other hand around Damion's slim hip and found his sweetly erect penis. He stroked it up and down, and Damion hissed, "Oh yes!"

It was happening. Damion was loving it.

Vanni was in a sort of dazed rapture, a land of utter nirvana where all the love was breaking up inside him in a good way, shattering into golden droplets of beauty that surrounded him, so many they outnumbered the stars.

He moved his hips. The dance went on and on until he could see nothing but the droplets, and hear the buzzing of all the stars in the universe at once. Sweet honey doused his veins. Everything crashed forward, straight to his groin,

176

pooling higher and higher until the flood could not be held back.

Somewhere far away, he heard a voice calling out Damion's name.

Vanni came and came. Hips thrusting back and forth, back and forth. He felt the wetness of Damion on his hand, his erection pulsing like a heartbeat against his palm.

As he shouted in his triumph, sharp teeth breached the vein at his neck. Never sucked his blood and if possible, Vanni soared even higher. Little sparrow. Bright angel. He didn't care. Whatever the fuck this was, he never wanted to come down.

Chapter Twenty

Vanni did not recall pulling out of Damion, or Never pulling out of him.

His neck ached. He lay back on plush pillows and half against someone's wide chest, knees spread, his thighs wet, his cock still slick and half-hard against his thigh.

Never had his arm under his shoulders and was pressing his hard wrist to his mouth, ordering him to suck. It was like drinking the ocean at first, a toxic taste, but then the liquid he sipped evolved to cloying enticement, sugar and salt combined.

As he suckled, he opened his eyes and was dazzled. Candles throbbed everywhere. He turned his gaze toward Never and saw Damion cradled in the curve of his other arm, suckling like babe at his other wrist.

Never still wore his white shirt. Not a drop of blood speckled it.

They were both fed this blood for a reason, but Vanni did not yet understand. Healing, maybe? More rapture? He'd asked Never every night why, but if he got an answer, he could not remember it.

"Enough," came Never's voice. Like a live thing, it scurried into Vanni's mind.

The wrist vanished from Vanni's mouth. He sucked air for a moment, then closed his lips, swallowing. He rolled away as Never rose, pushing himself to the foot of the bed and standing over it, looking down at the two of them side by side now on his wide, red bed.

"No more secrets. No more hiding." Never did not smile. "Sleep now. Bask in each other. You are safe. I have errands, and you are not to follow me."

Vanni turned to look at Damion.

Damion turned his head away, one arm wrapping tight about his own waist as if to hold himself back. His brown nipples were still taut against the cool night air.

His cock lay soft now, pliant between his legs, pink and lovely, fresh and young. Vanni could not stop looking at it—at him. He was so lovely; he wanted to enfold him in his arms, rub his face into his glossy hair.

Never's footsteps sounded as he went to the door, opened it and called for his servants. They came and dressed him in fresh clothing as Vanni watched sleepily. The servants ignored Vanni and Damion in the bed. It was as if they did not exist.

Damion, Vanni noted, kept himself turned away.

Finally, Never left. The candles flickered. The sea wind whispered about the windows.

Vanni sighed, turned in the bed. "Damion?"

No answer.

Vanni pulled up a warm blanket, covering them both, tucking it in around Damion's sides.

"Please tell me you're all right." He didn't want his voice to sound so plaintive, but failed.

Finally, Damion's dark head moved to face him. He breathed in deep, his nostrils flaring. He said nothing, but his hand reached out from under the covers and touched Vanni lightly on the shoulder. He drew his hand down to Vanni's wrist. Lifting himself up on his other arm, Damion bent forward and placed a soft kiss to the inside of Vanni's elbow.

He pulled back, eyes dark and glistening.

Vanni folded his arm, pressing that tentative touch into himself like a precious flower. Later, he would run his fingers over that place on his arm over and over, reliving the moment, tattooing the memory into himself for all time. For though they had kissed on the mouth, and elsewhere, it had only been when Never had been in their minds and commanding them. Now they were alone, and that private kiss meant more than words could say to Vanni.

179

Closing his eyes, Damion put his head down on the pillow and moved it until his forehead touched Vanni's shoulder.

*

For several nights, they all ate together, dreamed together, walked together in the gardens at dusk. They ran over the salt-damp lawns until their leather boots were soaked and cold.

They stayed outside in the evenings longer and longer. When Damion complained of the cold, Never gave him drops of blood from his wrist and it warmed him until he could no longer feel the cold. He threw off his cloak and unbuttoned his shirt to stand on the cliffs at the edge of the yard and let the ocean zephyrs have their way with him.

They took impossible late-night picnics in the woods, bringing blankets and baskets filled with thick bread, wine, and peaches smothered in translucent, sweet cream.

They took lanterns but did not really need them to see. Never told them his blood in their bodies enhanced their senses. Sight, sound, scent.

How that was possible, Vanni didn't know, but it was true. Everything at night looked backlit in blue and gold. He saw detail more clearly, from the cracks in the bark of trees to individual blades of grass. He heard every flutter of every sleeping bird above them in the trees, as well as the footsteps of foxes and deer even when they were too far away to spy.

Out in the woods in the deepening autumn-steel shadows, they would place their blankets on the ground and lie back half-drunk on blood and wine, never feeling the cold. They rested on blankets of bright-dyed wool staring up through tree shadows flickering silver in their enhanced vision.

Never would give attention first to one, then the other, the deep drinking, the pleasure of the blood rush through

180

every vein as he took from them. Now he bit at more than their necks. Sometimes it was the wrists. Sometimes it was the fleshy part of a calf or thigh, or the soft skin between underarm and shoulder-blade.

They repeated often their first night together as three. Fucking in the moonlight. Vanni in the middle rocking back and forth, filling, filled. The euphoria only grew between them. Damion asked for it now. Begged.

Everything felt like a dream.

Never fed them in more creative ways. He would lie back with his legs spread. With a knife, he made shallow cuts on the insides of his thighs. Vanni and Damion bent to him and licked the blood away. When the wounds closed, they continued to lick up his thighs until they encountered his erection. Together they competed for it, sucking, licking, their tongues and mouths meeting until Never rewarded them with another kind of liquid, white and pure as tangy ocean foam.

Slowly, over the course of days, Never answered some of Vanni's unspoken questions.

At one of their night picnics, while Damion dozed in the nude on his side, his arms wrapped about Never's naked thigh, Never turned to Vanni, who was sitting up, arms about his knees and staring into the beautiful night.

Never said, "You have guessed some things about me, have you not?"

Vanni bent his head. "That your blood is not like ours? That you aren't like us at all?"

"Yes. What do you think about that?"

"Once I thought you might be a sea-witch."

Never chuckled. "I did not come from the sea. But I am very old. I do not age."

"Where do you come from?"

"I was human once."

"Like me and Damion?"

"Yes."

"How did you change? How is all this possible?"

"An ancient magic. Older than dust. Someone shared it with me. And now I want to share it with you."

Vanni nodded. To be like Never. He wanted it, whatever that was. Vanni knew the lord was different, strange, stronger than human. And he'd just said he was old but he had yet to say how old.

"And Damion?"

"I am not sure yet. But you—you I chose from the very beginning because you defied my tempt from the start in Lord Percy's garden."

How well Vanni remembered that strange evening when he'd lost time. When he'd feared for Damion's safety.

"Tempt? I heard you use that word before. What is it? Is it like the way you put me and Damion into a sort of dream so we'll do whatever you say?"

"I shall never underestimate you again, Earl Giovanni. You are quite astute."

"But you never had to do that. Damion loved you from the start. And I—I—"

"You what?" Never asked.

"You never had to use the tempt to make me want you. Even when you're rough, I want it."

Never laughed again. "You are a mink, not an angel. My demon-sparrow, in love with his brother but wanting the stranger from the night in his bed as well."

"Damion's not my brother!"

"Yes. I see that. Such strength of will!"

Vanni grunted. Even now, he wanted to feel Never inside him.

"Your defiance makes you the one," Never continued. "I chose you for that mental restlessness of yours. The way you go in and out of the tempt. With humans it should never happen. That clarity of thought never leaves you even when you are in the fog, does it?"

"I don't know." Vanni lifted his head from his knees and stared at him with a wry smile. "All I know is I like to know what I'm getting into when a stranger comes into my father's home and takes over. I like to know what he might be up to, and that Damion remains safe."

"Of course. But it is more than that. Your bond to Damion supersedes yours and mine. It's a power stronger than you know. It's both enticing and lovely. And a problem."

"A problem?"

"I want to make you like me. I want you to come away with me. But you would never leave him, would you." It was not a question.

Vanni glanced at Damion, naked and innocent, sleeping curled against Never's exposed thigh.

"Why would we leave?"

"Because your father will be home soon."

"So?"

"So, if I make you like me, he'll notice. Become suspicious. We cannot be ourselves, you and I, and stay at the Keep."

"He's suspicious anyway. And he pays little attention to me."

"Your father has many secrets, too, did you know that?"

Vanni frowned.

"Yes," Never continued. "His own fears and paranoia contributed to keeping both you and Damion locked up here until you were eighteen. He is aware people like me exist in this world. Not all are as—civilized as I."

"But he is not aware that you are—like you are?"

"No. But eventually--. It's why we need to make a plan to leave."

"If you made me like you, would I still grow old?"

Never looked upward. "You would grow old but not in the body. You would stay young forever. And your strength will increase, your senses, everything about you enhanced, alluring. It is how you will attract others so that you can feed."

"On their blood."

"Yes."

"Hmm." Vanni looked at his knees, at his hands folded around them. The ecstasy of their evenings in the night had been unlike anything he'd ever known. He wanted it.

He turned his head again, meeting Never's eyes. "I want you to make me like you."

"It's settled then."

Vanni reached out, grabbing Never by the upper arm. "No. It's not. I want you to make me like you. But only if you make Damion like you as well."

"I cannot promise. Weaker willed beings do not survive the change."

"Damion is not weak! And I will be with him the entire time."

Never was very quiet. Vanni could not even hear his breath.

Finally, Vanni spoke again. "You have never told me. Not in words. What are you?"

Never took a breath. His chest rose. Damion stirred but did not open his eyes.

A word came out of Never's mouth and rose upon the breeze. "Vampire," he said. "I am a vampire."

Chapter Twenty-One

The word vampire crossed Vanni's mind again and again the following week as September washed the woods in amber and the sea grumbled blackly. He'd never heard the term before. It didn't matter. He wanted to be that.

Vampire. A being of eternal youth and strength. Never to get sick. Healing from every injury. A witness of the centuries to come.

He wanted to be with Never. The Keep held nothing for him but nostalgia. He didn't care about being an earl.

But Never hesitated when it came to Damion.

For Vanni, that was a huge problem.

Damion seemed more easily lost in the blood fevers and the tempt than Vanni was. He talked little. He did only a few hours of work a week on the ledgers, just enough to allow the Keep to function.

Most of the time, when they weren't playing games and pretending everything was normal, they were in bed together, all three of them, or in the woods at night on dark picnics. Or sleeping.

Today, Damion went to his bedroom after breakfast complaining of being tired. Vanni lingered at the table with Never, who seemed quite unconcerned, then said, "I'm going to check on him."

"He'll be fine. You should leave him to sleep."

"It's the blood. Maybe you took too much?"

Never sipped languidly from a goblet. "I take no more from him than I do from you."

But how much was that? Vanni didn't know. He couldn't really feel how much the bites bled. When Never took from his thighs, he still could not see, and his wounds healed quickly after Never licked them clean. He knew that

Never gave them only drops of his own blood. Did he take much more than that from them?

Vanni did not recall ever being dizzy, merely dreamy, or sleepy. And still always ready for passion. If the blood supply in his body went too low, how could he still get hard?

Vanni stood, tossing his napkin on his half-empty plate. "I'm going to check on him anyway."

A twisted smile formed on Never's lips. "Don't wear him out too much before nightfall."

Vanni rolled his eyes and left the dining room.

In truth, he and Damion had rarely been alone together since Never had arrived. And they'd not done anything sensual without Never in the room with them.

Climbing the hard steps, Vanni remembered how as boys he and Damion would run up and down the hallways, their laughter echoing with the cries of the wind about the rock walls.

At Damion's door, he thought to knock, but stopped. They had no secrets. There had been none since they'd first met as children. Any privacy between them was gone these last weeks.

He put his hand on the metal handle and opened the door.

The room was stuffy, dark. One askew curtain let in a blinding ray of light that striped the floor. The bed, in shadow, looked rumpled. Damion lay in a white dressing gown curled around a pillow.

Vanni went straight to him, putting his hand against the side of his head. "Hey. Are you not feeling well?"

Damion stretched a bit, turning his head face up, dark eyes opening. "I wanted to sleep more," he replied, yawning.

"I can have some more food brought up."

He shrugged. "Later, maybe."

"You can tell me if something's wrong." Vanni stroked the side of Damion's head.

"What would be wrong? I'm happy."

186

Vanni hitched himself up on the bed and sat, Damion's head at his hip. He continued to stroke his hair. "It's a lot to take in—these last few weeks."

"You say that because I'm younger than you?"

"No."

"Then, what about you? It's a lot for you, too, right?" Damion said.

"Yes, it is." *You weren't the only virgin at the Keep.* "We've done some growing up, I think."

Damion began to chuckle. Vanni joined in.

"Bet you didn't think it would be like this," said Damion.

Vanni said, "I wouldn't change things."

Damion's laughter stopped. He swallowed hard.

"Would you?" Vanni asked.

Slowly, Damion shook his head. "But sometimes it hurts."

"What hurts?"

"I don't know. Something deep inside, I guess."

Vanni thought he knew what he was trying to say. He'd felt it, too, a desperation of the heart, fear of vulnerability, fear of love because love brought loss. His hand stroked over Damion's hair to his shoulder, then to the center of his chest.

"Damion, I love you. You know that."

Damion's chest moved up as he took a breath and held it. When he finally released it, he said, "Stay. Sleep here with me. Just for awhile. Like old times."

Vanni scrunched down in the bed, messing up the covers. Damion pushed them away, then brought them over them both. He turned and put his arms around Vanni, settling his head on his shoulder. Warmth grew between them.

"Like old times," Vanni said, and closed his eyes.

*

Vanni cornered Never in the downstairs living area.

Never faced him, frowning. "What is it?" His tone came out annoyed. Impatient.

After everything, Vanni should not have been shocked. Never played with him as if he were but a toy. He did not profess love, but instead used words like "I chose you" and "you're the strong one."

A sort of confused fury rose up in him. Especially because the subject he wanted to discuss with him was Damion, who loved Never, too, but was forced to take most of his affections from Vanni.

Forced. Yes. That was the right word. It made Vanni question everything.

"I know you say Damion is weak, that he might not survive becoming like you. But you're not allowing him to show you his will. I know what you're doing with him, keeping him under the tempt, making him complacent."

A half-smile twitched at Never's full mouth. His eyes glittered.

"Well?" Vanni demanded an answer.

"You presume much." Never stood by a curtained window, all in black today, even his shirt. Lean and trim, he raised his chin putting himself at an angle that most showed off his beauty.

The daylight came around the edges of the curtains making them look lined in silver and pink trim. The light touched him with tentative fingers on one shoulder rippling to his elbow, his hip.

"You aren't letting him choose. He would be with you willingly, like me."

"You presume you are willing?" Never asked.

Vanni stopped short. Blinked. "Of course."

Never's smile grew. Casually, "The tempt simply works differently on you."

Vanni laughed. "I know what I'm doing. Besides, you said it doesn't take with me. I break out of it."

"Yes. I did say that. And it is true. Sometimes."

Vanni frowned. "Stop playing games. I have consented to you, and I want to go with you." He approached the vampire. "Damion, too. I know him. He loves you. He loves us. You don't have to use the tempt to see that. You don't have to make him seem so—so drunk all the time."

"You think that's me? You think he has no questions? No hesitation? That you yourself understand all that you are asking? You barely ask me any questions. You assume I have a plan. And of course I do, but is your mind truly clear?"

Never laughed as he added, "You're both so young. Damion is confused. Afraid. Has he not told you so? That drunken, dreamy silence is his behavior when I am not using the tempt. When everything seems fine to you, normal—that is when I am using the tempt."

Vanni pressed his lips tight to his teeth, feeling them dig in. "And myself?"

"You know the bliss of our arrangement. The strength you feel every time you taste my blood. What does it matter where that comes from? It's real to you."

"What does that mean? You think I don't want this? Or you?"

Never came forward and raised his hand to Vanni's face, cupping his cheek. "Of course you do."

"I—I love you." Why was it so hard to say?

Never slapped gently at his face. "That's my golden angel."

"Stop teasing. Be honest for once!" Vanni pushed his hand away, then stepped up to Never until they were chest to chest. "I do want you. It's all me. You can't convince me otherwise." He put his hands on Never's shoulders.

"Yes. I know." That infernal smile.

Vanni leaned in and kissed him. It was hot, deep, like a fever that started and would not let up. When he pulled back, he breathed out the words, "You're a complete bastard, but I want you all the time."

Never raised an eyebrow. "Yes. I know."

"And Damion, too."

"You would give your life for him, wouldn't you?"

"In a heartbeat," Vanni answered.

Never's eyes narrowed. His lashes made shadows on his cheeks. "Good to know," he said. "It makes the bond for all three of us more powerful."

"Just—don't underestimate Damion," Vanni said.

"I certainly do not," came the reply. "Nor should you."

Chapter Twenty-Two

There was no warning when the duke returned to the Keep. One late afternoon the sleek, black carriage arrived at the front steps and the estate ceased to be a privileged private playground for three.

It seemed wrong. All of it. The duke returned at the most inopportune moment. For Vanni was in bed with Never and Damion, naked, sandwiched between them, riding the wings of bliss straight up to the tops of the Keep's tower.

But amid that bliss, his preternatural sense of hearing acknowledged the coach's wheels crackling over rocks in the road long before it reached the entry to the front driveway. He could smell the horses' sweat, their hot breaths. The fog from the sea gave everything a tart edge.

"We have to stop. They're coming," he said. But he continued to rock his body, Damion so sweet in front of him, Never so rough behind him. It was everything he could ever want. On the verge of coming, held at the peek by Never's command.

His father could not find out!

"Who's coming? Because I'm about to," Damion gasped.

"The duke," Never said, thrusting with force into Vanni.

Vanni grunted at the fleeting sharp pain. Waves of pleasure washed over him, but his body could not hold onto them.

He kept moving, loving being in the middle of two beautiful men, but the intensity shifted. Lowered. He could not focus anymore. Anxiety reached out its ugly, sharp-nailed hands and tried to grip him. His mind, filled with the euphoric sensation of utter, wild abandon only seconds ago flooded with bleak shadows, shame, guilt, worry. Suspicion.

Vanni's breath stuttered in his throat. The shadows surrounding him now contained voices, thoughts, words of fear.

If he catches you, he'll disown you.

You can't trust Never. He says he has a plan but won't tell you what it is.

Do the servants know you've been drinking blood? Will they tell?

Where will you go?

What will you do?

A sharp smack to his rump made the voices stop. Vanni's head jerked up at the sudden sting. He let out a sharp groan. His wilting cock perked up at the pain.

"Fuck Damion harder," Never commanded. "He won't find us up here in my room. Besides, even now, my servants guard the door."

"Please, Vanni, more," Damion echoed.

"The duke will wait," Never added.

Damion laughed, then fell forward on his hands, his rear thrust up. All his dark hair cascaded over his head. His back muscles tightened, as did his ass around Vanni's cock. Vanni's hands clasped his hips, stroking down over the perfect, pale brown curves. One hand reached around and stroked his satiny, stiff cock. Damion gasped.

The carriage approached the driveway entrance, the sound of it rattling louder in Vanni's ears.

He'll know. We can't hide this.

Vanni lost his rhythm.

Another slap from Never. "Vanni!"

He pulled away from Damion, who gave a grunt of surprise. Vanni fell away from Never as Never withdrew. On the slippery red sheets it was easy to slide and fall to the floor. Vanni's knees hit the stone beside the rug. His palms smacked hard. He grabbed up his white shirt.

192

"Vanni, come here. Now!" came Never's order.

But he couldn't see the room anymore, or Damion so beautifully stretched out on the bed. He could not hear Never coaxing him to comply.

All he saw was his father's stern face, the constant disapproval. He could do no right, but this—this would end everything before he was ready.

They had no plan!

They had drunk blood. A lot of blood just this evening, trading wrists and necks and thighs, back and forth. They had shared a bed, the three of them, for weeks.

The servants would tell.

The duke would fear disgrace. Worse, he might find out what Never was.

Vanni's heart hammered. For a moment he could not catch his breath. He felt a touch on the back his neck. A hand raised to his lips. A pressing of skin. His lips encountered wetness. His tongue licked it away. Blood.

"Drink," said Never, kneeling by his side. As usual, Never was not completely naked; he wore only his shirt. His legs were long, dusted with fine dark hairs. The muscles clenched, cat-like, lean.

It made Vanni feel all the more vulnerable to be fully naked with Never still half-dressed. And it was so very arousing as well.

But right now he couldn't think. Couldn't understand. He didn't want blood. He wanted to go back to the beginning, deny Never's advances, make everything right again.

Softly, "Vanni, what are you afraid of?"

Vanni raised his head. Never's question lingered in his thoughts. He had to repeat it over and over in his mind before he could understand it.

Damion stared down at him, hunched into himself at the edge of the bed, his hair hanging forward.

Vanni took a breath. And answered.

"My father."

*

"What do you sense?" Never put on a long coat with tails.

"I don't know. Something—wrong." Vanni quickly fastened his belt.

"My blood gives way to certain gifts. I don't have the gift of long-distance sensation, but you may," said Never.

"But I'm not like you yet. You haven't made us like you. You've kept us on the cusp."

Never had made the final step of becoming a vampire remain a mystery for both Vanni and Damion.

"I don't feel it," Damion said.

"Your gift, little angel, may be different," said Never. He turned to Vanni. "Think harder. What is the danger you feel. Try to be specific."

"That's just it. I'm shaking but I don't know why."

Damion came to him, touching him on the shoulder. He was fully dressed, now, his hair pulled back into a ribbon.

"He beat you a lot. That's what this is. He never touched me, but you—you he treated worse than a servant. Now he's come back to disrupt your life, to spoil everything we have now. Between us."

Between us. Vanni wanted to smile at those words, especially since they came from Damion. But all he could feel was danger.

They left the room. Never's servants entered as soon as they were all in the hall.

"Clean the room as quickly as possible," Never told them.

The servants never spoke. They never showed any surprise at spilled blood or semen stains, or the fact that Never had just spent the day in bed with not one but two young men who were practically brothers.

194

As the three of them went down the stairs, the stone pulsed cold under Vanni's booted feet. Everything beneath him seemed filled with a dark iciness, as if he was descending to the bottom of the sea.

When they reached the first floor, the duke was coming in from the foyer to the front room, already shrugging out of his cloak. A servant took it and scurried away. Behind him were two male strangers, richly dressed, also shedding warm, woolen cloaks. Their hands and faces were damp. Their clothing shed droplets of water.

It must have been raining, but Vanni had been too busy behind closed doors to notice.

The duke looked up at the three of them. "Oh, you're all here. Good then. We have guests." He did not introduce them.

Andreas looked at Never and bowed his head. "I see you are still here. That is as I expected. We will discuss more about your future plans later."

Vanni knew the duke was cold, but this was not the sort of dismissive greeting he'd expected. He still sensed danger, and yet his father moved by them as if he'd been gone only hours and not weeks.

"Where's mother?" Damion asked, looking beyond them and into the shadowed foyer.

"She's visiting her Aunt Macy and will arrive back here next week," the duke answered. Even Damion, the duke's favorite, was dismissed. Andreas never even looked at him as he answered.

"I'll be in my study," Andreas said. "I have business to conduct with our guests. I expect to see you all at dinner."

The three of them stood at the foot of the staircase. Paused. Silent.

Finally, Never broke the silence. "Well, we needn't have hurried after all."

Both young men looked at Vanni.

"Something's not right," Vanni said. "He never sent word he was returning. Nothing."

"Vanni's right," Damion said. "Andreas is an excessive planner, very organized. He's returned home quickly for some reason." He took a deep breath. "But it might not have anything at all to do with us."

Never turned on Vanni. "What do you sense?"

"We need to find out who those men are. Why they are here. I don't recognize them."

"Yes," Never replied. "But tell me what you feel? What you sense? Exactly?"

Vanni frowned. "It's like a build up of quick energy, like I want to run. Run away. Fast. It's prickling the inside of my skin."

"Panic," Never murmured.

"Guilt, maybe?" Damion asked.

Vanni glared at him, suddenly defensive. "And don't you feel it, too? We've been sneaking around here for weeks! Doing… things. Things people aren't supposed to talk about."

Never smiled. "Hush. It's all right. Maybe people don't talk about it, but everyone does… things."

"Not like we have!"

Damion reached out to touch his sleeve. Vanni pulled away.

"Maybe a servant talked," Vanni said.

"They are all commanded by me right now. The tempt is strong."

"If you recall, I broke the tempt. It surprised you. Maybe you're not as strong as you think, Never!"

Never laughed. "Look how frightened you are. By what I am… and what you two are becoming. If you truly understood, you'd relax."

"So make us understand, then! You promised to tell us what the plan is, how we'll be like you." He didn't say that Never was unsure about Damion being strong enough to

196

become a vampire. "Tell us finally. Now! Because I still feel it. The danger."

"Let's go into the drawing room."

The candles in their favorite room for games and drinking were all new. The old stubs and melted wax hanging from shelves and end tables had been cleared away. The air smelled of beeswax.

Damion sat at the table where they played cards. Vanni wandered to the hearth where it burned low but warm.

Never sprawled upon the sofa.

Vanni turned to face him. "We need a plan now. And I don't care what you say; that plan must include Damion."

"What? I wasn't to be included?"

Never waved his hand. "I did not say that." He waved it again, his fingers tracing shapes on the air.

"You did. To me!" Vanni argued, but the fingers drew his eye. Made him want to agree with Never. Pretend he had mis-heard. "Stop using the tempt!"

Damion turned his dark gaze on Vanni. "He isn't—" Then he stopped abruptly and turned to look at Never. "Are you doing what you did to the servants to us?" He looked stricken.

Never tilted his head. He looked regal and handsome in that moment, with the firelight flickering on his face and in his deep eyes. The rain tapped the windows behind him.

Vanni's skin grew hot and he thought back on what all three of them had been doing just a half an hour ago. The red bed, Damion's slim hips beneath his palms, Never hard inside him.

"I confess, I did," Never began. "But only to cushion the difficult path we are all taking. You two, as close as you are, only needed a little urging to your happiness. And I, well I am breathless to witness you. Both of you. And as a vampire the flavors of your blood when in love are exquisite. You would not have understood if I approached you in any other way."

197

It occurred to Vanni that what Never was saying meant he'd actually forced all three of them into this situation. But he made it sound normal. Inevitable. As if there was nothing wrong.

It wasn't like this was new information. Still, as much as Vanni felt as if he were in love with Never and Damion of his own free will, Never's words and tone right now turned his stomach sour.

"And now you want to make us like you," Vanni said.

"It is a gift."

"When we become like you, will we, too, force people to our wills?" Vanni asked.

"You can of you wish. You can be the catalyst for great loves, great lusts, great seductions. And at the same time, you feed off that and become even more powerful. You won't age. You won't die. You'll be a god. It's one way to survive."

Damion looked a bit pale. His hands were fists upon the table. But he raised his chin. He pressed his lips together until they were a hard line. Then he said, "How is it done?"

Never laughed. "That's my boy."

Vanni felt hot and cold all over. His heart galloped. The sensation of imminent danger increased, yet he couldn't deny he wanted this, and had all along. He'd been fascinated by Never's explanation of being a vampire. Not frightened. It was Damion he'd worried about, because Never told him Damion was weak. And then Damion had come to him saying he was afraid but didn't know why.

Vanni's protective instinct for Damion rushed through him. He had the urge to run again. He wanted to go to Damion, grab him and vanish into the night with him. But even if Damion agreed to that, it could not happen. Never would always be there, behind them, between them, in the shadows.

"You have my blood in you right now. If you were to die, it would be like sleeping, and you would awaken."

The insides of Vanni's stomach flipped. They would have to die? He trusted Never, but not that far.

But Damion got a bold look in his eyes. "That's it?"

"No. That's the beginning."

The skin around Damion's eyes tightened. "And after?"

Vanni stared at Never, watching the handsome features widen with a flat smile, then harden as the jaw worked back and forth as he held them both in his gaze. As he drew out his answer.

Finally, it came. Two words. "You feed."

"On the blood of another." Damion did not hesitate to finish the thought. His words were not a question.

Never bowed his head in affirmation.

It was obscene, really, Vanni thought. A race of eternally young beings who drank blood. Yet he wanted it. More than anything. He had wanted to go with Never from the very beginning, when Never said he'd chosen him over Damion. He hated himself for it even now.

"Do you have to kill that person?" Vanni asked. And why were they finding out details only now? He began to suspect Never had not intended to fulfill all his promises, but he couldn't be sure.

"No. But the first time is difficult to control. Most fledglings do kill on their first feeding."

Damion sat back, hands sliding along the table.

Vanni came forward from the hearth. "You'll help us, then, right? So it won't have to be like that?"

Never stared up at him. Vanni saw a whirlwind in his eyes, and almost felt the cold of it. For that moment, Never's face looked frozen, unmoved by time or love or pretty boys. But then his mouth opened. "Of course," he said. "I'll be right by your sides."

"Then we have to do it tonight," Damion said.

"That is my plan now, since the duke arrived and Vanni sensed danger. We cannot risk staying longer."

"When were you going to tell us?" Vanni asked.

"I'm telling you now." Never's fury showed. "Vanni, the duke only just arrived."

Vanni crossed his arms over his chest and glared.

Never ignored him. "We should leave tonight. When the moon is behind the clouds and the winds are high. No one will see or hear us."

"How will we die?" Damion asked.

Vanni's throat closed. He was going to be sick.

"The easiest way is an overdose of sleeping draught. But not here. First we must get away. I have other places."

The admission surprised Vanni. "Then why did you come here after the fire?"

"My dearest angel, your father offered. How could I refuse the opportunity to get to know his boys better? You both made quite an impression at that ball."

"But—you—" Vanni had no words.

"You don't regret anything now, do you?" Never's smile did not widen, but remained sly.

"No." Vanni turned away. His heart ached. Inside, he was yelling his love. But deeper still, he wondered, *Is this still the tempt?* How could he ever know for sure?

"I have a carriage that survived the fire. It was brought here and is stored in the carriage house. We'll take that. My servants will have everything ready. I suggest we all meet at the carriage house at eleven. All you two need to do is pack a small bag. Only what you really want to take. And behave normally the rest of the evening."

"I'm ready to leave this place. I'll go pack now!" Damion said, getting up. He was out the door and gone in a blink.

Vanni turned away then.

"Vanni?" Never's voice found him like a tendril of smoke from the shadows going into him, tugging.

He fought the urge to go to Never, to embrace him, to hold him as if never to let go. Instead, he strode to the door

200

and opened it. The hallway glimmered in greens and oranges from the oil lamps. The air was cold, salt-laden.

"Vanni?"

"I'm going to pack, too," he replied gruffly.

He closed the door behind him, leaving behind warmth, beauty, love. He still felt the danger, paramount and growing. Could it be from Never himself? As he talked of their deaths?

But no, he felt it down below on the first floor as well. An emanation of foreboding from the people in the Keep, servants, the duke, his guests, a sensation as if they were all waiting. As if a storm were coming. As if nothing yet had been secured against prevailing winds, and they stood to lose much.

He stood in the center of the hall on the stone floor and listened. His hearing was acute now, almost preternatural. Voices drifted up to him through the icy walls. He strained to make out words. Who were the duke's guests? What were they here for?

"...the others..."

"...will of the..."

"...the stone cottage..."

He knew of a stone cottage about a mile away. It had been empty, as far as he knew, his whole life. It hugged the cliffs much like Cliffside Keep, but on a drastically smaller scale. His father joked once that it was haunted, and that little boys must stay far away from it. But unlike the sea-cave, it had never drawn him.

Vanni did not like the tones of the voices. Even if he could not make out complete sentences, the men talked quickly, almost scattered-sounding. The duke's voice drummed the loudest but too echoey to make out more words.

The cold creeped onto his fingers, and down the neck of his shirt. Damion could not die. Vanni could not die. He would not allow it. And yet he wanted eternal night. He could taste the blood-ink of it, peppered with stars, already upon his lips.

He moved to the stairs and took them downward, two at a time, until he reached the duke's study. He stood before it, taking several breaths, then knocked. His rapping was loud. His knuckles stung.

Vanni heard movement from within the room. Footsteps. The door jerked open. Andreas stared at him. His hair was messed, the ends still wet from rain. His eyebrows rose in a show of surprise.

"Vanni."

"I—I would like to be introduced to our guests," Vanni said.

Andreas opened the door wider. "I said we would see you at dinner."

"I know." Vanni wondered right then if Andreas could smell it upon him. Sex, blood, sin. All that they had been doing.

What servant had ratted them out? Never said he'd had everything under control, but Never wasn't perfect. He made mistakes. When Vanni thought of Damion and worried too much about him, the tempt became weak, even broken.

Who among the servants, Vanni wondered, loved Damion the most? Or himself? And suspected something was off? Worried they might be harmed? Was worry alone enough to break the tempt? For Vanni it had been, but he loved Damion fiercely, more than he'd allowed himself to admit.

"Come in." Andreas said the words without conviction.

Vanni stepped past the door's threshold.

The two men who'd rushed past them earlier at the door, rose. They wore rich suits, boots, and waistcoats. One was tall and slim, in his late forties. The other looked younger, rounder, with pale brown hair.

"The Earl Davin," Andreas said.

The taller man stepped forward, arm outstretched.

Vanni took it. "Giovanni."

202

"And," Andreas continued, "Count Felerre."

Vanni shook the smaller man's hand, feeling a tremble in the palm.

"It is a pleasure to meet you both," he said. "My father has guests sometimes, but not often."

The men nodded as if they knew this for a fact. They watched him warily, or maybe it was his imagination.

Vanni faced his father. Why not be bold, as if he had nothing to hide? "Why have they returned to the Keep with you?"

Andreas put his hands behind his back. "Business matters, that is all."

"What business?"

"Investments."

Andreas was evasive, but Vanni did not work with him, either, not on business, so that wasn't unusual. Damion did the books and sometimes correspondence. If this was business, Damion should have been in the room.

Vanni smiled. "That's wonderful. I'm sure Damion will be interested."

"Yes. His talent with numbers will be invaluable on these new ventures."

They all stood for a moment, staring about the room.

"If you will excuse us, then, Vanni," Andreas said. "We are in the middle of a meeting."

"Oh, yes, of course."

Vanni left. But he could not relax. The feeling of danger remained.

Chapter Twenty-Three

Everything at dinner glittered too brightly in Vanni's eyes.

Vanni had been the first to arrive. He toyed with his water glass, almost spilling it. Droplets dotted the back of his hand.

Andreas and his guests, Davin and Felerre finally arrived.

Damion and Never were nowhere in sight.

After meeting Andreas's guests earlier, Vanni did not go back to the drawing room. Nor did he go to his own rooms to pack. Instead, he went outside in the wind and the rain and helped the servants shore up the outbuildings and barns for the coming storm.

This was to be his last evening at the Keep. He wanted everything to look normal.

He'd changed out of his wet clothes for dinner. But though the ends of his hair had dried, the thicker hair at his nape, still rain-damp, chilled his skin.

"Have you seen Damion?" Andreas asked.

Vanni shook his head.

"Or Lord Neverelle?"

"No."

Andreas glanced at his guests with a quick wince. Vanni caught it. The sense of danger prickled beneath his skin once more.

Vanni bit hard at the inside of his lower lip. There was no way Andreas could know their secret unless a servant had told him. And most of the servants had not come near them for weeks. Never swore he had them controlled. In private, they had relied almost entirely on the skills of Never's private servants.

But he could not be sure. If Andreas knew, what might he be planning? Vanni felt cold all over at the thought.

"We needn't wait any longer," Andreas said to the servants. "Please bring the food now."

Just as the servants finished pouring the wine and filling their plates, a soft step came from behind Vanni. He turned.

Damion came into the dining room.

Andreas did not look up as he said, "You're late."

"I'm sorry."

Damion sat, hands in his lap, head half-bowed but gaze straight-ahead. His cheeks showed tints of pink. He looked as sweet and young as ever. Nothing showed in his dark eyes but the flicker of candlelight. His hair was loose, still, tossed over the backs of his shoulders.

Andreas began cutting his meat. "And Lord Neverelle? Have you seen him?"

Damion shook his head. "No, sir." He glanced at Vanni, who frowned at him, then away.

Where *was* Never?

The top of Vanni's stomach crawled with his nervousness. He was not at all hungry. But he forced himself to pick up his knife and fork and cut a small piece off the delicate chicken breast he'd just been served.

For the entire meal, Damion also picked at his food.

Andreas, Davin and Felerre made small talk about the weather, the food, the magnificent oldness of the Keep. No one knew how long the Keep had been there. It had weathered the greatest of storms over hundreds of years.

The meal seemed endless. Vanni wanted none of the good food and drink, but forced himself to eat. He kept looking at Damion, but Damion would not meet his gaze.

Vanni watched him from underneath half-closed eyelids. His entire body quickened for Damion. He wanted him all the time. Even more than Never inside him, he wanted Damion's silken skin beneath his hands, the scent of his storm-dark hair against his face. He loved how Damion was built, the gazelle nature of his movements, long-limbed and graceful. Damion was leaner than Vanni, but not much shorter. He was like the dancer of Vanni's mind, always spinning, always enticing.

Never was lean and dark, too, but more angular. His edges were sharper, his wit jaded, hurtful, cool. But his lustfulness, and that star-fresh scent of adventure and of the unknown pervaded whenever he was around. Vanni liked the way the vampire strode about as if he owned the world. Who wouldn't want that feeling, that euphoria to ride into the next years of life, into the next centuries? It was as compelling as water to a thirsty boy.

"Damion." Andreas's voice interrupted Vanni's thoughts. "How are the books?"

Damion let his eyelids lift, all calm. "Fine."

"Good."

Vanni cleared his throat. In truth, those books had gathered dust in the past week or so.

Andreas asked, "Are there more candles than normal in the rooms because of a scarcity of oil?"

"No," Damion replied, voice even. "I happen to like candles."

"I prefer the lamps. Use the candelabra for decorative purposes, a few per room, lit only at night. Cut your candle orders in half at least."

"Yes, sir."

Vanni breathed deep. Damion never got into trouble. The duke loved him more than Vanni. He never reprimanded him. Not at dinner. And most certainly not in front of guests.

"I'm sure Lord Neverelle's influence has been part of that," Andreas said. "But he'll have his own accommodations before long."

Damion nodded.

Vanni scratched at his neck.

Andreas turned to him. "Vanni? Something bothering you?"

"No, sir."

But he knew deep in his blood, now. Andreas was onto them. It was good they were leaving tonight. They could not get away soon enough.

*

Vanni lay on top of his bedcovers, wearing his favorite white shirt and black trousers, waiting yet again for Never to come. But tonight it was for different reasons. Not blood. Not sex. Not great fucking. Tonight was the turning point for his and Damion's lives.

He had already double-checked his carpetbag twice. Everything was there that he wanted to take.

He'd lit all the candles. The drapes on his walls and the polished wood of his bureau reflected the flames, sparkling. The room shimmered in fine excelsior. He drifted on it, closing his eyes, seeing a dozen colors he could not name.

The candles smelled sweet, the humid air of rain. He still tasted the sourness of a dinner he could not eat, and the bile of anxiety on the edges of his tongue. His every sense was heightened. Every emotion. Every thought like little stars burning up his mind.

It would be like this forever, Never promised him. The wonder. The rapture. The fulfillment of all hunger and desire.

By eleven this evening, the three of them would be gone, out into the world on a new adventure, a new life. They would become vampires like Never and remain young, become strong. Be like gods.

He worried about what Never had said, though, that Damion was too weak, that he might not survive the transformation. Though he'd once had thoughts of leaving Damion behind, he now knew that had been the tempt. Now, he could not imagine surviving without him.

His mind wandered pleasantly; the untrimmed candle-light gleamed.

In the back of his thoughts everything was still unfinished, still gesturing toward an unseen future. He'd carefully wrapped every nostalgic thought he had for his life here at the Keep and placed it to the side of his mind marked: PAST. With Never and Damion at his sides, he wouldn't need those memories anymore. He expected to have no more room inside himself, or time, to miss this place.

Low voices in the hall brought him back to reality. Someone rapped on the door. It was crisp and hard, not like Never's usual soft knock.

He jumped up and opened the door.

A grounds servant named Lar stood some feet back looking nervous. Vanni had worked with him a lot outdoors. In fact, they'd worked together today.

Lar was a large man with dark bangs that curled over his eyes. He wore faded black trousers and a stained white shirt, work clothes, no ruffles. At this hour his job was done. He should have been in the servants' quarters taking the evening off.

"Master Vanni, I am sorry to disturb you." Lar's hands came together in a nervous gesture, palms rubbing.

"Lar, what is it?"

But before Lar could answer, Vanni's sensitive ears heard the sound of carriages, at least two, coming up the drive, thin wheels splashing through puddles. He heard the front doors three floors down open. At this time of night, and during a storm, the activity was unprecedented.

He heard at least half a dozen voices. One of them was the duke's.

Had something happened in one of the nearby villages?

That dangerous feeling from earlier in the day had caught up to him. His bones ached with it.

He edged past Lar and ran up the hallway to Damion's door, opening it. The room sat empty and silent, the hearth cold. Had Damion never returned after dinner?

He listened for sounds of Never and Damion in the Keep. The hurrying of shuffling feet on the stairwell distracted him.

Vanni ran to the end of the hall where he saw several men on the stairs. They passed him by, going to the fourth floor. Andreas trailed behind them.

When Vanni met his father's eyes, Andreas narrowed his gaze. "Go back to your room. Stay there!" His voice came harsh.

"What's happening?"

"I said go back to your room! Now!"

Vanni had locked horns with his father so many times he'd lost count. He was not about to obey him this time, either. As Andreas moved ahead, Vanni came onto the stairs behind him.

He knew where they were headed. He could barely breathe at the knowledge that somehow Never had been found out. Andreas had obviously brought reinforcements to confront him. But how much did they know? That Never drank blood? That he was an immortal?

If they knew everything, what would happen?

Vanni had to do everything in his power to thwart this. Make them all understand this was ridiculous, that there had been a mistake.

When he got to the fourth floor, there was such commotion, people everywhere, servants running down the corridor.

Vanni looked for Never's servants but didn't see them.

At Never's room, Andreas's two guests, Davin and Felerre, pounded on the door.

"Open at once!" Felerre yelled.

Vanni ran, pushing through the crowd, and came to a dead stop at the door. He ignored his father and went up to the two men.

"What's the meaning of this? This is a private room. The man inside is a guest of the Keep!"

"Step aside!" Andreas yelled. He came up to Vanni and put out his hand, shoving him back.

Vanni fought the push. "Father, what are you doing?"

Andreas raised his hand toward Vanni, but before he could do anything, a yell came from within the guest room. First it was an exclamation, like a shout, but soon the tone lengthened, and turned into a shrill keening.

Vanni knew that voice well. Damion.

Two male servants ran forward carrying heavy axes.

"Break down that door now," Andreas ordered.

They both heaved back with their tools to swing. The axes ground into the wood and against the lock.

Vanni stood back, mouth open. After only moments, the door swung away.

Never, in an unbuttoned white shirt and black trousers, lay writhing on the floor, eyes shut, oblivious to what was happening around him.

Damion stood beside his bed, shirtless, yelling, "Stop! Stop!" There was fresh blood at his throat. Vanni smelled a strange odor, acrid like burnt sage.

Shouts from the hall accused. "Vampire! Vampire!"

Davin and Felerre ran into the room toward Never as he continued to writhe.

Damion was in tears. He cried out, "What's wrong with him? What's wrong?"

Andreas went to Damion and roughly grabbed him by the arm. He yanked Damion forward, staring at the blood at his throat.

"How long has he been feeding on you!" Andreas asked.

Vanni strode forward, furious. He did not have time to wonder what Damion and Never were doing on the very evening all three of them were to leave the Keep forever. Instead, he pushed his father away, turning all his anger on him.

"How dare you accuse Damion of anything!"

"Look for yourself," Andreas said, unmoving, his hand still gripping Damion's naked arm. "He's knows exactly what is happening."

Damion struggled to pull his arm away. Tears streamed down his cheeks. He said, "Make them stop. Stop that! Never didn't hurt me!"

Damion pulled back again, trying to get at Never on the floor. Andreas held him tight. Vanni tried to get between them.

"Let go of him!" Vanni demanded. He could already see where the duke's fingernails were cutting into Damion's skin.

"Vanni! Do something!" Damion screamed.

Vanni turned to see the men, three of them now, grappling with the writhing form of Never. From somewhere they'd gotten chains, thick and heavy, and wrapped them about his feet and hands. They put a muzzle over his face and dragged him, still writhing and moaning, from the room.

Andreas, clutching Damion, gave the orders. "Take him to the carriage and put him in the stone house with the others."

Vanni stepped forward, panic rising. "Father? You can't do this!"

Andreas turned on him.

"You would defend this? After seeing the blood on Damion's neck? Did you both know, then? You and Damion?" His hand came up from Damion's arm, letting him go, and grabbed Vanni's throat, pushing him hard against the wall. "I thought more of you, Vanni. I really did."

Vanni's head cracked as his father slammed it against the wall a second time in uncontrollable anger. The fingers at his throat tightened and he started to gag.

This was it. Andreas was going to kill him here and now in front of everyone.

But the pressure decreased. Andreas pushed away and Vanni's knees bent. He slid slowly down the wall watching in shock as their dinner guests along with several strangers dragged Never away.

The crowd rushed down the stairs, following the trapped vampire.

Damion, stunned, stood trembling in the middle of the room.

At the sight of him, Vanni leapt up, turning his fury on him now. "What the hell happened?"

"Father put something in our food. Something poisonous to—to Never's kind. A combination of herbs or something. When I ate dinner—"

"But nothing can kill Never."

"He'd not dead." His voice came fast, panicked. "He's in pain, but not dead. When he tried to drink from me he was poisoned. I'm sorry, Vanni. It's all my fault."

"It's not," he said testily. "You couldn't have known."

"But it is my fault!"

"No..."

"We were supposed to be leaving," Damion said. "But Never told me he was only taking me, and he needed one last taste of my blood to cement the bond between us for the journey so we could never be parted. I wanted to do it. But I wasn't going to leave you, Vanni. I promise. I wasn't!" He put his hands to his face.

Downstairs, people shouted. Then came a roar, inhuman, like a beast caged. The roar was loud even with the muzzle. Never's agony rolling through the Keep.

Vanni slammed his fist into the wall. "What an idiot! Damn it, Damion!" As he said those words, he knew his anger was misplaced. Never had used the tempt on Damion. It was obvious. It was really Never he was angry with.

Damion came around to face him, eyes liquid, brimming. "I'm so sorry." He grabbed his shirt from the floor and shrugged into it, rapidly buttoning it up. "We can go after him. We have to. We have to save him, Vanni!"

"How?"

"The carriage they are using to transport him has to use the side road toward the nearest village. We can go along the cliff, bypass the bend right before it gets to the village road, and catch up to it. We'll jump the driver and let him out. "

"Can you even fight in your condition?"

"I can fight," Damion quipped, wiping the fresh blood from his neck. "Come on."

It sounded good. He couldn't think of a better alternative. They had to move quickly.

They took the back stairs that led out to the cliff top behind the Keep. No one stopped them.

They didn't even pause to don coats or hats.

The early autumn night was cool and damp, the wind still filled with leaves and stray raindrops. A bigger storm was on its way, but for now they had a reprieve.

Soon they were sprinting through the briars that lined the road, their white shirts billowing behind them. The wind blew through Vanni's hair. The moon scoured the skies in dimmed gold as wispy rain clouds veiled it with their lace.

He couldn't believe he was doing this! Going to rescue a beautiful, magical monster that loved Damion more than him. And yet Vanni loved Never, and couldn't seem to stop himself even now that he knew Never had been lying to him. Betraying him.

Would they really have left him behind? He could not believe it.

They ran fast, of course. They were two young men in love. They had vampire blood in their systems which made them strong. Their will propelled them over large rocks, through thickets of weeds and stands of spindly trees.

With the road to their right and the cliff on their left, they made their way with perfect balance and the fortitude and dedication of love. They beat the carriage at a bend in the road by a full minute and hid behind a clump of tall sea grass, waiting, breathing hard.

The damp air coated Vanni's lungs. The ocean undulated blackly, pulling back its tide and rushing forth with an almost constant clamor. Like thunder.

A skiff of wind blew against Vanni's face, peppering his forehead with sprinkles of water, though it was barely drizzling anymore.

In the shadows, lying side by side on the sandy ground, Damion stammered his words. "I'm so—sorry. So so sorry." Again and again, he tried to apologize.

Vanni was angry even though he knew they had both been influenced by Never, by the compulsion of his predatory tempt.

He wanted to ask why he was the one left behind. Instead, Vanni just said, "Shut up."

At that moment, the carriage came into view. It was a prison carriage, the back and windows barred. Slowly, it came closer; they could practically feel the horses' breaths on their upturned faces.

It all happened in a blur.

There were times Vanni thought back on this scene and wondered what might have been the result if they had just let Never go, not gone after him, and lived their lives as ordinary men.

But of course neither of them could have let him go. They had his blood running through their veins. And both were still under the residual effects of Never's tempt. Their future had been fated from the moment he had laid eyes on them and chosen them for his prey.

The two men, one driver and one passenger did not see them coming. Vanni and Damion jumped them from either side of the carriage and pulled them to the ground before they knew what hit them. The horses reared to a stop, whinnying.

Tight arms around the neck held for thirty seconds and both men were unconscious.

One of the men had keys to the barred back door on his belt. Vanni grabbed them and unlocked the door.

Never, shirt hanging off his shoulders, stumbled out the back of the carriage and fell to the ground. They unlocked the chains, took off the muzzle.

"I should have known." Never snarled for a moment, on his hands and knees, then gave a short laugh. He did not seem the least bit panicked. In fact, he sounded bored.

"My two heroes. Is there anything in this world you two wouldn't do for me?"

His reaction did not really surprise Vanni, nor did his pouting look of being put out, as if all of this were a mere nuisance at most. At this point nothing Never did surprised Vanni anymore. Including when he began to laugh again as voices from the bushes on the forest side of the road wafted toward them.

There were shouts, running footsteps, the sound of something fast whooshing by Vanni's ear.

"You have to run," Vanni urged him, confused at Never's lackadaisical reaction. But it was too late. Men came out of the bushes further down the road and ran toward them.

Shouts rang out from behind them, along with the sound of another carriage.

Vanni heard more thrumming sounds on the air and knew what it was. Arrows. Then he heard gunshots.

Never yelled as if he'd been hit.

Vanni started to lunge for him. He felt a sting, then an explosion in his chest. Everything slowed. He found himself floating or flying; he couldn't really tell the difference. Whatever it was, his entire being felt like it was breaking apart into misty pieces drifting on the sea winds. All he could do was watch it happen. All he could do was fall toward the edge of the cliff.

He lost his balance. And then there was only air as he flailed for the land, hands out.

Everything was dreamlike, slow. Damion stayed in his line of vision, tall, strong. Vanni watched Damion turn, his dark hair a wave behind him; watched his mouth open, his lips form his name as if shouting it, but Vanni could hear nothing.

Then he saw Damion's white shirt turn red, and two arrows tremored against his chest. His best friend's body—no, his lover's body—was pushed back from the velocity and made a slow sort of arc, arms coming slightly up from his sides.

He was still able to stand, to move forward. He reached for Vanni as if to save him. Vanni reached back. But it was too late. He was already going back and when Damion grabbed his hand, Vanni's weight pulled him along with him until they were both falling together toward the rocks and the beach and the sea.

Everything went white.

Chapter Twenty-Four

The whiteness rushed at him with a million cold arms. It was sprinkled with black stars, and a warm wind pushed furiously at his hair.

Vanni fell, tumbling, through this negative space. His heart burned in the center of his chest. He could not seem to breathe. There was no scent, nothing but the roar of the wind as he fell at a speed he could not comprehend.

Frantic, he glanced about as he continued to roll as if caught in the depths of a pale sea but with no friction to slow him down.

Shouldn't he have hit the rocks or the beach by now? But no. This was a different space and time. Like a dream. He wasn't falling through air.

He wondered if he fell like this forever, would he break apart until he slowly ceased to exist? Was this death?

Just as that thought came to him, the loud rush stopped, and the black-starred, empty space vanished.

Now Vanni stood in a white room, completely square in shape, with a low ceiling and no obvious light source. Never, dressed all in black with a red waistcoat and a red, fur-lined cloak, stood before him. His hair fell to his waist in sheets of dark brown silk. His eyes were blue lights, wide and round.

"Vanni, my angel, my little sparrow from a crumbling keep. Here you are, at long last." His voice sounded as if it originated from an echo.

"What? What's happening?"

"I've given you a gift. Now is the time for you to embrace it."

"I don't understand."

"Of course you do. We discussed this."

Still dazed, he shook his head. "You were leaving me—
"

"My plans are much more far-ranging than you and Damion alone. I was coming back for you both later. It was all in the letter I was going to leave the two of you."

Never held out his hand. "Now, it's too late. I will not return. Take the gift. Some day, in another place, we will meet again."

"No."

"You must listen now. And do as I say, or all will be lost for you and Damion."

Damion. That was what was important now. Vanni could comprehend that.

"What do I do?"

"Take my gift. It is a great one, and it comes with great danger, secrecy, and responsibility. You will not age. You will not need food or drink, only blood. A lot at first. Less as you grow older with the centuries."

"But—"

"Do not talk. Take what I offer." Never, face less harsh than usual in the soft, white light, his image more breathtaking than ever, shook his closed fist at Vanni.

On instinct, Vanni held out his hand. Never's hand opened and he pressed something hard into Vanni's palm. It pricked him. Vanni looked down and saw blood welling. Beside the beads of blood, an abalone comb just like the one he'd found as a boy, lay against his fingers.

He closed his hand around the precious treasure.

Never vanished.

*

Vanni woke to another roar, and hard, pitted sea-rock beneath him. His body shivered, soaked in salty mist. He opened his eyes.

218

He lay in the sea-cave by the stony pool where anemones grew, where little silver fish darted into shadow, where the sea-witches had once lived.

He sat up, remembering all at once the gunshots, the arrows. He looked down at his white shirt, touched his chest. There was no wound, but the shirt was stained with blood, and torn as if something sharp had caught it.

How had he gotten here?

He glanced around in the dimness seeing only shadows, the shapes of the uneven and curving rock walls, and something else—something that was not a rock or a smaller tide-pool.

He reached out in the dimness and encountered still-warm flesh—an arm, a thigh—and moved closer to it. His hands roamed over the motionless chest, fingers catching in long tangles of hair. There could be no mistake.

"Damion!"

Damion had taken two arrows. Both in the chest. Vanni felt around but everything seemed clean; there were no wounds. Vanni reached upward to clasp his shoulders.

"Damion!"

Vanni jerked his body as if to wake him.

Nothing happened.

After a moment, he put his head to Damion's chest, cheek against his throat, lips close to the underside of his chin. He didn't realize he was weeping uncontrollably until the body beneath him began to stir.

Vanni cried out, tugging him up, hugging Damion hard to him.

Damion sputtered, took a few deep breaths and tensed. "What? What happened?"

"You're alive. You're alive," was all Vanni could manage over and over. He gasped for air, gulping it in, realizing he was sobbing.

Damion put a hand on his shoulder and said one word. "Vanni."

As Vanni calmed, he leaned back. His eyes were growing used to the darkness and he could see the figure of Damion now, and the paleness of his shirt. He watched as Damion looked about.

"Where are we?" Damion asked.

"The sea-cave."

"How did we get here? I remember seeing you fall—" His voice trembled.

"We both did."

"It's Never's gift to us. Why we woke," Damion whispered. "But how did we get down here?"

"The sea-cave must've been right below the road where we stopped the carriage. We went over the cliff and probably landed on the beach. Someone must have carried us," Vanni said, wiping at the dampness on his face.

Damion reached out and clasped his hand tightly in his. "Never's still alive, then. He did this."

"I don't know—" Vanni leaned forward, pushing at the hard rock with his hand to get his balance. His hand encountered something small and sharp.

He closed his fingers around the object and brought it up and said to Damion, "You're right. He was here. I just found this on the ground next to me."

Damion took the comb in his free hand. "The sea-witch's comb."

"It's his," Vanni said, feeling in his pocket for its mate and finding it. "I have the other one in my pocket. Now there are two."

Still trembling, Damion leaned into Vanni. "He saved us."

Holding Damion's hand, Vanni encircled him with his other arm. "I had a dream before I woke here. I remember now. Never gave me this second comb."

"I had a dream of him, too," Damion said. "But he didn't give me a comb."

"Do you think it means he's all right?"

"He said he would see us again some day." Damion replied.

Vanni's breathing hitched. Tears rolled down his face again, burning. "Well, how long is that going to be?"

"I don't know, but remember what he told us. If we're to survive now, we have to feed. Or we'll die for real this time."

It was as if they'd traded minds. Damion was the calm one, now. No sorrow. No tears.

Damion leaned closer to Vanni, rubbing the side of his head against his shoulder. "He brought us both here. He did not leave us behind."

"But he told you he was leaving me. And you were ready to do it."

Damion interrupted. "It's true, what you say. But I was under the tempt. I couldn't argue. I would never leave you, Vanni." Those last words came out soft, breathy.

Again, Vanni wiped at his tears. Practically slapping them off his face.

Damion said quietly, "Anyway, didn't he tell you the same thing? That you should leave me behind because I was weak?"

"How did you know?"

"I knew he was playing both of us, I just didn't know how to stop it."

With a coldness he didn't feel, Vanni pulled away from Damion's embrace and pushed himself to stand.

Damion followed.

"We have to go back to the Keep," Damion said.

"They know about us there."

"We can scout it out. See what's going on first. If your father thinks he rescued us, we'll be fine. We can keep this secret forever. We have to."

Vanni nodded in the darkness. It made sense. He felt Damion's hand come up and brush briefly across his still-wet face before turning away.

221

"Forever," Damion repeated.

*

Together they rushed to the Keep.

When they came around to the front, in the dark and the wind, servants in black shawls holding lanterns stood huddled by the steps to the entryway.

Vanni and Damion approached.

"What's going on?" Damion commanded loudly.

The circle of servants parted. No one looked at them suspiciously, which was good. So far.

"We don't know," someone said.

Another: "We just found him like this."

Vanni looked at the area where they huddled, forming a circle with their bodies.

There, Andreas lay limp and unmoving on the front step, neck torn out, blood in a puddle by his head. The blood looked black in the lantern-light. Still running out of him and pooling, still warm.

Vanni froze. He couldn't think or speak. He just stared at his father as chills washed over him.

Damion said, "Do you remember what happened tonight? Anything?"

They all shook their heads. And yet the whole house had been awakened with Never's abduction. All the servants had been running up and down the halls. Yet none of them remembered.

Vanni frowned.

Damion leaned toward him and said, "The tempt."

"Never?" Vanni felt as if he were falling again.

Damion nodded. Then he turned to the servants.

"The duke has been killed by an animal attack. That much is obvious. We must be vigilant. Post more guards. You know what to do. Wrap him and lay him in Cliffside's crypt. Treat his body with honor and care. And send someone into all the villages. Tell them the duke is dead. Warn them to stay indoors at night. There will be more hungry wolves than ever this winter. Tell them their new governor is the duke's son, the Earl Giovanni."

Most of the servants nodded agreement. Many began to weep aloud.

Damion turned away.

Vanni looked at Damion as though he were a stranger. When had he grown up so much? When had he gotten so decisive?

"Vanni?" Damion looked at him hard.

Vanni kept staring at his father's corpse.

"Vanni." Damion's voice grew more insistent. "Come inside. We have a funeral to plan."

Vanni broke away from the crowd and followed Damion inside.

They had to look a sight, shirts bloody and torn, hair wind-blown into witch-knots. But the servants took no notice.

This had to be a nightmare. His father and he had not gotten along much throughout his life, but this was never the plan. The duke was not supposed to die!

"Come." Damion led Vanni into the Keep's main living area.

In the front room a crackling hearth, candles and warmth greeted them. Never's two silent and obedient servants, Raiden and Anastasia, sat on an ornate sofa with their hands folded in their laps as if waiting for something.

As Vanni and Damion came into the room, the ethereal servants both looked up and smiled the same open smile.

Vanni exchanged confused looks with Damion. But before he could even think what to say, Damion stepped forward, again taking charge.

"Where is your master?"

For the first time, one of them spoke. The male, Raiden, said, "We are here at our master's command." His voice came out dulcet, sending a stab of pleasure into Vanni's midsection.

"Why?" Damion asked.

"For you."

"For us?"

"Yes." Raiden took a slim, shining silver knife from his sleeve. As if it were nothing unusual, he pushed up his sleeve and ran the blade up the bare flesh of his arm. Red blood flowed up in a line.

Vanni winced.

"Stop that!" But as Vanni spoke, a strange and unusual hunger rose inside him like an unbearable ache starting at the bottom of his stomach and ending at his chest. The hollowness grew until it became overwhelming.

Damion was already kneeling before Raiden.

Vanni knew it was the only way, but so much had happened this night. Too much too fast.

He heard Never's voice in his head. *I've given you a gift. Now is the time for you to embrace it.*

But his father lay dead on the front steps. And Never was gone. What did he have to keep living for?

He turned and saw Damion, head bent now, licking at the red stripe on Raiden's arm. Drinking. Feeding. That dark hair like a torrent haloing him. His back straight, his hips canted, his buttocks beneath his damp trousers slim yet rounded in the sweetest way.

He remembered the sweet, smiling boy, how more nights than not Damion came to his room to sleep with him until dawn, afraid of nightmares, afraid of the dark.

Now he looked at him with a new gaze. This boy—*his boy*—was a man now. Ready to take life on. Strong, capable, and right now before Vanni's eyes transforming into the most beautiful immortal vampire Vanni could imagine.

Anastasia smiled up at Vanni, taking Raiden's knife, running it up her own arm until the flesh gave way to the veins and the blood flowed.

"For you," she said, voice as sweet as Raiden's. "All for you."

"Take all you need," Raiden said to Damion.

"All you need," Anastasia said to Vanni, holding up her arm.

"I don't—" He paused.

Damion lifted his head up, his lips red and glistening. "Vanni?"

"Not yet. I can't."

Damion sat back on his heels, licking his full lips. Vanni had the urge to go to him, to lick those lips himself.

"Vanni, you must. Never said he would see us again. It's the only way!"

Vanni took a step back. He wanted this. But tonight had gone all wrong. Everything was a jumble in his mind. What had started out weeks ago as harmless flirting, and erotic fun, had led to this. He'd always felt the danger. Always. But he had not listened to his own instincts. And now tragedy surrounded them.

"Vanni, I know it's hard. You're mourning. But you must feed!"

Damion's dark eyes held tears now. His voice pleaded.

"Don't you love me anymore?" Damion asked.

It was the final straw. The statement Damion had to know would win Vanni's obedience. For Vanni loved Damion the way the tide loved the shore, the way the moon loved the night. And he always would.

He stepped forward.

Anastasia held her arms out to him as if to embrace him.

He was still angry at Damion for meeting Never without him tonight, for that secret alone, even though he knew Damion could not fight the tempt like he could.

He scowled at the thought, and the torment of the evening rippled through him. But the scent of fresh blood drew him down. He heard Damion let out a rush of air.

"There," Damion said softly. "Yes. There."

Vanni licked at the tartness of warm blood. Before he realized it, he had fastened his mouth over the deepest area of the long cut and sucked hard. Blood welled into his mouth, salty and sweet, creating within him a deep longing like endless autumn nights. He heard the haunting cry of an owl and kept drinking. He saw stars. He lost time.

He knew he needed to stop. Anastasia might be strange, and a product of Never's world, but as far as he knew she was human. She could die.

He fell back, breaking the seal of lips on skin.

He looked about. Everything blurred. The room too hot. The fire in the hearth like explosions in his ears. His skin tingled. His heart thrummed. His veins held a sweetness of pleasure, like the afterglow of sex.

He could hear servants moving about the grounds, the wind as if it lived inside him, the sea chanting in its hoarse voice. Even the clouds—he heard their soft billowings, their puffed breaths.

Everything smelled wet and new, jungled and sea-green. The candles gave off scents of roses. Of turned earth. Never's scent.

Vanni's heart broke into a million pieces at that fragrance, then put itself back together as the human blood inside him invaded every cell, turning him, changing him, making him a never-ending thread of time itself.

His vision cleared and he saw every fiber of the material of the sofa, and the rug he knelt on. He looked at the hearth. The flames appeared as translucent beings doing a wild dance. Damion rose up, lips crimson, like a young god before him, eyes dark as eternity.

Vanni's throat threatened to close at such beauty.

He saw the servants on the sofa relaxed as if sleeping. Had he and Damion killed them? But no. His preternatural vision saw their breaths like tiny mists of fog coming from their noses and mouths.

Vanni wanted to reach out to them for more blood. He swayed back to keep himself from indulging in more.

Never might be a murderer, but Vanni swore he would not become that sort of being… that sort of monster. He stood, almost falling as dizziness overtook him for a few seconds.

Damion stood as well, smiling, glowing. Reaching out to him.

Vanni turned away. It shouldn't have been this way. Nothing about this night was right.

*

The day was overcast, but still the sun hurt his skin. White flashes exploded in his peripheral vision. Light slanted like shards of pink glass upon the churning sea.

Vanni pulled his cloak hood over his head and wrapped himself in the strong cloth. He sat on the sea-weed strewn beach. Broken shells and dark rocks littered the wild shore.

Over and over his mind replayed recent events.

It had been two days since he had become a vampire. As another storm blew through, he had remained alone in his room. He took his meals there. Food. It was a habit to eat, though he no longer needed that sort of sustenance. But eating and drinking gave an illusion to others—the servants, mainly—that he was not seriously ill, just in mourning for his father. That he was normal. Human.

Though there were times Vanni longed to see him, Damion stayed away. Vanni wanted to be with him more than he could say. And yet he needed time. Damion must have sensed it.

That night, out on the dark road, after being shot and left for dead, he had experienced so many emotions at once. Fear. Peace. Love lost. Life settled.

The death-dream of Never had been so real. A gift, the lord called this immortal, vampiric state of being.

Vanni was still trying to process all the new sensations, the way his body hummed as if singing aloud, and how he felt now as master of the Keep.

When he finally emerged from his room this morning, everyone came to him for decisions. Orders. Damion stood like a shadow at his side, but they still hadn't talked.

Vanni missed Never so badly he had woken himself up crying out in the night. In those moments, he wished he really had died on the dark road that led to the village—or in the sea-cave.

Now, alone beside the ocean, he thought again of the sea-witches. How truly he had believed in them when he was a child. How he'd wanted to meet one, dreamed of it.

The sound of the waves became a siren tune in his head, part of all the beautiful scents and songs that life made. The Keep might be old, and the cliff craggy, but this was a gorgeous area here on the beach, a perfect resting place.

Vanni lay back in the sunlight letting it warm his skin through the cloak, but inside he was so cold. He wondered if the day had not been overcast would he would simply burn up and die? Never again could he allow himself to be in direct sunlight. His innocence was gone. His light. And maybe even his love.

He sat on the lonely beach, wrapped in his cloak, and mourned.

Epilogue

Vanni lay on his side in his bed, eyes wide open, watching the curtains on his windows flash white, then black, as silent lightning far out to sea performed its dance upon the horizon.

He'd already drunk blood three times since his new state of being. Once from Anastasia on that fateful night. Twice from Raiden just today. Never's two servants both revived quickly, as long Vanni gave them his own blood—only a few drops needed—in return for their service.

Damion used them, too, but away from Vanni's eyes. Still giving him space.

Damion.

Vanni's heart skipped at the thought of him, of how he loved him even now in his sorrow of half-blaming Damion for everything that had happened. He needed to know Damion was all right, even if Vanni was avoiding him.

Now he strained to hear him in his room one door down, making sure Damion was still there, still close. He did this every night, but tonight he heard nothing from the neighboring room. Not even a breath.

He sat up. Where was Damion?

The door to Vanni's room swung slowly open.

Damion stood in the doorway in a white dressing gown. The look on his face, striped with shadows and golden light from the hall oil lamps, was one of utter despair. His eyelashes glittered, damp with tears.

Vanni sat up.

"Please don't hate me." Damion stood on the threshold. "I can't live in this world without you." He paused, bowing his head. "Are you going to be mad at me forever?"

Vanni scooted further up in his bed, scowling. If they were careful, forever was what they had. Or at least a very very long life.

"I'm not mad at you, Damion. Don't you know that? I could never be mad at you. And I believed you when you said you were never going to leave me."

"Nor will you ever leave me," Damion replied. "But you're suffering so. And I'm the only person in the whole world who knows why."

Vanni shrugged.

"You miss Never. I miss him, too."

Damion took a step into the room, advancing toward the bed. The door shut with a click behind him. When he came up against the mattress edge, he climbed under the covers.

Damion reached out to Vanni, drawing him to him. For one who was no longer human, Damion was so warm. He still smelled of summer and wonder and childhood.

As Damion softly began to talk, Vanni felt tears burn beneath his eyelids.

"It isn't so bad, is it?" Damion said. "This feeling, this vampire feeling… it's like nothing I've ever experienced before. It's amazing. It puts everything into perspective. Vanni, we'll do this together, won't we? And we will see Never again. He promised."

Vanni didn't know who he missed more, Never or Damion. And because of that, Vanni had wanted to die a hundred times over the past three days. He wanted to just black out blissfully remembering only the good things he'd loved in this life, spring days in the woods as the sun set and the sky turned darkly orange, or curled up under quilts with Damion on winter nights reading stories of ancient heroes.

He wanted the crisp taste of fall apples, the scents of chestnut and mountain laurel wafting up through the valleys and woods surrounding the Keep. Finally, he still desired that heady feeling of falling utterly in love without hope for redemption.

Damion…Vanni was so angry with him for keeping Never's secrets three nights ago. This boy, his best friend, whom he loved more than anyone….

But he had told the truth just a minute ago. He could never be truly mad at Damion. Not really.

The whole world shimmered. And Damion, too. Beside him, now. Like an angel about to spread his gossamer wings.

This was a new kind of drunk and yes, Damion was right, being a vampire was amazing. Explosive. He loved it. He wanted to wallow in it. He certainly didn't feel like he wanted to die any longer.

Still, not everything was fixed by this cold, cold gift.

Damion was different, changed, no longer the innocent little boy, no longer afraid of his own shadow, of witches in the wood.

After a while, it was Damion who said, "Vanni, everything with Never, all of it…I regret nothing."

Vanni's hand came up and combed through the cool black tresses, pulling Damion's face closer.

Damion rolled into him.

This was what Vanni had been waiting for all along.

They kissed. Lavender. Spun-sugar.

Damion's tongue delved sweetly, the probe a promise of more. His body moved against Vanni just right, just enough to make the constant fluttering of Vanni's arousal for him increase.

They fit together perfectly.

Vanni's heart still hurt. But Damion made it hurt less. Damion made it whole.

Vanni reached between them and pulled the edges of their gowns up until their bodies met skin on skin.

Damion groaned, his strong, slim cock pushing hard against Vanni's abdomen. Vanni's hands brushed down his back and over his slim hips, gripping the smooth, muscular buttocks.

So beautiful, he was. It was easy to understand why Never might have loved him more.

Damion whispered, as if reading his mind, "It was always you I loved most."

But Vanni knew they both still cared almost as much about Never. Even as he pulled the younger man into his arms, he felt an errant stab of jealousy. Then stark possessiveness. Damion had always been his. And now he wanted him more than anything he'd ever wanted in his life.

He yanked Damion's gown over his head and threw it to the floor.

"Vanni!"

Vanni didn't wait for more words, or explanations. He pulled Damion up hard until his thighs straddled his chest and took his pretty sweet cock into his mouth.

Damion, on his knees now over Vanni's, arched back. He let his voice cry out, a strangled sound that pierced the soul.

Vanni fed, both hands on Damion's smooth hips, caressing slowly down the fronts of his thighs and toward the inside.

Damion leaned a little forward and clutched Vanni's head with both hands, thrusting just a little, always gentle, always sweet. Vanni teased him with just his tongue. Caressed the insides of his thighs.

"Please. Yes. Please," Damion begged.

They were alone now. They didn't have to do what Never said. They could be themselves. But Vanni found he liked prolonging the pleasure. Making Damion quiver and plead. He would make him come hard now, then rouse him again and take him from behind.

His cock ached so pleasantly as he made Damion groan louder. As he placed Damion's cock on the edge of his tongue and held it there, he then put his mouth all the way over it without sucking.

Damion was sputtering sweet nothings. No longer the innocent he once was. "You're so warm. Feels so good. I love it when you suckle me. Please suck harder."

When Vanni finally succumbed and sucked him down hard, Damion whispered, "Love it. Love it. Love you."

Damion came beautifully, lithe muscles taut, back straightening. He stood all the way up on his knees as his beautiful manhood spurted over and over again into Vanni's mouth and then onto his face. Vanni swallowed. The semen was like honey to his vampire taste buds. As a vampire himself, Damion's pleasure gushed fierce and strong, double the amount the most virile of humans could give. Vanni fed on it as if it were blood, and felt his vampire hunger yearn for more.

When Damion was spent, he fell back, legs splayed out, erection still throbbing against his abdomen. Vanni came up and over him, flipping him onto his stomach.

Just like when they were with Never, only without the psychic *tempt* overriding him now, Damion raised his hips, jutting his beautiful ass in Vanni's face. Inviting.

Vanni caressed him gently, then licked him there, over and over against the sensitive hole. When Damion was good and wet, he spread him with his fingers, watching in the candlelight as Damion's hole open and closed, opened and closed, seeking him. He greased a finger and made sure Damion was slick, ready.

Damion sighed loudly. "Put it in me already!"

Vanni rose onto his knees and lined up his cock against the hole. He was already wet with arousal and knew he would not last long. To be inside Damion… it was better than anything. The best. With or without Never, he had wanted Damion like this. All the time.

He thrust in all the way.

With Damion it was hard to be gentle not because he didn't love him, but because he loved him too much. He had difficulty holding himself back. Never's control over them was all that kept him in line.

The first time he'd plunged himself into Damion only weeks ago had been pure ecstasy, and that never changed. Even as Never had chuckled at his fumbling attempts that first time, he felt no shame in his actual love. Love-making skills could be learned, but the love he felt—that could never be faked, and none of Never's teasing could take that away from him.

Still, with all his heart, he longed for the powerful vampire. Missed him more than he could ever articulate. But Damion filled those mournful spaces beautifully. In truth, it was Damion he'd always wanted from the beginning. And now he had him.

Damion thrust up beneath him. "I love you inside me. Move," he whispered. "Just move."

Vanni obeyed, now knowing just how Damion liked it, knowing how hard to press, and which angles felt best.

He held Damion tightly to him, running his hands all over his naked body.

Vanni's own gown fell around them both, the hem bunching at Damion's lower back. His thrust became a staccato of jerks as both men quivered in pleasure.

Vanni reached around Damion's waist and grasped his cock, pumping fast.

Vanni's cock burst inside Damion again and again. Damion's second orgasm made his cock throb beautifully in Vanni's grip. He squeezed and milked him until Damion was pounding the bedcovers with his fists.

When he pulled out they were both damp with sweat and semen. They turned and fell onto the bed in each other's arms.

"You can feed on me if you want," Damion offered, tucking his head under Vanni's chin. "I had a servant earlier. She didn't even know. Wasn't even sick after. Just walked away."

234

"You can use tempt already?"

Damion nodded.

"Better than me. I haven't learned that yet. But I don't need to feed on you right now," Vanni said. "I drank my fill from Raiden."

Damion chuckled.

For a while they lay sated and silent in each other's arms.

Finally, Damion turned, naked in Vanni's arms, and kissed him lightly on the neck. "Can I stay?"

"Of course." Then he added, for old time's sake, "Nightmares?"

"Not anymore. When I dream, I dream of you. So when I wake, I just want to be sure you're real."

Vanni blinked hard.

Damion drew his lips up from Vanni's neck to his ear. "Let me stay and you can have me again later."

"Oh, I will."

Their embrace tightened. They both fell to sleep at the same time.

The End

Dear Reader:

Thank you for reading my vampire fantasy romance.

This book is very close to my heart. I love all my characters I write about, but Vanni's voice while writing this one was very distinct in my head. He had a lot of beautifully rich observations to make, and I love him for it!

Even long after the book was done, Vanni continues to be a large presence in my mind.

Wendy Rathbone

Connect with Wendy:

Newsletter: https://www.subscribepage.com/c7y0t5
Amazon: https://www.amazon.com/Wendy-Rathbone/e/B00B0O9BMS?ref_=dbs_p_ebk_r00_ab au_000000
Facebook
Page: https://www.facebook.com/wendy.rathbone.3
Facebook Reader
Group: https://www.facebook.com/groups/718074255 203918/
BookBub: https://www.bookbub.com/authors/wendy-rathbone
Twitter: https://twitter.com/wendyrathbone1
Instagram: https://www.instagram.com/authorwendyrat hbone/
Goodreads: https://www.goodreads.com/author/show/3 52636.Wendy_Rathbone

ALSO BY WENDY RATHBONE

The Kingdom of Slaves Series (contemporary fantasy mm romance)

The Slave Palace
The Slave Harem
Master of Halloween (short story)

The Omega Misfits (Omegaverse mm romance)

Trust No Alpha
The Alpha's Fake Mate
Alpha's Embrace
Single Omega Dad
Omega Chattel
Omega Untamed
Alpha Daddy (novella)
Alpha Snowed In (holiday novella)

The Imposter Series (fantasy mm romance)

The Imposter Prince
The Imposter King

The Moonling Prince Series (fantasy, sci fi mm romance)

The Moonling Prince
The Coming of the Light

The Foundling Series (contemporary billionaire mm romance trilogy)

Rescue Me
Sacrifice Me
Remember Me

The Fantastic Immortals Series (fantasy/myth mm romance)

Ganymede: Abducted by the Gods
Zeus: Conquering his Heart

Stand Alone Novels

Sci Fi MM Romance

Solstice Gift (holiday)
Not Another Hero
Cocky Virgin Prince
Prey
Scoundrel
The Android and the Thief (Second edition)
Letters to an Android

Fantasy MM Romance

Lord Vampyre
Lace (vampire fairies)
Snow of the White Hills (mm fairy tale)
The Elves of Christmas (holiday magical)
Santa's Reindeer Shifters (holiday magical mpreg omegaverse)
Santa's Naughty Boy (holiday magical daddy/boy)

Contemporary MM Romance

Romantically Incorrect
Snowfall and Romance (Christmas/holiday)
The Bodyguard's Valentine
Buying You

WENDY RATHBONE'S
TROPE CHEAT SHEET

Omegaverse non-shifter:

Trust No Alpha, The Alpha's Fake Mate, Alpha's Embrace, Single Omega Dad, Omega Chattel, Omega Untamed, Alpha Daddy, Alpha Snowed In

Omegaverse shifter:

Santa's Reindeer Shifters

Daddy kink:

Alpha Daddy, Omega Untamed (light), Santa's Naughty Boy

Master/slave, indentured servant:

The Slave Palace, The Slave Harem, Scoundrel, The Android and the Thief, Letters to an Android, Prey, Solstice Gift, Ganymede, The Imposter Prince

Captive rescue:

Trust No Alpha, Alpha's Embrace, Omega Chattel, The Imposter Prince, The Imposter King, The Foundling Trilogy (Rescue Me, Sacrifice Me, Remember Me), Ganymede, Zeus, Prey, Scoundrel, The Android and the Thief, Letters to an Android, Lace, Snow of the White Hills

Single dad:

Single Omega Dad

Fated mates:

The Omega Misfits series, Lace, Santa's Reindeer Shifters

Gay Harem:

The Slave Harem

Fake identity, fake mate:
The Alpha's Fake Mate, The Imposter Prince, The Imposter King, Not Another Hero

Hurt/comfort, healing:
The Kingdom of Slaves series, The Omega Misfits series, The Imposter series, The Moonling Prince series, The Foundling trilogy, Zeus, Prey, Lace, Snow of the White Hills,

Mafia, underworld kingpin:
The Foundling trilogy

Vampires:
Lace, Lord Vampyre

Friends to Lovers:
Cocky Virgin Prince, Letters to an Android, The Android and the Thief

Famous, model, actor:
Buying You, Romantically Incorrect, Not Another Hero

MMM scenes:
Lace, Lord Vampyre, The Slave Harem

First time, virgin:
The Slave Palace, Trust No Alpha, The Alpha's Fake Mate, Alpha's Embrace, Omega Chattel, Alpha Daddy, The Imposter Prince, The Moonling Prince, Cocky Virgin Prince, Ganymede, Zeus, Not Another Hero, Prey, The Android and the Thief, Letters to an Android, Lace, Lord Vampyre, Snow of the White Hills, Santa's Reindeer Shifters

OMEGA UNTAMED
The Omega Misfits Book 6
Wendy Rathbone

Kee is a beautiful Omega and popular rent boy living in a part of Old Town called the Trenches. He's also an untamable addict. Wild and troubled, Kee is kidnapped by Alpha drug lords who think he knows too much.

Trapped, Kee longs for a way out of the hole he's dug for himself...but who would rescue a crazy Omega sex worker?

One Alpha will. His name is Bast. Bast knows he can't tame Kee through kindness, but he still wants him for his very own.

Kee needs an Alpha who will take control, hold him down, keep him from the worst of himself. Turns out, Bast is the very man for the job.

Non-shifter omegaverse, mpreg, rescue, an uninhibited Omega, a tough Alpha with a heart of gold, daddy care, bonding/knotting and HEA.

SINGLE OMEGA DAD
The Omega Misfits Book 4
Wendy Rathbone

My new financial guardian, Mathias, is a cold, self-centered, rude-ass Alpha and the son of one of the wealthiest men in the country. To him, I am a burden on society, only fit to live on a chattel farm.

It doesn't matter that I'm drawn to him, to his ominous presence and chiseled jaw, his muscular body in his fitted silk suits. I'm a single dad with kids and responsibilities --I don't have time for that rich bastard.

He keeps coming by the house so I can sign documents, fine. But then he's got cute gifts for my kids.

It's got to stop. I don't have time to fix him. Don't have time to fall in love with an Alpha right now.

A non-shifter Alpha/Omega love story with mpreg, a single widower Omega dad, an Alpha who cannot knot, emotional issues, two adorable identical twin boys, and an HEA.

Some characters from "Trust No Alpha" make appearances in this novel, however, this book is a standalone read.

TRUST NO ALPHA
The Omega Misfits, Book 1
Wendy Rathbone

It's a world gone mad. The Alphas are out of control. When you discover you're not who you thought you were, the nightmare begins.

KRIS
At age eighteen, life as he knows it is over for Kris. A secret to his nature he was not aware of has been revealed.

Now, kept as a prisoner in a locked room in the mansion of his wealthy father, Kris is at the mercy of Alpha laws and Alpha domination.

Things take a turn for the worse when his own litter mate threatens him, and his father starts behaving strangely around him.

Escape is his only hope. But where can he go in a world that allows him no rights?

THORNE
Marked as a dangerous Alpha, and living a secluded life alone and unloved, Thorne still grieves for the mate whose death he feels responsible for.

Years have passed, and he refuses to even try to function in normal society.

One day he discovers a young man on his property, disheveled, desperate, and scared. He acts like a runaway Omega, but he doesn't smell like one.

What is this boy? And why does Thorne feel an immediate need to protect him? To bond him? To make him his?

A non-shifter, Omegaverse love story of rescue, first time, fertility issues and an HEA. Standalone read. 65,500 words. (While Omegas are birth-fathers in this universe, there is no on-page mpreg in this book.)

THE ALPHA'S FAKE MATE
The Omega Misfits, Book 2
Wendy Rathbone

The Alphas think they own everything. Including people. Well, I'm here to say they don't own me, and I will never let one of those bastards touch me again.

The frenzy of their Burn cannot be trusted. I know from experience. My first time with an Alpha nearly ended in my death. And because of the laws which favor Alpha rights, and place a large number of unbonded, adult Omegas on chattel farms, my abuser can never be tried for his crimes against me.

Omegas are being hurt. Omegas are dying.

All Alphas are violent. Or so I believe. Until I meet Orion.

Ori is everything a guy could want in a mate. Six foot three. Beautiful brown wavy hair. Bright, dark eyes. Muscles like chiseled marble. He even says "please" and "thank you" at all the right times. He's got it all, except he's an Alpha.

Though he has given me a room in his home free of charge, and has signed fake paperwork saying we are bonded so I don't have to answer my attacker's claim, can I trust him?

But now I'm in danger. If I don't take a real mate, my life as I know it will be over. Can I believe in the goodness of Ori? Can I learn to love again?

A non-shifter, fake mate, Alpha/Omega love story. Rescue. First time. Omegaverse. Mpreg. Healing from sexual trauma. (All books in The Omega Misfits series are standalone reads and can be read in any order.) 61k words.

OMEGA CHATTEL
The Omega Misfits Book 5
Wendy Rathbone

At Zilly's Chattel Farm, Alli is seen as an upstart Omega. But in reality, he is the victim of a brutal house-dad who wants to control him. Threatened with being institutionalized when he turns eighteen, Alli runs away.

Tarin is an Alpha who runs a small school from his own home for wayward Omegas. Three or four students at a time are all he can handle and his home is full. But when he meets Alli on the streets, he is compelled to bring him home.

Alli wants a better future for himself, better than selling himself on the streets, so he agrees to be a student, when what he really wants is Tarin himself. Tarin doesn't sleep with his Omega students, and the one exception he made broke his heart.

But Alli is persistent. And not only does Tarin have a weakness for broken young men, there seems to be a spontaneous bond forming between them. The combination is turning hotter faster than they can keep up.

Non-shifter omegaverse, fated mates, mpreg, age gap, virgin, knotting/bonding, high steam, HEA.

ALPHA'S EMBRACE
The Omega Misfits Book 3
Wendy Rathbone

I am Misha. My name was given to me at birth by the doctor who delivered me. I have never known my parents. I live in a ten by ten space with one window, a sink and toilet, a bed and a locked door. Once a day I'm taken to an outdoor exercise area. I am allowed a limited access tablet and tutored online by computer programs. I have one friend I talk to through a tiny crack in the wall. His name is Cedric and he has trouble keeping himself quiet. When he isn't talking to me about monsters and demons, he screams all the time.

Why is my life so isolated and depressing? Because I am a Sylph. Sylphs are the byproduct of illegal Omega to Omega matings. We are all beautiful, but 99.9% are born insane. The rarest of Sylphs, like me, show no outward signs of madness or brain damage, but we live in institutions because we cannot be trusted.

All of us Sylphs who have lived long enough to pass through puberty have hypersexual disorder which makes life even more difficult for us, let alone our keepers. It is like something Alphas call the Burn, a mating urge Alphas experience once every couple of months.

But we're Sylphs, not Alphas, and this Burn thing? We experience it all the time. It's a huge problem and why we are kept isolated. Most of us don't survive through our teens because of it.

One day, a handsome Alpha comes to interview and study me. He calls himself the Chief of Staff but his real name is Geo. Like magic, I fall in love with him instantly. I do everything I can to seduce him. He will have none of it because touch between an Alpha and a Sylph is taboo. But I have plans. No matter what, I intend to bond him and make him mine. Forever.

A non-shifter Alpha/Omega-Sylph love story of forbidden love, rescue, and HEA. Standalone read. No Mpreg. 58k words

SONS OF NEVERLAND
A Deliciously Dark Male/Male Romance
Della Van Hise

Set against a backdrop of contemporary culture, *Sons of Neverland* explores the universal questions of love, sex and death - the three most crucial challenges every human being must face. Stefan London is a grieving man, suffering through the loss of his young daughter. When he goes to a science fiction convention in the hopes of meeting her friends, he encounters instead a man who is dangerously seductive. Lured into the night, Stefan soon discovers himself in a world where vampires are real, and immortality is only a kiss away.

But the price of eternal life is high, and as his handsome maker warns, "Through my blood you will learn a secret that will compel you to live forever, yet a secret so sinister it will haunt you for that same eternity."

The secret will haunt you, too.

―――――

A deliciously dark male/male romance. First time, enemies to lovers, love/hate relationship, HEA.

YEAR OF THE RAM
Della Van Hise

Year of the Ram was described by one reviewer as... "A space-faring gay romance full of love, angst, and longing."

Only after Star Commander Morgan Diego becomes an exile as a result of a Galaxy Corps political blunder does he begin to realize how much he valued the companionship of his second in command - the mysterious Lucien, an Alfarian who is more elfen than human, with peculiar powers & abilities which begin to unfold as he, too, realizes what he has lost.

Separated by circumstance from his former life, Morgan is thrust into a world where he must survive by his wits. When he meets a peculiar little old man calling himself Kim Le, Morgan finds himself in a situation where he is required to master The Art - not only a form of human & extraterrestrial martial arts, but a way of living that will alter his life forever.

At the temple, he is introduced to his new teacher, another Alfarian man who begins to steal his heart - a heart which is already promised to Lucien. Torn and conflicted, Morgan struggles with the world he left behind and the world he now inhabits.

Beginning to believe he may never again return to his ship and to the friends and loved ones he left behind, he is all the more frustrated and heartbroken when a new Master arrives at the temple: a man to whom Morgan is immediately drawn both mentally and physically, a man who is strikingly familiar... yet utterly alien.

M/M and M/M/M. An epic love story with a HEA.

www.ingramcontent.com/pod-product-compliance
Lightning Source LLC
Chambersburg PA
CBHW032036240626
47154CB00003B/938